"And with Dad's situation, I won't make big decisions for a while. But I'm certain I'm not going back to Denver."

Surprisingly good—and scary—news, as her rapid heartbeat demonstrated. It shouldn't matter, but it did. Lucas would need some support from Sloan for a while. She cleared her throat before speaking. "So that's why you keep insisting that you can stay for as long as he needs you."

"Exactly. Besides..." He stopped talking and stared down into the fire.

"Besides what?" Bethany asked, too curious to hold back.

"Oh, nothing. I'll tell you about my decision another time. Complicated reasons."

Bethany couldn't help but wonder if a woman was one of the complications. But she wouldn't go near that topic. "What will you do here—or anywhere else?"

Sloan chuckled as he lifted his shoulders and extended his hands to the side. "I don't know. It's up for grabs."

"Really?" She was now more curious than ever about Sloan.

Dear Reader,

Welcome back to Adelaide Creek, a thriving small town in Wyoming. After a long absence, Sloan Lancaster, a wealthy attorney and a veteran, is in town to see his dad at a care and rehab center. He arrives as rain is flooding the lobby, and when he jumps in to lend a hand, the first person he sees is Bethany Hoover, the person in charge of this run-down center—and Sloan's secret high school crush.

Bethany's husband has died and she's focused on raising three-year-old Heidi, along with fulfilling her vision to rescue the Winding Creek Rehab and Care Center from the neglect that led to bankruptcy. She has no time or inclination to fall in love again, but in Adelaide Creek, circumstances—and people—change. Sloan becomes a hard-to-ignore presence and Bethany's heart begins to open. Sloan's donations will help save Winding Creek, but his insistence on anonymity has unexpected consequences.

Christmas is coming. In Adelaide Creek that usually means romance is in the air. It's possible Christmas has more than one surprise in store for the familiar group of friends and family.

Sign up for my newsletter and updates at virginiamccullough.com. I hope you'll have a look at more books in this and my other Heartwarming series.

Virginia

A WYOMING FAMILY HOLIDAY

VIRGINIA McCULLOUGH

HEARTWARMING

If you purchased this book without a cover you should be aware that this book is stolen property. It was reported as "unsold and destroyed" to the publisher, and neither the author nor the publisher has received any payment for this "stripped book."

ISBN-13: 978-1-335-46021-9

A Wyoming Family Holiday

Copyright © 2025 by Virginia McCullough

All rights reserved. No part of this book may be used or reproduced in any manner whatsoever without written permission.

Without limiting the author's and publisher's exclusive rights, any unauthorized use of this publication to train generative artificial intelligence (AI) technologies is expressly prohibited.

This is a work of fiction. Names, characters, places and incidents are either the product of the author's imagination or are used fictitiously. Any resemblance to actual persons, living or dead, businesses, companies, events or locales is entirely coincidental.

For questions and comments about the quality of this book, please contact us at CustomerService@Harlequin.com.

TM and ® are trademarks of Harlequin Enterprises ULC.

Harlequin Enterprises ULC
22 Adelaide St. West, 41st Floor
Toronto, Ontario M5H 4E3, Canada
www.Harlequin.com

Printed in U.S.A.

Virginia McCullough has enjoyed a long career as an author of fiction and nonfiction books, often working behind the scenes as a ghostwriter, editor and coach. She's lived in many places and currently makes her home in Northeast Wisconsin, where she writes multigenerational romance and women's fiction. *A Wyoming Family Holiday* is the fifth book in her Back to Adelaide Creek series. Virginia's characters could be your neighbors and friends, and her stories always promise hope, healing and plenty of second chances.

Books by Virginia McCullough

Harlequin Heartwarming

Girl in the Spotlight
Something to Treasure
Love, Unexpected

Back to Bluestone River

A Family for Jason
The Christmas Kiss
A Bridge Home

Back to Adelaide Creek

Finding His Wyoming Sweetheart
The Rancher's Wyoming Twins
The Doc's Holiday Homecoming
His Wyoming Surprise

Visit the Author Profile page
at Harlequin.com for more titles.

For readers.

You inspire me to keep telling stories and will always be at the heart of my writing life.

CHAPTER ONE

SLOAN LANCASTER RAISED the hood of his jacket and raced through the downpour, skirting the water overflowing dips and deep potholes in the asphalt parking lot. This, plus the run-down brick-and-wood exterior, was all he needed to conclude that the Winding Creek Rehab and Care Center was past its prime. Especially dreary was the aging paint job, once white, but now a dull, dirty gray. Sloan summed up his first impression of this facility in one word: neglected.

As he ducked into the slow, hands-free revolving door, a commotion in the lobby caught his attention. Women and men in scrubs or lab coats were pushing and pulling furniture across the carpeted floor, while a couple of burly guys in maintenance uniforms dragged an oversize tarp into the far corner of the room where rainwater ran down the wall.

Two women a few feet in front of him struggled to pull a couch across the middle of the entrance that split the lobby into two sections. He approached from behind and called out, "Wait, let me help with that. Tell me where you want it."

A woman spun around. "Thanks. We can use the help." Her eyes opened wide in surprise. "Sloan?"

"Bethany?" He struggled to find his next words as he grasped the wooden armrest on one end. "I'd know you anywhere." It was true. She'd barely changed at all.

She pointed to the other side of the split lobby. "We're trying to get the couch over there. Out of the way for now. We'll figure out a better solution later."

Not the time to ask a lot of questions, Sloan thought, making his early-morning workouts at the gym pay off as he dragged the couch to the only empty spot on the other side of the lobby big enough to accommodate it. The space was already filled with a hodgepodge of tables and armchairs that had escaped the leaks.

Bethany pushed the couch from the other end. "I thought the voice offering help sounded familiar—a blast from the past." Her expression turned serious as she straightened up and put her hands on her hips. "You're here to see your dad, I assume. Medical transport brought him here a couple of hours ago."

Her burgundy pantsuit and crisp, tailored white shirt gave her a professional look in the style of the women lawyers at his firm. That led Sloan to guess that his high school friend Bethany Hoover was an administrator in this place, where, for better or worse, his dad was now a patient. The worn-out exterior and general disarray in the lobby weren't filling him with positive feelings about that. The opposite, in fact.

"I was surprised the hospital released my dad to another facility already." He waved toward the rain-streaked wall, his gaze traveling to water-damaged spots on the ceiling. If his dad had to be confined in a rehab facility for the next several weeks, maybe Sloan should intervene now and find a better arrangement. "It looks like you've got a situation, Bethany." He pointed to the end tables and lamps a few feet away. "Do you need help getting those out of the way?"

Bethany raised an index finger in the air, a signal for him to wait. Although a grade ahead of Bethany, Sloan had gone to school with her all the way through to his high school graduation. The way she held the attention of other staff, who stood in place, presumably waiting for directions, reinforced Sloan's sense that Bethany was now in charge.

"Thanks, everyone," Bethany called out, raising her arm to acknowledge the staff. "The roofer will be here later to assess the damage. Finish clearing the tables and lamps from that side of the lobby. The maintenance crew will keep an eye on the walls and carpet. We've done all we can for the moment."

On the outside, Bethany truly hadn't changed much over the years. Tall, with the posture of an athlete, she still carried herself with confidence. Back in high school, Sloan and his buddies had teased her about how she made an entrance. Her height added to her ability to walk into a room like she was royalty ready to address her subjects. Miss Queen they'd dubbed her when they joked around with the girls they'd grown up with. Watching her in action, Sloan concluded her ability to command a room hadn't changed over the years. Not one bit.

"Are we going to get a new roof or what?" The no-nonsense question came from a young woman in a floral nurse's top and blue scrubs. "My weather app tells me we're supposed to get even more rain later in the week."

"I know, Chloe. That's why we won't be moving the lobby furniture back in place right away. Arrange the pieces to look as neat as possible and we'll block off the leaky side so everyone can see it's off-limits." She put her palms together in front of her chest and aimed her words at every one of the dozen or so people assembled. "I appreciate your patience on this—and with everything else. But we *are* making progress."

Sloan looked on as the group of a dozen or so quickly dispersed, with a few staying behind to finish rearranging the lobby. He was more than ready to fire questions at Bethany—or someone—about his dad's condition after he'd had a stroke a couple of days ago. He'd been reassured that the stroke was deemed relatively minor, as these things went, and that there'd be a straightforward, clearly defined treatment plan. After some rehabilitation therapies, his father would likely regain his ability to walk on his own again. Even from a short phone conversation with him, Sloan had surmised, with enormous relief, that his dad's mind was as sharp as ever.

When Sloan had packed his SUV earlier that morning and started the long drive from Denver, he'd been surprised that his dad was already being transferred to the rehab center. He trusted Bethany could fill in the blanks about that.

When Bethany pivoted to face him, she wasn't smiling. Not that he'd expected her to be cheerful in the face of a badly leaking roof. But he had no trouble recalling her smile, the kind that took over her whole face. That pretty image was framed with wavy, blond, chin-length hair. But it was her distinctive light blue eyes that he remembered over any other feature. Without a doubt, she'd become the beautiful woman the teenager's face had promised.

"Thanks for waiting, Sloan, and for your help. I'll take you to your dad now." She gestured for him to follow. "The rehabilitation unit is this way."

"Uh, why don't you point me to his room, Bethany? I can take it from there," Sloan said. "Maybe we can talk later when you're not busy handling what's obviously a crisis."

"Hey, don't argue with me," she said, smiling broadly as she led him along the corridor. "Of course, I'm going to take you to Lucas. I promise you'll get the grand tour of Winding Creek later. For now, you can catch up with your dad. I'll be here if you have questions."

Sloan had plenty of questions lining up in his mind already. He didn't have to look closely to see that the exterior wasn't the only shabby part of this facility. The more he saw of it, the more he doubted this could possibly be the right place for his dad's recovery. But Bethany was an old friend, so Sloan held his tongue. For the moment.

They soon arrived at the open door of the room at the end of one of the four corridors that started at a common area behind the now chaotic and damaged lobby and housed a reception area and a patients' lounge. His dad was sitting in a large, cushioned chair near the bed. "Look who's here, Lucas," Bethany said, stepping aside to let Sloan approach.

"'Bout time you got here, Judge." His dad's wrinkled forehead matched his gruff tone and the overall picture was stern.

"Judge?" Bethany gave Sloan a pointed look. "Wow. I hadn't heard."

Sloan waved away those words and turned to his father. "Please, no Judge stuff, Dad. See? You've already confused Bethany." He met Bethany's eye. "I'm an *attorney*. Dad's only joking around, giving me what he thinks is a promotion." The usual nonsense from his dad.

"Yeah, so? You grumbled as much when I called you Ace. Nothing much changes with you."

Or Skater Boy when he was about twelve, or Sharpshooter when he played basketball, poorly. The best he could do was block shots, not make them. Then Sloan graduated to Brainiac when he took off for college. Ace came later when he flew medevacs in the army, not the more impressive and mighty fighter jets his crusty old dad thought would have given superior bragging rights.

"How about I call you Dad and you call me Sloan?" Sloan paused to stare at his dad. "A little dull, maybe, but let's give it a try."

"If you say so." His dad flashed a sly grin. "Better than Skater Boy. Since you're not a boy, maybe I'll start calling you Old Man."

"We'll see about that," Sloan said. "For now, I think I'll be the one giving you that Old Man moniker." Sloan grinned and shook his head. Enough of this. "What happened, Dad?" He gave Bethany a sidelong glance to include her in his question. "On the phone, the doctor said you had a stroke, but it didn't affect your mind at all. I can see that for myself. You're the same old grouch."

"Bum left leg is all." He used his right hand to pat his left thigh. "And maybe my left arm is a little off, too." As if he forgot, he tried to raise his arm and frowned at it, perhaps surprised it didn't respond to his force of will. "They sent me here to keep an eye on me. Gotta keep my blood thin and do some treatments that will get me up on my feet and walking again. No sense taking up space in the hospital."

"I see." Sloan noted that what his dad said was a fairly accurate summary of what the doctor had told him.

"They already rolled me in and out of those tubes they use nowadays—you know, the ones where they scan your brain looking for trouble. I swear they check my blood pressure every few minutes."

Sloan glanced at Bethany, who didn't add anything to his dad's explanation. Instead, she stepped back toward the door and gave him a nod. "I'll see you in a bit, Sloan. You can come to my office and I'll fill in a few details. But you can talk to the doctor yourself when she comes around in a couple of hours."

"Hey, I'll be the one doing the talking," Lucas insisted. "Don't need my kid asking all the questions."

Sloan didn't respond, primarily because it never made sense to argue or contradict his dad. Bethany must have agreed, because she slipped out of the room without further comment. Other than the dark circles under his eyes and his thinning head of white hair badly in need of a trim, ol' Lucas Lancaster didn't look much different than he had the last time Sloan saw him in October, exactly five years ago to the day.

His stomach lurched. That was guilt grabbing his attention. Doing the math, he realized his last trip to Adelaide Creek really was that long ago. Sloan had spent these last years paving his own path headlong into a state of burnout. Three huge and complex liability cases, a win, a loss and a win. The loss still stung. The consequences of burnout included an inability to figure out what was next for his career, or for anything else in his life. What happened to his dad handed him the perfect excuse to put aside his own concerns. They could wait for another day, or weeks, or even months. What counted now was what was next for his dad.

"Turns out you went to high school with that

Hoover girl, Bethany. You better watch out, Judge. She runs this place now," Lucas said. "She's a mother herself. I heard that from a nurse. And a widow. I don't know anything about what happened, though."

Those facts intrigued Sloan more than he cared to admit. He had to laugh at himself. High school left marks, after all. Sloan dated some, but Bethany had barely known he was alive. He could blush thinking about it, but he'd had a thing for the tall blonde girl with long legs and blue eyes. Even before her braces had given way to her perfect white teeth, he'd caught himself staring at her more than once. Must have been those mesmerizing eyes. "C'mon Dad, you need to rest. You can fill me in on the gossip later."

His dad grimaced and swatted the air. "Later? There won't be any later."

"Huh? What do you mean?"

"Now that you've seen I'm alive and kickin'... half-kickin'...you'll rev up your engines and head back to wherever you came from. Still Denver, I suppose. You haven't said otherwise." Lucas cleared his throat. "And by the way, what I said about Bethany was *news*, not gossip. Never did take to whispering about other people's problems."

Sloan stepped closer and rested his hand on his dad's shoulder. "Listen to me. I'm not going anywhere. I'm staying right here in Adelaide Creek and you're going to have to put up with me."

Ignoring Sloan's words, his dad blurted, "You remember Bridget?"

"Of course, I do. She's my cousin." Sloan rested a hip on the corner of the bed opposite his dad, making it easier to look him in the eye as they talked.

"She's been taking care of Flash. You'll have to go to her house to pick him up." Lucas narrowed his eyes in thought and scratched his cheek. "I've got lots of food in the mudroom for him."

"I'll look after him. Don't worry about Flash." A text had come in from Bridget last night about the dog, who, from photos his dad sent now and again, was a good-looking combination of collie and German shepherd. His dad had rescued Flash a few years ago, long after he'd sold his cattle to Bridget and her husband, Clint. He'd also leased some of his acres to another Lancaster relative before declaring he'd put the ranching business behind him once and for all.

Flash had replaced a border collie, also a rescue, who'd been Lucas's companion for many years. When Sloan was in the army and stationed in Texas, Afghanistan and Germany, a lot of his dad's emails had been tidbits about what that border collie was up to.

"What are you driving these days, anyway?"

"Change of subject, huh?" Sloan chuckled. "An SUV. What's it to ya, old man?"

A hint of a smile appeared. "Nothing, Judge. Had to find out if you still had a vehicle capable of handling a little snow."

"What a question." Sloan feigned an incredulous look. "You may have heard of Denver. It snows there." Smiling, he added, "I've hiked and camped up in the mountains, so you can be sure I've got the right kind of wheels." Back when he had time, he'd camped. It had been a good long while since he'd pitched his tent and enjoyed his morning coffee in the woods and let himself be mesmerized by the views of the mountains.

His dad lowered his gaze. "Good. I want to be sure you're safe driving around while you're here. Once Halloween is over, the snow could start. Maybe you forgot, but it can pile up."

The soft tone was new and brought a pinch in his chest. Even when Sloan was stationed in Afghanistan his dad had avoided any direct mention of his safety in that war zone. That would have shown a weakness Lucas Lancaster wouldn't admit to—and maybe even a deeper affection for Sloan than he was willing to reveal on the outside. "I'll be fine, Dad."

"When are you going home?"

Sloan wasn't sure how to take that. Was it fear that he was heading out in a few days or maybe

Dad worried his only kid would stay too long? "Not for a while. I'm definitely not leaving until I know you're on the mend. For real. Besides, I kinda like being in the country in the fall. October is the best month in Wyoming." It was pretty spectacular in Denver, too, but that was beside the point.

His dad waved his good arm at him. "Listen to me now, I don't want you losing your job because you stayed away too long. A man has to work. Can't be slacking off."

Sloan debated if he should tell his dad he'd taken a leave from the firm. It was an open-ended leave, more or less, so he'd have time to visit his dad for as long as needed. But he also welcomed the distance from both the city and his office. He'd use these weeks, or months, to gain clarity about his next move, but for now, he'd keep this need to himself. Sloan couldn't predict how a practical, thrifty man like his dad would react if he mentioned that money wasn't an issue. Better to stay away from that topic, at least for now. "The firm is doing fine, Dad. That means I'm free to take all the time I need."

Lucas looked past him at the open door into the hall, where a man in a white uniform lifted a tray off a cart. "I'll see how the food is and report back to you, Judge."

"We are known for our *cuisine*, Mr. Lancaster.

A little light on the salt, though." The man, who looked like he'd only recently left his teen years behind, had more to say. "My name is Andre. I'm going to be with you for a while in case you need help."

"Suit yourself, Andre," Lucas said, "but you can see I'm doing pretty good."

Thinking that he wanted to find Bethany before she left for the day, Sloan stepped out of the way. "I'm going to hunt for coffee and a sandwich."

"Go say hello to Bethany," Lucas said. "I know you, Judge. You've got lots of questions rolling around in your noggin."

The old guy could be amusing, all right. "Okay, Dad, I'll leave and let Andre put up with you. When I come back, though, you better drop the Judge stuff and call me Sloan. Mom always said you're the one who gave me that name. Start using it."

His dad looked puzzled. "Is that so? I could have sworn it was Polly who stuck you with that name. Hmm...guess it doesn't matter now." His dad gave him another sly grin. "Get outta here. I need to sample this so-called cuisine and Andre here has to earn whatever they pay him."

Sloan was halfway out the door when the sound of his name stopped him. He turned back. "What is it, Dad?"

"Wanted to tell you I'm glad you're here."

He hadn't seen that coming. He swallowed hard. "Me, too, Dad."

"But don't be fretting about hanging around. You know us. It doesn't take long before we start getting on each other's nerves."

Sloan grinned, but he didn't argue. How could he? It was the truth, and pretty much always had been. Given the look on Andre's face, though, Sloan was obligated to say something. "I'll keep that in mind, Dad." He hurried out the door before his old man had a chance to elaborate.

WITH THE RAIN still beating against the extra-wide picture window in her office, Bethany ended her call with Quincy Lancaster, her collaborator and mentor on all things related to Winding Creek. He also happened to be one of Sloan's numerous uncles. Unlike Bethany, whose relatives could fit around a table set for eight, the Lancasters were more of a clan than a family. But the call hadn't been about Quincy's much older brother Lucas, or about Sloan. She'd also decided to pass on the latest news about their grant application. Turned down again. But for today, she'd used the time with Quincy to fill in the details about the disaster in the lobby. More than her ally, he was her liaison with the governing board of Winding Creek. The board she helped to assemble and answered to.

It had been a stress-packed day, but somehow seeing an old friend lifted her spirits, or maybe Sloan reminded her that she hadn't always been a weary single mom with a demanding job. Some might call it an impossible job, made more stressful because forming a not-for-profit to take over the management of this rehab and care center had been her idea in the first place. She could blame only herself when things got tough.

With the call over, Bethany pivoted to face the window and tilted her desk chair back. She closed her eyes and let her hands hang loose over the armrests while she listened to the rain hit the windows and batter the roof. She'd always enjoyed the sound of the rain, but today it was her nemesis. She attempted to change her focus, remembering that although she was no yoga master, she'd learned the value of deep breathing. One of the benefits of having Heather as her lifelong best friend was learning new things. Heather had insisted on passing along some easy breathing exercises and insisted Bethany practice them to help her manage her considerable load of stress.

She'd reached a light meditative state when the rapping on her open office door startled her. In a split second she was upright in the chair and alert as she swiveled around to face the door.

"Sorry, Bethany, I didn't mean to...you know... break your concentration." His voice both low and slow, Sloan was studying her through his curious and super-warm brown eyes, dark brown like his thick hair, which was cut conservatively, in a style befitting a serious trial attorney.

"Come in, come in." She hadn't anticipated the quaver in her voice. She gestured to the chair. "Have a seat." Normally, running into Sloan or any of her high school friends would have been a pleasant interlude in her day. Not this time. Instead, seeing him had triggered a bad case of nerves. Probably because this was no casual encounter. It didn't take sharp observation skills to note the skepticism in Sloan's eyes when he'd glanced around the shabby rehab center. Seeing the place through his eyes brought home the magnitude of the job ahead. "Other than feisty, how did you find Lucas?"

"He's insisting he's absolutely fine, except for what he calls his bum leg," Sloan said. "I'll ask the doctor what's next for him."

"Physical therapy is next," Bethany said, her confidence making a comeback. "He'll be monitored to make sure his blood is thin and his blood pressure is under control." She filled in other blanks about his medical condition, which was surprisingly good for a man who by his own admission didn't pay much attention to when and what he ate. On the other hand, when she went to Lucas's room to greet him and ask a few questions about his life, she was glad to hear that he spent a lot of time walking the fields and woods near his house. According to Lucas himself, he and his current canine pal, and the ones who'd come before, enjoyed roaming around in all but the most extreme cold and blizzard-like conditions.

Sloan didn't seem surprised when she told him that regular checkups had never been a priority for his dad. Despite that, Lucas was fit and trim. Years of demanding ranch work and now walking had paid off, at least until now, when he was in his late seventies.

Bethany was close friends with numerous members of the extended Lancaster family, a gregarious bunch except for Lucas, who was known for keeping to himself. But he'd been talkative when his only child showed up. Sloan himself had always been a bit of a wild card. Once he'd left Adelaide Creek, he seldom visited. And two of his many cousins, Bridget and Willow, whom Bethany counted among her good women friends, rarely mentioned him.

"Lucas opened up when he saw your face." Bethany patted the tablet on her desk. "I looked at his chart before he arrived. The nurses noted he was quiet, a little withdrawn. But I saw no sign of that once you showed up."

"His mind is clicking along," Sloan said, obviously amused. "He's sharp enough to bring out a couple of the nicknames he'd made up for me—he's been doing that for as long as I can remember."

"You didn't like him calling you Judge, did you?" Bethany wanted to hear more about that from Sloan. Maybe he was testing her memory of his dad's monikers. She still winced at a memory from way back in high school when she'd heard Lucas call Sloan "sharpshooter" at a basketball game. It especially stung because Sloan had missed an outside jumper he'd been forced to take before the shot clock hit zero. As loquacious as Lucas had been with Sloan, Bethany had noted that his tone still carried some attitude. Thinking about Lucas and Sloan's past brought back her own many missed shots on the high school basketball court.

Sloan dismissed her question with a quick air swat. "Let's just say Judge is only one more sarcastic nickname he uses to needle me a little. But that's not important now."

Bethany took the hint and changed the subject. "He'll get physical therapy here for a period measured in weeks to months. Then, after he's home, he'll continue to come back for regular therapy for an as yet undetermined time. He'll learn to maneuver with a walker, then a cane. And then..." Bethany shrugged "...we'll see if he'll recover his ability to walk unaided. It's too early to say. But his release date likely will depend on him having someone who can give him the help he needs until he's able to get around completely on his own." She paused before adding, "I don't want to push, Sloan, but how long do you plan to stay? And can you hire someone when he's released?"

Sloan took a couple of seconds before answering her question. "I haven't discussed any of this with Dad yet, but my plans are open-ended. At this point, I'm not even thinking about a schedule for going back to Denver. I've handled arrangements at the firm that allow me to stay flexible and be available to my dad," Sloan said. "If he's ready to come home, but still needs more help than I can give him, I'll hire a caregiver." Sloan chuckled. "As it is, at the moment my most important job is picking up Flash, Dad's dog, from Bridget's house."

"Here's some good news. You can bring Flash here on Wednesday and Saturday afternoons." One part of Bethany's brain was on autopilot, while another part was figuring out what Sloan actually meant by open-ended plans. "We have a full unit of patients in permanent care, so we have regular animal therapy visits. Lots of people in town bring their dogs around on the designated days as part of our program. We don't need research to prove that patients perk up when they see their own canine buddies, although we have all the data we need to back up our program." She was proud of the dog visit policy she'd put in place when she took over. It was a common practice in care centers, but new to Winding Creek. It was popular with patients and their families whether they had pets of their own or not. "We have lots of activities here. You'll see."

"Really? What kinds of things, other than rehab?"

"As it happens, we're a source of community service hours for the high school students." Bethany smiled thinking about the teenagers she'd talked to on her last visit to the school. "They remind me of us back in the day. Anyway, they're coming in soon to decorate for Halloween and then on the day itself, they'll bring cookies. We don't have enough staff as it is, so we can't spare the time to do things like decorate for holidays. We take all the service hours from the teenagers we can get."

"I remember those projects in high school." The thoughtful look in Sloan's eyes led Bethany to conclude that pleasant memories had come to mind. "We might have grumbled a little about the service requirement, but it was good for us. I'm sure that's still true for kids today."

"We're having a family-style Thanksgiving here, the first one. On Christmas Eve afternoon, we'll have some Christmas caroling led by Dr. Tom, you know, your cousin Willow's husband. He's a pediatrician and his sister sings and plays fiddle with a local band. If you stick around a while, you'll eventually meet some of our hometown's newcomers."

"I think I'll start by reconnecting with Uncle Quincy and my cousins."

"That big Lancaster clan of yours is involved in most everything that goes on in Adelaide Creek." As she'd done her quick rundown of things going on at the center, Sloan's expression revealed an uptick in his interest.

When her phone buzzed, she immediately picked it up and looked at the screen. She sighed but didn't answer the call. "I was hoping that was the roofer. As you can imagine, I'm eager to find out how soon he can get started on the repairs. So far, these leaks are confined to the lobby," she said. "We haven't been forced to move patients around." She detected fatigue seeping into her voice. That wouldn't do. She shifted in her chair. If she needed to perk up her tone, she could start by throwing her shoulders back and sitting up a little straighter. That usually did the trick.

"So this is an ongoing problem?" Sloan asked. "I mean, what's the story of this place? Decorations and caroling are fine, but a leaky roof and an otherwise run-down look are kind of jarring."

Bethany's sigh came out more like a groan.

"I guess that was pretty rude, huh?"

Bethany leaned forward and plunked an elbow on the desk and rested her chin in her palm. "Let's call it frank. I was getting around to filling in some background info about Winding Creek. But just so you know, your dad had a choice. There was a room for him in a facility on the other side of the county. Admittedly, it's shiny and new, and it's also owned by a well-known chain of rehab and care centers." Bethany maintained a matter-of-fact tone and had nothing to hide. "But given a choice, Lucas decided to come here. For one thing, it's close to home, and that means it's easier for Quincy to visit, as well as Willow and Bridget. And now you."

"Why do I think there's more to the story? I remember this building from when we were kids." Sloan's forehead wrinkled in thought. "It never looked like an upscale kind of place, but wasn't an eyesore, either. By the way, if I remember correctly, you're a nurse practitioner. But according to Dad you run this place now. Is he right?"

Valid questions about Winding Creek and her. "It's a long story, but I'll give you the shorthand version. The previous owners let the place deteriorate and then go bankrupt. But we came up with a plan to salvage it, and thanks to people like your uncle Quincy, we've been able to keep it open. Our goal is to preserve it as a town—and county—resource."

Sloan tilted his head to one side and then the other as if considering this idea. "No chain of nursing care or rehab centers wanted to buy it?"

Bethany scoffed. "Oh, we could have a buyer by tomorrow morning, if we chose that route. Lots of people would write big checks to take it off our hands, including a couple of developers who want it for the acres we're sitting on. They'd raze the building and replace it with a mansion and sell it for a few million dollars."

"Right," Sloan said, nodding. "A familiar tale."

"The building may be worn-out and drab, a few walls may have cracks, but it's a stone's throw from Addie Creek." She gestured back at the window. "Walk down to the creek when it's not raining. You'll see the gorgeous fields and woods. So, sure, we could always sell it. But I—*we*—didn't want to miss a chance to try something new that could be good for the town."

"I see. This was your idea?"

Why be modest? Or on the other hand to try to deflect what could very well turn into a colossal flop. "Yep, it was my idea initially, but luckily, your uncle Quincy helped me spearhead the project. He's willing to take a risk on what he envisions as a public ownership model. Lucky for me, your uncle has the know-how to jump-start big ideas, and the personality to coax others to hop on board with us."

"So, Dad's right. You're in charge now."

She shook her head. "Not exactly. A board is in charge, but I handle the day-to-day management. I oversee patient care, which is the most important work I do. But the board hires and fires the director. For now, that's me." She gave Sloan a quick update on her degree in public health, which, along with her clinical background, added additional qualifications, at least on paper. Her office phone interrupted her when she was about to talk about the funding. It took only a couple of seconds to get the message. "That was Candace at reception. Dr. Abrams is here. She's heading to Lucas's room." She stood and picked up her handbag. "I have to go, so I'll walk you out."

Bethany stepped away from her desk and grabbed her raincoat off the hook by the door. "I'll fill you in another time about how the situation here at the center came about. Your uncle Quincy can recount the painful details of how close we came to losing this facility altogether. It's a long story." She snickered as she started toward the door. "Well, maybe it's more like an *old* story. Lack of funds."

"Sure, we'll talk another time." Sloan's expression turned serious. "What's happened to my dad is top of my mind right now, anyway."

She closed her office door behind her and she and Sloan started down the hall toward the lobby. "I'll see you soon, then. And welcome home. Lots of changes since you left."

"Uh, Bethany, a quick question. I noticed a picture of a little girl on your desk. Is she your daughter?"

"Oh, yeah, that's my Heidi. She's three, but she'll tell you she's almost four." Bethany didn't need a mirror to know that her automatic smile at the mention of Heidi had replaced the all-business expression she'd worn most of that day.

"I guessed that, of course, because she looks like you, despite her darker eyes and hair."

"She gets the red in those auburn waves from her dad's side of the family." Bethany wasn't used to explaining any of this, not anymore. "Charlie's been gone almost two years now. He was killed in an incident…an explosion…overseas." She spoke faster with every word to get through the basics. "He was on assignment doing contract intelligence work."

"Oh, I'm sorry. I shouldn't have brought it up," Sloan said.

"You didn't," Bethany said, slipping into her coat. "I did. Losing Charlie was awful, but I will always have Heidi." Suddenly, talking about Charlie, his work, and how he died so young brought on a heaviness that enveloped her like a shroud. Feeling weighed down, she needed to escape. She picked up the pace to the lobby, where she gave Sloan a quick wave goodbye. "I'll check in on your dad first thing in the morning."

She didn't wait for a response but hurried out to her car in the employee lot. After starting the engine, she reached for the phone in her handbag and without stopping to mull over her decision, she sent a text to Heather canceling their dinner at the Tall Tale Lodge. Bethany wouldn't get away with that quick text, though. Heather, her best friend since before kindergarten, would call her later and demand to know the reason she'd backed out. At least she wasn't leaving Heather in the lurch. A few other friends would be there for what had become a once-a-month women's meetup, almost always held at Tall Tale.

Heather's immediate response was a text with nothing but a row of sad face emojis. Bethany called her mom next. She explained that since she wasn't going out to dinner as planned, she could pick up Heidi in a few minutes.

"Uh, I see." Her mom spoke in a hesitant tone. "Why don't you let her stay here as planned, sweetie? We're just about to sit down to have our mac 'n' cheese dinner." Her mother chuckled. "You know it's Heidi's favorite."

Bethany couldn't argue with that. It was everybody's favorite. "Okay, I'll wait until after she's had her dinner. I need to pick up groceries anyway."

Silence. Then, "Uh, I meant let's go with the original plan." Her mom was no longer tentative. "I know what your days have been like recently. And your dad promised Heidi he'd play the new alphabet game with her after dinner."

Right as usual, her mom. They'd worked out a system and Heidi knew what to expect after preschool and on the few evenings or weekend days when Bethany made other plans. Her parents had fixed up Bethany's childhood bedroom and Heidi looked forward to a sleepover with Grandma and Grandpa. She couldn't deny that an evening of solitude had some appeal. Bethany shouldn't feel guilty about that, but she did, as if she was shirking mom duty.

"Okay, Mom, you're right," she said. "I'll go on to the market. But I thought it would be easier for you if I took Heidi home."

"Not really. Your dad and I like our routines with Heidi, and she likes her time with us." She paused. "Come down and have breakfast with us in the morning. I was going to make the blueberry waffles she likes, anyway. Then you can drive her to preschool from here."

"Sounds good, Mom. Give her a kiss for me." Bethany ended the call, accepting that her mother had wisely discouraged her first impulse to disrupt a plan already in place. Heidi might not have a dad, but she had doting grandparents.

Bethany rested her head on the back of the seat, relieved the rain had let up to a light drizzle. A hint of regret seeped in about canceling her plans with Heather and the others, but it didn't last. She was bone-tired after her day. It didn't help that the handsome and apparently successful son of a new patient had walked in on such a mess. Maybe it was good that Sloan wasn't a stranger, or it could be that it was easier to be more vocal with an old friend about expecting better for his dad.

As she sat in the car reviewing all that had happened that day, the roofer texted. He'd stop by the center that evening to assess the damage and be back early in the morning to talk to her about the logistics—and the cost—of repairs. One more item she could stop thinking about. Somehow, the day was drawing to a close whether she'd accomplished all she'd wanted to or not. After her abbreviated explanation to Sloan about what happened to Charlie, she was having a hard time shaking him from her mind.

After Charlie died, her parents, who had busy lives of their own, had showered her and their only grandchild with attention and the support needed to endure those awful early days and weeks. Disbelief came first, followed by Bethany's profound, paralyzing grief. She and Charlie had been hoping for a second child. It was supposed to have been his last overseas assignment and he'd already taken himself off the rotation schedule. Instead, he'd decided to push the company for assignments that allowed him to work from home all the time. If the contracting company had objected, he'd have changed jobs, or even careers.

Bethany steered toward the market on Merchant Street, her thoughts drifting to the little bungalow in town she and Charlie had bought right before they were married. Not wanting to live in it anymore without him, she'd packed up some favorite things and moved back to the bunkhouse on her parents' once-large sheep ranch. For the last many years, her mother had kept only a couple of dozen sheep and made a name for herself as a wool supplier and spinner for the fiber arts market. After college and nurse practitioner school, Bethany had moved into the bunkhouse, which her parents had converted into a two-bedroom cottage. It sat about a quarter mile behind her parents' farmhouse and offered spectacular views of the ridges and mountains and deep woods in the back.

Bethany approached the center of town, but on impulse she made a couple of turns and ended up on O'Malley Street, where she soon found herself in front of the little place she and Charlie had once called home. She got out of the car and stared at the now vacant house. "Hey, Charlie. Here I am, thinking of you and our life together. Our bungalow is dark now, but your parents will be here in a few weeks. Ed and Cheri like staying here—like us, they like it because it's small, cozy."

Not quite two years had passed, but it seemed her life with Charlie had taken place in another era. She could almost hear Charlie teasing her a little about moving from one compact nest back to the bunkhouse, which also fit that description. She and Charlie considered it their country house, a place to have picnics and watch the sun set.

With Charlie gone, it seemed only natural that she'd go back there with Heidi and live closer to her parents. They helped Bethany out with dropping off and picking up routines for Heidi, but they also had outings and sleepovers that helped Bethany build the sense of security for Heidi that came with having family nearby. Bethany had made a conscious choice to change her life. If she hadn't, her grief for Charlie had posed a risk of becoming chronic. For Heidi's sake she couldn't let that happen.

At the same time, the safest path forward was to maintain the status quo. She was single and the two grandpas would be the important men in Heidi's life. Bethany couldn't see herself falling in love and marrying again—ever. Out of the question. She'd been lucky enough to find that kind of happiness once, and that would have to be enough.

Leaving her job at the hospital and permanently moving out of the bungalow had been concrete steps in the direction of healing and stabilizing. "We were happy in our little nest, Charlie," she whispered, "a lifetime ago."

CHAPTER TWO

BETHANY WAVED AT the familiar checkout clerk and filled her cart with the staples that kept Heidi, and her, well-nourished, but not bogged down in the kitchen. The market had delicious take-out dishes, the main reason Bethany gave it rave reviews, especially the market special and family favorite, mac 'n' cheese. As always, Bethany made room in her cart for an extra container for her parents. She bought a thick turkey-on-rye sandwich from the deli. That would be her dinner, along with a container of the market's coleslaw and a giant package of homemade pub chips that would last the week.

By the time Bethany got back to the bunkhouse, some of the bad and frantic feelings about the mini-flood had faded. She even patted herself on the back for the way she'd handled it, confidently and with a take-charge attitude. With that sense of satisfaction she arranged her food on a tray and carried it to the couch in the newly added family room. Finally admitting that the bunkhouse was a tad *too* cozy to be a permanent home for her and Heidi, she'd paid for an addition to create more open space, along with large bay windows on either side of a second fireplace. It meant an expanded living room, and the new windows added so much light she'd taken to calling the addition her solarium family room.

She tuned into the local weather report on TV and as she munched her sandwich and chips she absorbed the bad news about the weather. Normally, she'd welcome the autumn rains as needed to replenish the earth after the summer drought. But the roofers couldn't start temporary repairs in pouring rain. Patching the walls would be futile until the roof was secure and ready for whatever Mother Nature delivered next.

She'd finished her dinner and had taken a few bites of a saucer-size oatmeal cookie when her phone grabbed her attention. Heather. Of course, Heather. She immediately muted the TV and answered the call. "I know, I know, but canceling was a last-minute decision."

"You were missed," Heather said bluntly. "We all wanted to see you, so why did you back out?"

Bethany transferred the tray from her lap to the coffee table and curled her legs under her. "I was so down over what happened today. The roof is leaking badly—"

"At the *bunkhouse*?"

"No, at Winding Creek." She filled in the details about the problem and the solution. "We hope the repairs will last through the winter, but come spring, we'll need a new roof, full or partial." She described the flurry of moving the furniture from one side of the lobby to the other.

Heather groaned. "I'm so sorry to hear that. That kind of damage can be distracting. It risks detracting from what you're doing to give that place a new lease on life."

"Which Sloan Lancaster pointed out—the look of the center, I mean."

"Oh, right. Sloan is back. Willow mentioned that when she told me about her uncle Lucas's stroke. Her dad is keeping her posted."

"Quincy and I talk almost every day. He's the one who contacted Sloan." She let out a frustrated groan. "He drove in from Denver and arrived in the midst of the mess, but in time to help us move a heavy couch out of the way."

"Do you think that because of what he walked into he'll arrange to transfer his dad to another rehab facility before he heads home?"

"I suppose that remains to be seen. Sloan didn't mince words. He came right out and asked if I thought he should move him," Bethany said. "But Lucas himself chose to come to Winding Creek for his rehab. He wants to be close to home. Sloan is staying in his house. He'll take care of Flash, Lucas's dog."

"But for how long?" Heather asked.

Sloan had mentioned his lack of firm plans, but he'd spoken in confidence, so she wouldn't repeat what he'd said. "We didn't talk for that long. He only arrived a few hours ago, so I doubt he's finalized anything."

"So our old pal's homecoming happened in the middle of a downpour, huh?"

"And when he walked inside his first impression included me and the staff in a frenzy. You know, burly guys pulling tarps, and the rest of us dragging lobby furniture across the carpet. That's why he jumped in to help. Then he wondered how I happened to be in charge, so I gave him the short version of trying to save Winding Creek." Bethany sighed. "Sloan was curious and blunt about the dismal conditions—the cosmetic stuff. But it doesn't follow that he'll want to move his dad."

"Probably not." Heather chuckled. "I always knew Sloan was kinda sweet on you. If he moves Lucas, he won't see you."

"Me? Oh, please, way back then I thought he was out of my league. You know, a year older, an athlete, *and* smart." Not to mention his thick dark hair, which, along with his height, were signature Lancaster traits.

"What are you talking about?" Heather said with a snicker. "The tall skinny kid played basketball on the varsity boys' team. You played on the varsity girls' team. Yes, the cute guy was smart, but no smarter than you."

Bethany groaned. "I played basketball because I was the tallest girl in the class. Turned out I wasn't especially good at it."

Heather snorted. "Ha! Neither was Sloan. Remember? We used to joke that he couldn't manage a free throw to save his life, let alone make a shot from the floor. But there weren't many six-foot-plus boys. Hmm... I think your would-be romance with Sloan was thwarted by teenage shyness." In a teasing voice she added, "Can't be because of looks. You're gorgeous, and well... so is he!"

"Oh, stop," Bethany said, laughing at her best friend's assessment—and hyperbole. Putting good looks aside, Heather was right about the basketball skills, hers and Sloan's. Sloan was a few inches over six feet tall, for all the good it did him on the court. He could block a shot now and again, but his biggest skill had been deftly passing the ball to players who actually made shots and scored points. "I've told you the story of my day, now tell me how you are. How's the baby bump?"

"Growing a little every day, or so it seems,"

Heather said. "And like clockwork, I feel yucky around six a.m., but it passes and I'm okay the rest of the day. Until I lose steam and crash."

"Sounds about right. Between being a mom, a sheep rancher and seeing kids all day at Dr. Tom's office, you need R and R at the end of the day." Bethany accepted that she could be simultaneously happy for Heather, but green with envy over her pregnancy. Heather and Matt were already raising his late sister's twins, a boy and a girl who'd recently turned nine. Now the two were adding their own child to the family.

Heather and her brother, Jeff, had struggled through some hard times, including the loss of both parents and their ranch when they were still in their twenties. Bethany had been thrilled when her best friend had fallen in love with Matt, who'd been Charlie's best man at their summer wedding in her parents' front yard. No one had done more to help and support Bethany after Charlie's death than Heather and Matt. But the green-eyed monster still managed to pop up and taunt Bethany now and again. She'd really wanted another child.

"I've been sitting in the lodge's parking lot all this time, but I've got to get myself on the road and head home," Heather said. "Tell Sloan I said hello."

"I will. If he's sticking around for…uh…more than a few days, you'll run into him," Bethany said. "He'll probably be in touch with your brother. As I recall, Sloan and Jeff were pretty tight."

"I suppose, but once Sloan left, he was really gone. He even kept his distance from his Lancaster relatives," Heather pointed out. "Kind of odd for that family. What's the story? I can't help but wonder."

At the moment, Bethany had no comment, but she had a feeling that whatever the reason for Sloan's loose ties with Adelaide Creek and the people he grew up with, his dad was likely a pivotal part of the story.

SLOAN WAS DONE skirting the issue. Small talk wasn't his style, and it didn't fit Uncle Quincy, either. "It appears you have a stake in this place," he said to Quincy as a preamble. "Still, be honest with me. Do you think I should move Dad to another facility? Do *you* think he'd be better off in that newer place across the county? It's likely the rehab equipment is more up-to-date."

Quincy pushed the cafeteria tray aside and gestured around the room. "Let's be clear. I have no *financial* stake in Winding Creek, if that's what you were implying."

"Okay, okay, bad choice of words," Sloan said, leaning back in his chair.

"That's not a mere detail," Quincy said. "We've

done mountains of legal paperwork to create a not-for-profit so we can buy ourselves a couple of years to turn this place around." In a softer voice, he added, "And under the same circumstances as my brother, I'd rather be here than over an hour away. That new place is closer to the Utah border than to Adelaide Creek. And another facility in the county is full—it almost always is. That's why we need Winding Creek."

Sloan raised his hands in surrender. "Okay, got it. And Bethany told me I can bring Flash for visits. That's likely all my dad needs to hear."

Quincy gave the table a determined pat. "Don't judge this particular book by its cover."

"Point taken, Uncle Quincy. I'm concerned, that's all." Maybe the center was a touchy subject for his uncle, but Sloan had no intention of backing down. For one thing, who, besides Bethany, were included in the "we" and the "ourselves" Quincy referred to?

"You won't find better staff anywhere," Quincy continued. "The place might appear old and neglected, but I've done the research and our rehab equipment is state-of-the-art. That was a nonnegotiable item for Bethany when she took over."

Sloan stood corrected. "Okay." He hesitated a couple of seconds, but then decided to satisfy his curiosity. "Speaking of staff, is it true that you and Bethany came up with the idea of preserving Winding Creek?"

"If that's what Bethany implied, she's being modest. *She* came to me with the idea of forming a not-for-profit to take it over. We didn't know if it was even possible. Her biggest concern was that the building would be bought and torn down, and our chance to save it would be gone forever." Quincy frowned. "I'd been preoccupied with other projects for a couple of years, so I hadn't been paying attention to the deteriorating conditions. But since Bethany worked in the orthopedics department at the hospital, she had better information about the state of rehab facilities around here, including this one. She wasn't surprised when the rumors became a reality and the owners declared bankruptcy."

Narrowing his eyes in thought, Quincy leaned back in the chair. "Bethany is a lot like you in some ways, Sloan. Good ways. She's idealistic and has excellent instincts. Unapologetically ambitious, too. She likes to see the possibilities in things, same as you."

"You flatter me, Uncle Quincy."

"Not really. I happen to know a fact or two about you. First, you've used your law degree to take on cases other firms wouldn't touch. A couple of those cases made national news."

"And I've done very well in the process," Sloan

said, to deflect any outsized notion of generosity. "Our firm takes risks, but most have paid off handsomely."

Quincy shrugged. "Okay, fair enough. But you flew medevacs in Afghanistan. If I'm not mistaken, that's a job that carries some risk."

Sloan conceded the point. "I was lucky."

"Well, Bethany had a vision of what could be good for Adelaide Creek. She gave up a secure job to make it a reality."

"And you backed her," Sloan said. "Maybe I get my idealist streak from you."

"Maybe so," Quincy conceded. "In this case, though, when you boil the vision down, it's simple. With a population closing in on five hundred fifty, the town's growth streak of the last few years shows no sign of slowing down. That's primarily important because the same trend is occurring for the even smaller surrounding towns. More people means we need more rehab and nursing care facilities. Having one of the few available places collapse into bankruptcy delivered a blow.

"Fortunately, we got ourselves a board and were able to keep Winding Creek's doors open without interrupting patient care. As Bethany constantly reminds us, we could also use more affordable independent and assisted living setups. As it is, many people have to drive a couple of hours to see their family members in care centers."

"Isn't that why national chains are eager to buy a place like Winding Creek?" Sloan asked. "Those corporations pay big bucks to track population growth—and trends." Sloan chuckled. "By the way, speaking of growth, in his typically grumpy tone, Dad told me he doesn't even recognize some of the folks he sees at the market. Like it's an affront."

Quincy rolled his eyes. "That sounds like my big brother. But the good news about Adelaide Creek's growth has been the way it's thriving. Exactly why Bethany came to me with her idea." Quincy started to elaborate but something across the cafeteria caught his attention. "Hang on a minute, Sloan. A friend of mine is waving to me from the coffee machine. I'll go see what he wants."

Sloan took advantage of Quincy's absence to consider his surroundings, along with his uncle's words about Bethany. Sloan gave her credit for knowing exactly who to go to with her idea. Unlike the more taciturn Lucas, Quincy was one of the public Lancasters, immersed in community affairs, gregarious and well thought of in town. It was sad, Sloan thought, that people new to Adelaide Creek probably never heard of Lucas Lancaster, once a successful cattle rancher. Today, if known at all, he'd be described as semi-reclusive and stingy with smiles and greetings. Only a few old friends and some family would see through the tough hide Lucas showed on the outside. Even Sloan had a hard time remembering that on the rare occasions when his dad chose to show it, he had another side that was more like velvety soft leather.

Glancing around Winding Creek's cafeteria, Sloan had to admit that *old* and *plain* were words that best described the space. On the other hand, the plate of beef stew and homemade rolls he'd had for lunch with Quincy was as good or better than what he'd pay top dollar for at a high-end Denver restaurant. According to Quincy, in the spirit of encouraging public service, Bethany had lured a chef from one of the better restaurants in Landrum to consult with the dietician and kitchen staff about bumping up the quality while not increasing the budget. Excellent decision.

After Quincy came back to the table, the two of them carried their trays to the kitchen's receiving window. A smiling young woman thanked them and whisked away their dirty dishes. "The place has a friendly energy, Quincy, and I'll give the cafeteria's stew five stars."

"Glad you noticed. We're starting a fund to raise money for a new roof, by the way. We have some cash reserves we could use, but that money was supposed to be set aside for general repairs and to spruce up the place."

"How much do you need?" Sloan blurted as they started walking down the hall.

"Don't have a final figure, but many thousands of dollars, even after insurance." Quincy grinned. "Why? You want to make a contribution?"

Now was as good a time as any, Sloan thought. "I might be able to help out. But first, tell me how you plan to raise money. Are there big donors around?"

Quincy's scrutinizing expression left no doubt that he took Sloan's questions seriously. "Matter of fact, we're starting in a couple of days at Harvest Saturday in Landrum. We have the mayor and the town council in a tent to promote Adelaide Creek itself and our events, things like Spring Fling and our annual Holiday Market on Merchant Street. This year, we'll add information about Winding Creek in our booth. The major health network in the county also has our information, and since Willow runs the Tall Tale Lodge booth, we're covered there."

"Sounds like you're talking about donation jars." To Sloan, that sounded like a small and likely slow-as-molasses way to raise thousands of dollars.

"That's the quickest thing we can do to kick-start the new roof project. We don't have the final estimate yet, and work won't start until spring, but we need to launch the campaign now." Quincy dropped into the technical side about insurance and riders that involved the roof. "The board met online for a quick vote to give Bethany the green light to arrange emergency repairs. We have to get through the winter."

Sloan mulled over his decision, but not for long. "Go ahead and pass the word that an anonymous donor will pay for the emergency repairs." He and Quincy were alone in the corridor, but Sloan kept his voice low, anyway. He could add some money to start the funding for the new roof. "Then you won't need to deplete what you put aside to spruce things up a little."

"You're serious?" Quincy stopped walking, his expression showing both surprise and curiosity. "You can do that without, oh, I don't know, checking with your accountant?"

Sloan nodded but ignored what he chose to treat as a rhetorical question. "Keep it between us, Quincy. I haven't talked about this with my dad or anyone, but like I said, the firm took on big, complex product liability cases in the last few years. With sizable settlements. Plus, we had a few smaller cases that went our way. So, yes, I can do this." Sloan left it at that. Other ideas about using his money to do some good could wait.

"Do we need a bigger conversation about Winding Creek and what you're prepared to do?" Quincy asked when they reached the lobby. "I mean, a few minutes ago you asked me if you should move your dad."

Quincy was so positive about Winding Creek that Sloan had decided to put aside his concerns and keep his dad close to home. Besides, it was clear Lucas was sharp and could make his own decisions about where he'd land. "We can talk about that later. I'll be here a while, so we'll have time." Sloan took a minute to gather his thoughts. "Nothing is wrong with Dad's mind, so who am I to interfere with what he wants? Besides, his dog is everything to him. Meanwhile, go ahead and put Bethany's mind at ease about the repairs. And your board, of course."

Quincy stopped walking again. "You're sure?"

"I'm sure. But maintaining my anonymity is my only condition. Not a word to anyone." Sloan had to laugh at how quickly he'd acted, but no matter how long between his visits or how distant he was from his dad, this little dot on a map was his hometown and family was family. "What can I say? Maybe I'm warming up to the big picture of what you and Bethany have in mind." He put his hand on Quincy's arm. "Also a conversation for another day."

"Definitely," Quincy said, his eyes widening. "I'll keep your name out of everything."

"Good. That's all I want." Sloan would bet his uncle was planning to open his own checkbook for the cause, but he probably hadn't expected his nephew to do the same.

"Okay, then, don't forget to bring Flash around on pet day," Quincy said as he turned in the direction of Bethany's office.

Sloan wished he had an excuse to stop by Bethany's office. Odd thought. But he couldn't deny she'd been on his mind. "I won't, Quincy. I'm going to check out Harvest Saturday and then bring the dog here."

Quincy smiled. "Lucas will perk right up the minute he sees Flash. You wait and see."

"I hope so," Sloan said. "So far, he's been all about lobbing lame jokes and barbs at me."

"Give it time, Sloan. My big brother has been keeping to himself more and more every year. Being here now, he has to interact with other people. And that might be the good thing that comes out of all of this." Quincy pointed down the hall. "I better go. I need to tell Bethany about the *anonymous* donation to cover roof repairs. That's one less thing for her to worry about."

Sloan left the building thinking about the tunnel vision he'd had during his cases, and in the army and in law school before he joined the young firm. He'd been admired, but was considered a little on the brash side. Laser focus was great when preparing for the next deposition or methodically absorbing critical data gleaned from hundreds of pages of research, and especially when writing opening and closing statements. However, his years of tunnel vision had, unfortunately, left him out of touch not only with his family, but even with what friends he'd had outside of work.

He hoped Bethany had someone, or many people, other than her little girl, who could break through her shell when a to-do list and unanswered questions consumed her. His train of thought led him to think about Lonnie, one of the few people who could coax him out of the tunnel and remind him there was more to life than a case. He missed her. He owed her a call—one day soon.

CHAPTER THREE

BETHANY EXTENDED TWO fingers of her hand to Heidi. "Take my fingers, sweetie, and hold on tight."

"Do I *have* to?"

Thankfully, Heidi's tone fell short of a whine. Bethany ordinarily liked her daughter's Miss Independent act, but not in the midst of the hordes of people wandering around the Harvest Saturday event. Downtown Landrum was overrun with visitors enjoying the reprieve in the weather. Nature had provided an overcast but rain-free day, unseasonably warm, too.

"Absolutely. I'm not turning you loose." Too many people, too easy to get lost. "Come on, we promised to help Grandma Jen in her tent." That happened to be one of Bethany's favorite things to do, made even better because being around her mom's wool and herbs bore no resemblance to orthopedic nursing, managing a staff, or squeezing spare dollars out of a tight budget.

"O…kay." Heidi wrapped her hand around

Bethany's fingers and they navigated left and then right and then left again around clusters of people. When they closed in on the Cold Country Wool tent, Heidi shouted, "Hi, Grandma!"

Jen spun around at the sound of her name, her face was already bright and happy. Bethany enjoyed her instant shot of pleasure in the way Heidi's voice never failed to bring the same response from Grandma Jen. "I've been expecting you," Jen said, "and I'm going to put you to work." She glanced at Bethany. "I thought she could sit on the end of the counter and help us give away my brochures."

"You have a donation jar?" Bethany asked, surprised at the sight of a glass gallon jug on the folding counter her mother set up at fairs. She hadn't yet had a chance to tell her parents about the plan to fund a new roof, or about the anonymous donor. "Wow, Quincy and the board got this project underway so fast." And it happened without the need for her to be involved in the rush of planning.

"Quincy was here earlier to give us the jars. And these." Her mom handed her the sheet that explained what the fund was for. Quincy had added a band around the jug that said: ADD YOUR DOLLARS AND PUT A NEW ROOF OVER OUR RESIDENTS' HEADS!

Bethany approved. "Nice. And to the point."

"Do you think the so-called anonymous donor is Quincy himself?" Jen asked in a low voice.

"I'm not sure how widely the repair issue is known outside of the board," Bethany said. "Of course, he refused to name the person, but I wouldn't be surprised if your hunch is right and it's Quincy. In fact, I more or less assume it."

"I had a hot dog, Grandma Jen," Heidi interjected.

"No kidding? Was it good?" With that quick change of subject, Jen motioned for Heidi and Bethany to come around the counter and into the tent, while Heidi added her accolades about mustard and pickles.

Her mom's company, Cold Country Wool, was a familiar sight at town and county events. Jen Hoover's wool, along with her herb blends and teas, drew lots of attention—and many repeat customers. At the moment, half a dozen women were deep in her tent going through baskets filled with wool from her Shetland and Icelandic sheep. Two customers were ready to check out and Bethany stepped in to take over that job.

Bethany soon fell into a rhythm of straightening the stock and chatting with customers as she bagged their purchases in her mother's distinctive shopping bags stamped with her logo, two sheep and the outline of mountain peaks behind them. Bethany had known many of these shoppers most of her life. Even Heidi was starting to recognize people she'd regularly see around town at festivals and other events. Pediatrician Dr. Tom had described Heidi as strong on verbal skills. He'd said it with a teasing drawl, obviously using doctor language for what Bethany and her parents called Heidi, a chatterbox.

Watching her three-year-old sitting on the table swinging her legs and pointing to the picture on the brochure showing her Grandma Jen and her sheep, Bethany relaxed into a moment of uncomplicated pleasure.

The time in the booth passed quickly, but during a lull, Bethany stepped back and listened to the tinny carnival music coming from the carousel. She watched the turn of the Ferris wheel that towered above everything else on the far edge of the square. The mixed aromas of burgers and hot dogs, pizza and barbecued ribs competed with her mother's lavender sachets and the dried herbs tied in bunches, items that were her mother's top sellers.

Then, absorbed in filling a basket with the raw wool from the Icelandic sheep, she was jolted by her mother's sharp voice calling her name. "What is it, Mom?"

"Come up to the front, honey. A man named Andre from Winding Creek wants to see you."

Must be important. She'd staffed Winding Creek's

section of the town's tent with employees equipped to answer questions about the center's current status, with an emphasis on the positive features, and the funds needed. Bethany caught Andre's eye and waved him toward her and into the narrow space between her mom's booth and the next one in the line.

"You need to come with me, Bethany," Andre said. "A couple of guys are hanging around the booth. They're trying to persuade the new mayor that Adelaide Creek would be better off with their company in charge of the center."

Bethany smiled to herself. Alice Buckley, the former mayor, had joined Winding Creek's board as soon as her term was over. She'd warned Bethany and the other board members that private companies would try to court the town council and the center's employees. Starting with the new mayor, Zoe Lerner, made sense. Bethany turned to her mom, whose amusing shoo-shoo gestures were not ambiguous. No words needed.

"I'll be right back, Heidi." She and Andre hurried down the block-long row of tents. She took a look at her forest green blazer and slim black jeans. She'd chosen her good boots. Casual professional, the right image for a Saturday fair, whether helping her mom or being the face of Winding Creek.

"It was getting tense," Andre said. "Mayor Zoe was trying to stay friendly and hoped they'd move along. But they stayed put and kept asking a string of questions she couldn't answer—or wouldn't address."

"I get it. It's okay." When they reached the town's tent, Bethany nodded to Zoe as she approached the two men around her age, late thirties or so, and introduced herself. "I'm the director of Winding Creek. What can I do for you?"

One of the men, classically handsome and dressed in a buttoned-up kind of style, handed her his business card. Todd Webber, of the Ashley Group, headquartered in Oregon. "I don't believe I've had the pleasure of meeting you, Ms. Hoover."

"I think you're right, but why are you here today?" She adopted a neutral and professional tone and dipped her chin to acknowledge the other man, who stood silent.

"We're getting a feel for the town." Todd nodded to the donation jar, filled with many singles and fives, and a couple of $10 bills, along with a layer of loose change. "I see you're raising funds for a roof. How's that going?"

"Very well, thanks," she said, wishing there was a way to subtly mention the anonymous donor. On the other hand, the less she engaged, the better. These weren't bad or evil guys, she reminded herself. They had their jobs, and she had hers. If her vision for Winding Creek failed, then Todd himself could end up being her employer.

"You know, if the Ashley Group were in charge, you wouldn't need to waste your valuable time raising funds," Todd said. "We'd immediately put our resources into updates and repairs."

Bethany eyed Zoe, who was observing the scene from a few feet away. She was trying not to be obvious about it, but her deep frown put her concerns on full display. The recently sworn-in mayor certainly didn't want a public argument at a crowded autumn festival, which was always a fun family event. Fine. Bethany had no intention of starting a ruckus.

"But, Todd, you're not in charge." The arc of her arm included Mayor Zoe and the new town council member, Eve Bennett, an attorney in town. She'd taken Quincy's place on the council when his term was up. "Adelaide Creek's town council and the board governing Winding Creek are making the decisions now."

Todd held a quizzical stare when he spoke. "What are they paying you?"

Bethany gave him what she hoped was an unmistakably withering look. Todd couldn't possibly expect an answer to such an inappropriate question. In public no less.

"Whatever number you'd give me, I'm sure we could do better." Todd pointed to Andre and another employee, a night shift nurse at Winding Creek. "That goes for all the employees. Ask around. We're known for our outstanding employee relations."

"This isn't the time or place for this discussion," Bethany said, "but you already know that. I suggest you make an appointment with the board or attend the next town council meeting. State your case. See what happens. I never miss the monthly meetings myself."

"Eventually, everyone in this business of serving an aging population learns that it's all about funding," Todd said, widening his stance. "Profit and loss. A cold reality. Annoying perhaps, but no less real."

"Why don't you enjoy the festival?" Bethany inhaled deeply as if taking in the scents surrounding them. "Get yourself some barbecue—it's the best in the state."

"Like I said, Ms. Hoover, it all comes down to profit and loss."

Bethany backed away, her body language making it clear the conversation was over. Suddenly, a familiar voice came from behind her. "Hey, Bethany, got a minute?"

She turned to see Sloan with a big smile on his face. He held two giant orange-and-green, pumpkin-shaped cookies in each hand.

"As a matter of fact, I do," Bethany called out, nodding to the staff and to Zoe and Eve. "Thanks, everyone." Looking at Sloan, she picked up the donation jar from the counter and shook it to rattle the change. "Not bad for day one, huh?"

SLOAN CHUCKLED WHEN Bethany held up the jar and flashed a self-satisfied smile. The way that guy and his sidekick were slinking away amused him, too.

"Nice diversion, Sloan." Bethany tilted her head in the direction of his hands. "I assume you're offering me one of those cookies as part of your rescue scheme. Saving me from a potential argument, are you?"

"You were holding your own. No rescue needed. But the cookies are for you, your daughter and your mom," Sloan said, "and one for me. I had a friendly chat with your family and thought they might enjoy one of these giant cookies. I'm heading back to them now."

"Oh, really. Then you know Mom remembers you—the lanky, basketball guy."

"Whose claim to fame was blocking a shot now and then."

"Hey, that was *my* talent," Bethany quipped. "Don't mess with my only skill on the court. Any...*way*, I feel like I abandoned my mom."

"I think your daughter is entertaining the customers in line." He glanced around at the people coming and going from the town's tent. "I wouldn't worry."

Bethany explained how she happened to end up talking to Todd. "Andre thought if I came around and introduced myself, the two guys would move on. Turns out he was right."

"You can probably expect a lot more sales pitches—visits, phone calls, letters." Sloan held out one hand. "Here, take these two cookies. Let's deliver them to your mom and your cute little girl."

"Did she talk your ear off?"

"What? Are you kidding? If she put her mind to it, she could talk me into taking up a new hobby, spinning wool." The laughter in Sloan's voice showed how much Heidi had amused him. "Being a stranger, though, I kept my distance from her until your mom formally introduced us." The child so closely resembled Bethany, down to the charming way she talked with her hands. "Besides, she was busy educating a couple of people about the two kinds of sheep who give her grandma wool."

Bethany's face lit up. "That's my girl."

"Heidi is quite the storyteller," Sloan said, "and very entertaining."

"And she loves cookies, especially ones with thick frosting."

As they made their way to Cold Country Wool, Sloan took in what was going on around him. Adults pushed strollers or carried babies in slings or back carriers through the line of tents. The whistle of the kiddie train sounded in the distance, and the aromas of barbecue and funnel cake and popcorn permeated the air.

One tent sold handmade wooden stools and small tables, and the one next door featured leather belts and vests. A couple of jewelers had what Sloan guessed as hundreds of pairs of earrings on display between them, some made from Wyoming's grayish green jade. In the Tall Tale Lodge tent, Willow and others were talking up the spa services and the regular entertainment the place offered. And one row of tents featured the farmer's market regulars.

"Look at my cousin," Sloan said, nodding toward Willow. "I'm told she's a real PR pro. When I stopped by to say hello, she was handing out postcards about Tall Tale's Halloween parties. Plural. One for the kids on Halloween, and another one in the restaurant-bar on the weekend with costumes and music for their regular customers. Sounds like fun." Sloan chuckled. "She's got a lot of enthusiasm, too. And she's mighty proud of the nearly full donation jar." He was curious about the amount of money this one fundraising event would bring in. Maybe he'd underestimated the crowd's response.

"I'm not surprised. Willow, Bridget and I are really good friends, so I see Willow often. She's the voice of Tall Tale Lodge, and don't forget the spa part."

"I can see she's good at it," Sloan said, watching his cousin, animated and happy as she spoke with a couple of visitors.

"Heather and I joined the book club your cousins are a part of, and we have a women's dinner once a month. And Willow arranges discounted spa days for us, too." Bethany sighed. "I'll never forget the way Willow and Bridget rallied around me when Charlie died. They were amazing."

"I'm glad to hear that. With your little girl still a baby, it must have been hard." Now that he was here, Sloan was hit by the reality that although he'd rarely thought about Willow or Bridget over the years, he was proud to call them family.

"Yes, it was a terrible shock," Bethany said. "I had many dark days."

Intrigued. That was one word for his reaction to seeing Bethany again after so many years. In only the few days he'd been in town, he'd seen her many demeanors. Upset about the water damage, but professional, directing other people, defending Winding Creek's quality rehab services. She'd given his dad a warm welcome, and her face beamed when she talked about her child. That was only a start. When she spoke to him or to anyone else, he'd noted she always looked the other person directly in the eye. All that put together explained why his uncle Quincy had deep faith in her.

"So much has changed," Sloan said, his tone unintentionally wistful. "Like Adelaide Creek, Landrum is growing and looking good. This October festival is at least twice the size of the ones I remember."

"You've been gone a long time, Sloan." She scanned the busy scene in front of them. "Haven't you missed any of this?"

Missed it? It rarely crossed his mind. "Nah, not really."

"Whoa. Don't hold back, Sloan." Bethany snickered. "You didn't even need to think about your answer. Are you always this blunt?"

"Uh, you expected a different response? I haven't been back for five years, and that was more or less a drive-by visit." Once he'd left for college he'd never considered, not for a minute, settling down in Adelaide Creek.

"I suppose I did," Bethany said. "Unlike me, you have a big family here—aunts, uncles, first and second cousins all across the county. And Lucas, of course."

"I suppose, but nothing was keeping me here. Certainly not my dad." He paused, regretting the cynical way he'd phrased that. In a softer voice, he added, "We were never close. Not like you and your parents. Or, look at Quincy and Willow. In between talking about Winding Creek, he told me the story of Willow's decision about adopting Naomi on her own. He had tears in his eyes talking about it. And his reaction when she and Tom fell in love."

"I'm sorry about you and your dad," Bethany said. "I didn't know. Over the years I haven't seen him or heard much about him. I was in the orthopedics department at the hospital before taking this job. According to his medical history, until now Lucas had kept himself out of the hospital."

When they reached Jen's tent, Sloan handed one cookie to Heidi and Bethany gave one of hers to Jen.

"Everything okay?" Jen asked, glancing back and forth between him and Bethany.

"I suppose," Bethany responded before taking a big bite out of the cookie. "The guys from one of the companies that are looking to buy Winding Creek stopped by to talk to Mayor Zoe."

Jen gave Sloan a long look. "At least it wasn't someone looking to raze the place."

"Bethany doesn't seem too worried," he said to Jen. Bethany was now talking about the cookie with Heidi, but Sloan had a feeling she was putting on a casual face for her mother. On the other hand, from a distance he'd seen her stiffen her spine and raise her chin. Her way of making an entrance hadn't changed since high school. He'd still call her Miss Queen.

"Oh, she's worried," Jen said loud enough for Bethany to hear, "but she hides it well."

Bethany grinned. "C'mon, Mom. Don't give away my secrets." She tilted her head toward Sloan. "Besides, I can't fool him. He knows me from way back."

Sloan smiled, but his recent remarks to Bethany about his dad had reminded him that he had to be on his way. "I need to get going, Bethany. My dad's expecting me, or I should say he's expecting to visit with his dog today."

"Good to see you, Sloan." Jen held up what was left of the cookie. "Thanks for the treat."

"Yes. Let me know if your dad needs anything," Bethany said, "anything at all."

"Thanks, I will. So far, so good, though." Then Sloan singled out Heidi. "It's been an honor to meet you, Heidi. I hope to see you again soon."

With a mustache of orange frosting, Heidi gave him a shy smile. "Are you Mommy's friend?"

Sloan hadn't seen that question coming. "Why, yes. From a long time ago. When I was just a little older than you."

"I'm almost four."

Bethany laughed. "I told you that's what she'd say."

Heidi followed up with a little windshield wiper wave, which he returned as he left.

Walking toward the parking lot, he sensed three pairs of eyes watching him. He wished he could've stayed, and maybe learned more about Bethany and what motivated her to take on Winding Creek. And with such an air of confidence.

He was still thinking about Bethany and the festival an hour later, when he kept a tight hold on Flash's leash and walked past the damaged and roped-off section of Winding Creek's lobby. There were a few patients with visitors, both human and canine, gathering in the residents' lounge opposite the reception desk, where Sloan headed. Marla, a young person he hadn't seen before, greeted him. After he introduced himself and Flash, she wrote both their names on a badge for him. She explained that covering the reception desk on the weekends was her part-time job. Not surprisingly, the teenager also told him that Ms. Hoover had visited the school to recruit both volunteers and a few part-time workers for Winding Creek.

Marla leaned over the desk to say hello to Flash. "I'm lucky I get to work on Saturdays when the dogs visit."

"I can hear a couple of them now." Sloan pointed down a corridor reserved for the permanent residents. It was generally quieter there, the visitors more subdued. But not that day. A couple of dogs were barking, likely at each other.

"There's a really sick lady in a room down that hall," Marla said, her cheerful facade fading. "Her grandsons bring her two terriers to visit twice a week."

Flash saved Sloan from dwelling on the notion of his dad ever living in that part of Winding Creek. Sensing something was about to change in his world, the dog pulled at the leash all the way down the hall to his dad's room. Sloan didn't let go of the leash until they were on the threshold of Lucas's room. Then the dog raced to Lucas, who was sitting in the chair. He wrapped his good arm around the dog whose tail was wagging wildly. Sloan laughed along with Lucas at the dog's excitement. Too big to be in anyone's lap, he managed to cram his front paws on the seat and stretched his body so Lucas could lower his head and rest his cheek on the dog's head.

"There's a good dog," Lucas said once, and then again and again, until he finally added, "Okay, Flash, time to sit now." The dog obeyed, but when he settled down he leaned against Lucas's bad leg and put all his weight against it. "Isn't it something? The dog knows that side of me is hurt. He wants to fix my leg."

Sloan stared at his dad, and the brown-and-tan dog, whose eyes were soft, but earnest. The bond between the two didn't surprise Sloan, but his own tender reaction to it moved him in unexpected ways. Not a hint of grumpiness remained in his dad's demeanor. If it were up to him, he'd leave the room so his dad could enjoy his best friend and companion alone, the way he did at home. But that would be breaking the house rules, so to speak, which were clear. Beyond checking in at reception, he had to be present with his dad and Flash. He could already predict the affectionate dog wasn't going to like it when Sloan had to take him home.

"They tell me I'm doing pretty well," Lucas said, including Flash as he spoke. His left arm and hand weren't as damaged as his leg, so he moved three of his fingers slowly and a little awkwardly across the dog's fur. "That doc, Neela Abrams, claims I'm really lucky. She says I'll be as good as new, but it might take a while."

"Good thing you have a while, Dad," Sloan said. Dr. Abrams had said as much to him on the phone earlier that morning. "She also likes your good attitude about physical therapy. She sees you're motivated to get better."

"You bet I am." He stared down at the dog. "This critter needs his regular exercise. I can't let him down."

"I took him for a long walk early this morning," Sloan said. "We crossed the field to the ledge with those outcroppings Mom used to say looked like a row of crooked teeth."

"Good, Judge, that's good."

Sloan sighed. Even the dog turned to look at him when his dad called him Judge. Maybe the best path was to let go of his objections and resign himself to this latest nickname.

"How much do you remember about your mother?" Lucas asked.

What? That came out of the blue. And threw Sloan for a loop—a phrase his mom had used when Sloan was a little kid. His dad had never once asked that question before, not even when he was a teenager. But at the sudden mention of his mom, memories from thirty years ago flooded into his consciousness and brought tears to his eyes. His mom, and her death, became real all over again.

Sloan blinked to stop the tears. He couldn't cry now, not with his dad watching him. He took a deep breath. "I remember a lot, Dad. Right this minute I recall the time I told her she smelled like pine cones. She must have been making a new wreath for Christmas. Why do you ask? She's been gone since I was nine."

"Don't know exactly," his dad said, his gruff tone back. "Do you remember that Quincy was on his own with Willow? You both lost your moms. But Polly and I were a lot older when we had you."

"Yes, of course I remember Willow's mom." Almost a teenager when her mom died, Willow had been visibly sad for a while, but didn't talk about the loss, not with Sloan, anyway. "I was a year ahead of my cousin in school. There weren't many of us who didn't have moms. A few kids had stepmoms, though."

"Seems Quincy is a lot like me. I never thought about marrying another woman, and neither has my baby brother. Near as I can tell, anyway." Lucas looked up at Sloan and then flapped his good arm dismissively. "But why would I? Your mom, well, she was…" Lucas shook his head sadly, but he'd apparently run out of words.

"She was special, Dad. I always knew how much she loved us, you and me." He closed his eyes and wished away the wave of bittersweet emotion, but he didn't get his wish. Sloan wouldn't be the one to change the subject, though. It had been years since his dad mentioned his mom. At one time, Sloan wondered if his dad even thought about her. That had troubled him, but he was too afraid of how his dad might react to ask him.

"Like I said, we were older. Your mom, well, having you made her real happy." Lucas looked at the dog, who'd curled up in a ball at his feet. "She'd have liked Flash. That's for sure."

Sloan doubted that. He didn't recall his mom being especially fond of the ranch dogs, certainly not as house companions. She hadn't taken to cats, either, but she'd fed strays to keep them in the neighborhood, as she called it, because she despised seeing mice in the barn. On the other hand, she had a soft spot for calves and their mamas, but she directed her true passion to their horses.

His dad hit the armrest with the heel of his good hand. "I wonder if your old classmate, you know, Bethany, would ever marry again. From what I hear she and her fella were really happy. Probably knows she'd never find another guy like that, so she'll be like Quincy and me."

His heart sank. And why? He didn't have a claim on his old classmate, as his dad called her. But it seemed like such an odd thing to say. Sloan was trying to come up with a response, but his dad spoke first.

"But I hope not. She's still so young, has lots of life left in her." A silence passed between them before his dad chose another topic. "Okay, you've been here a few days now, so it's time for you to tell me the truth. Did you lose your job?" His eyebrows knitted in a fierce frown. "Is that why you're not in any hurry to get back to Denver? You need any money? I might be able to manage a loan."

The reversal in his dad's tone shook Sloan as much as the change of topic. And the implication that he'd come back to Adelaide Creek broke astounded him.

Sloan got up from the corner of the bed and slid the straight-backed chair from the corner of the room in place across from his dad and Flash. When he sat down, he took his dad's good hand and pressed it between the two of his.

"I'm stunned by your questions. And that's an understatement. I've never hedged about my situation. Or lied. I'm a partner in the firm, Dad, so no, I haven't lost my job."

"Did you tell me you were a partner? I don't recall that."

"I'm sure I did," Sloan said. "It's a small firm and I was part of the expansion. And my team won another huge case a few weeks ago. So no, I don't need money." Even better, the team had settled that case in the hours before dawn on the day the trial was scheduled to begin. It had taken Sloan's team over a year of nearly nonstop work to prepare the ugly mountain of evidence to present at trial. Fortunately, a cool head on the defense team had prevailed. The case came to a close and avoided some bad publicity for the company being sued, and worse, losing. It also added to the freedom Sloan had to take a leave and be here with his dad without hesitation. Sloan made a quick decision to avoid adding more specifics about his finances. That could wait. "I took a leave of absence from the firm so I could be here with you."

Sloan left out the part about burnout and his realization that he had to step away for a time. No more long stretches of twelve- or fourteen-hour workdays, seven days a week, for months and months on end.

"What kind of job lets a man not work for months? I don't get it." His dad looked down at the dog. "What do you think, Flash? Sounds a little strange to me."

Sloan chuckled. "It probably sounds strange to lots of people. But you know what, Dad? It's time you accepted that I may not be a judge, but as an attorney, I'm a big success." He paused, hoping his amused expression to go with the deliberate, and light, boasting might help the facts sink into his dad's head. "That's why I'm able to take a few months off. I'm resting up, getting ready for the next big project." That wasn't exactly a lie. If he failed to make some kind of life change, he'd risk ending up back at the firm and diving into the same old grind. Indecision would guarantee that nothing changed. But he needed more than rest. He was after a new direction, one that didn't require him to stay in Denver. Not that Adelaide Creek was included in any vision of his future life.

"I'll be good as new in a couple of months,"

Lucas said. "I don't want you thinking I'm trying to keep you here. Bridget would take Flash for a while. You could get back to your life."

"What's this? Are you trying to chase me away, sending me packing back home to Denver?"

"Denver? You call it home?"

"It is for now." He spoke quickly, clarifying it as a temporary location for himself as well as for his dad.

"I don't know about that." Lucas narrowed his eyes as he gave Sloan a skeptical look. "Can't be much of a home if it's only for now."

That thought was precisely what Sloan had been avoiding since he passed the Welcome to Adelaide Creek sign on the road into town. "You got me there, Dad. I can't argue with that."

Flash stirred and got to his feet. Distracted, Lucas sweet-talked the dog and rubbed his jowls and neck with his good hand. Sloan looked on, amused, but his mind drifted to the morning at Harvest Saturday with all its sounds and smells. And hanging out with Bethany and Heidi, and Jen, too. Adelaide Creek hadn't been his home for years, but for today, Denver was far away.

"I suppose if you were meant to be a one-woman man like me, you'd have married by now," Lucas said. "I thought you had a girlfriend. But I guess not. You must like the bachelor life."

Sloan suppressed a groan. He could explain

that Teresa had left him when he was so immersed in a case he'd forgotten her birthday and canceled one date after another. Better at apologizing than following through, he deserved what had happened with Teresa. He'd been an awful boyfriend. Even he was shocked by how little it hurt when she told him he was so unreliable she wasn't interested in seeing him anymore. But he had no inclination to recount his dismal history with women and romance with his dad. Instead, he said, "Not so fast, Dad. Don't give up on me, yet."

Lucas stared at him, but Sloan couldn't read his expression or even guess what he might be thinking. Then his dad shrugged one shoulder and said, "Suit yourself. You're all grown up, so I don't expect you'd take your old man's advice, anyway. You turned out okay, I guess." Then his dad's face broke into a beaming smile. "Can't thank you enough for bringing Flash to see me, Sloan."

"You're welcome, Dad. I'll bring him for another visit on Wednesday." Sloan smiled to himself. Well, well, his dad had actually called him by his name. Progress.

CHAPTER FOUR

BETHANY LED THE two teenagers past a row of old metal shelving crammed with boxes and plastic crates in the storage room. She stopped in front of a pile of cardboard boxes stacked against the far wall. "This obviously isn't one of our regular supply rooms. When I took over in January, the custodial staff told me this is where they stash things they don't need day-to-day, and old stuff no one knows what to do with."

The kids scanned the items and noted the variety of odds and ends packed in the boxes and crates.

"Lots of emergency battery lanterns. Maybe two dozen." Cooper, one of the teen volunteers, pulled one off the shelf and turned on the switch. When the light came on, he held it up in triumph.

"I'll bulk-order some batteries and when we're done with the decorations, maybe you'll check them all," Bethany said, pulling open the top folds of a second carton. Huh? She picked up a stub of a candle. "Good grief. Why would anyone save a box full of mostly burned down candles." She rifled through the box, finding only a hodgepodge of now yellowish candle stubs. "I'm declaring this fit only for the trash." She patted the top of another pile. "I'm told that these cartons contain whatever holiday decorations we have. But I don't know what condition they're in."

A girl who'd introduced herself as Tori planted her hands on her hips. "What? They aren't even labeled."

Bethany found the girl's tone of indignation quite entertaining. And she needed a bit of that kind of fun.

Bethany responded with an impish grin. "Whaddya know? I guess that's one of your challenges. To inventory what we have. And toss stuff that's so worn out, tired and shabby it would bring attention to how worn out, tired and shabby the building itself is."

Bethany was acquainted with both Tori and Cooper, juniors at the high school, from town festivals and events at the lodge where they put in their volunteer service hours. She didn't know Tori's family, but Cooper's parents were both teachers who also lived on O'Malley Street.

She gestured for the kids to backtrack out the door. Then she showed the way to the designated area in a corner of the reception area where she'd set up tables. "I'll come up with a little petty cash if you find there's not a pumpkin, ghost or black cat fit to call itself a decoration." She paused. "Same goes for Thanksgiving turkeys and holiday wreaths and Santas and other Christmas stuff. Then we'll make a shopping list."

"Co...ol," Tori said.

"I've got patients to see, but I'll check in later. When you're done, I'll call the custodians to haul away whatever has seen better days." She turned toward her office, but called out, "Have fun." From the way the two kids were already scrambling to get boxes open, she doubted fun was going to be an issue.

When she got back to her office, she slipped out of her blazer and into a lab coat and grabbed her tablet. This was one of her favorite parts of the day. By midafternoon she'd usually worn out her capacity for paperwork, and she'd also made a habit of scheduling staff meetings for early in the day when possible. But the familiar interactions with patients were what kept her energized through big things like replacing the roof and all the little things like tossing out boxes of candle stubs.

She glanced at the collection of renderings of Winding Creek hanging on the wall opposite her desk. She kept them there as a reminder that this place was once new and fresh. Despite its age, the design of the center worked well for the range of services provided. The units were laid out in spoke-like fashion from the lobby-reception hub. The administrative offices, including hers, and the cafeteria took over the first wing to the left of the front door. The one next to it was the quietest wing, which included patients needing twenty-four-hour nursing care, and who were unlikely to leave the center and live independently again. That was where Bethany was heading. She crossed the lobby and walked to the far end of that corridor, where the last four rooms were largely overseen by the county's hospice staff and volunteers. Another one of Bethany's ideas the county hospice service had welcomed.

Bethany slowed down, giving herself the space to clear her mind of the roof and water damage and of teenagers and decorations. Local hospice nurses mostly worked with people in their homes, but these four rooms often were used for short-term stays. Bethany wanted her mind as quiet as the nurses and family members caring for these patients.

Earlier, Bethany had perused the notifications she'd received about weekend admissions, patients whose data appeared in her tablet now. Based on her review, she made decisions about whom to visit and when. She'd been saddened to see the name of one of her former teachers on the list of three new patients. Mrs. Kingsley had been admitted to hospice, and Bethany understood that palliative treatment had been ordered for her fourth grade teacher. That meant Mrs. Kingsley's comfort was the priority.

She approached the half-open door to the dim room, knocking softly so she wouldn't startle the two women standing on either side of the bed. She didn't recognize either one of them, but they were considerably older than Bethany. Moving closer, she quickly introduced herself and confirmed her hunch that the women were her former teacher's daughters. "I wanted to stop by to make sure you have everything *you* need."

When the sisters indicated they wanted to talk in the hall, Bethany led them out. The two middle-aged women appeared tired, which was true for almost all hospice patients' families. But in this case, they admitted their relief that after three years, someone else had taken over the task of keeping their mother comfortable while they said their goodbyes.

"Your mother was one of my teachers," Bethany said. "Another one of her students happens to be in the building today, because his father is in the rehab wing. Your mother taught school here for a long time, so I suppose you've run into other former students, huh?"

The older of the two chuckled. "We arrived

yesterday and you're former student number three."

"That's the kind of comfort we need now," the younger woman said, folding her arms across her chest. "Whose dad is it?"

"Sloan Lancaster."

The woman smiled and pressed her index finger on her chin. "Hmm...let's see. I wonder how many Lancaster kids Mom taught. At least twenty, I'll bet."

The exchange took a serious turn when the younger sister spoke up. "We've called the rest of our family, all the grandchildren. They'll be arriving, along with our pastor."

Bethany nodded. "I'll alert reception. We can bring in extra chairs. You can keep the door closed for privacy." Bethany pulled a trifold brochure from her lab coat pocket. "Here's a list of steps we can take and services we offer to families in your situation. Cafeteria hours and who to call with your questions. Things like that."

After working in a hospital setting, she'd developed a sense of what families of patients would likely ask. When she took over as Winding Creek's director she'd produced a series of FAQ brochures, one of which she'd written with families of hospice patients in mind.

Bethany left with the promise to return and then checked the remaining three rooms. She sat with a hospice volunteer and chatted with the patient, who was sitting up in the chair while the volunteer braided her hair. It was another half hour later when she retraced her steps down the hall, having made the rounds of the first wing.

Bethany joined Candace Archer, the regular weekday receptionist at the check-in desk, who stood watching the two teens sorting large and small items and banners by holiday and quality. Next to the tables, cartons were already at least half-full of items to be recycled or fit only for the dumpster out back. Scanning the piles, Bethany concluded that most of what they started with would never see the light of day again. Better to know that late in October than deep into December. Her mood was lighter now that at least she'd made some headway in making sense of what had taken up space in the storage room.

"I've been having the best time watching the kids," Candace said, with a laugh in her voice. "They take this job very seriously, I can tell you that."

"So I see. Good thing tomorrow is trash day."

She looked up to see Sloan coming from the rehab wing wheeling Lucas in a wheelchair. He hadn't yet seen her when Lucas waved toward the table and the kids. Cooper and Tori approached Lucas and Sloan and introduced themselves. Bethany couldn't hear every word, but she was quite sure Lucas used the word "junk" when he pointed to the boxes on the floor. He also seemed to have an opinion about the items left on the table. Whatever he said made the teenagers laugh.

"Uh-oh, I think it's time I kept an ear open," Bethany said. "If we're not careful Lucas might tell the kids to haul the whole kit 'n' caboodle out the door." Not necessarily a bad idea. She'd like to start a one hundred percent new decoration collection. But she was obligated to keep track of every dollar. Where was an anonymous donor when she needed one—again?

"This I have to see," Candace said, but then made a quick pivot. "Oops, or maybe not." She greeted a group of visitors walking toward the desk. One wore a clerical collar, leading Bethany to think he was the Kingsleys' pastor.

While Candace addressed the visitors, Bethany positioned herself near Sloan and Lucas. "Giving your opinion, Lucas?" She glanced at the kids.

"Seems like this place could do better than these old shabby things." As if he hadn't made himself clear, he dismissively flapped his hand at the tables. Nothing subtle about Lucas. Meanwhile, the energetic teenagers continued to find Lucas's crabby ways quite amusing.

For his part, Sloan nodded his agreement. But he also gave the kids a dose of reality. "You've identified the problem, so now it's time to come up with a plan."

Tori planted both hands on her hips. "You already have a donation jar for the roof, so maybe we could put out another one for a little...you know...beautification."

Bethany shook her head. "I'm afraid I can't do that right now. I don't think my bosses would approve of raising money for another project, and one that they might label as frivolous. We need all those dollars in the jar for our new roof. Besides, I've got a slush fund for minor *beautification* projects." She grinned at Tori.

"How could brightening up holidays like Halloween and Thanksgiving in a care center be considered frivolous?" Once again, Tori's indignation was on display in both her posture and in her voice. "Everybody likes ghosts and witches and pumpkins. Decorations lift people's spirits."

Sloan cast a pointed—and amused—glance Bethany's way, but before she could respond, Tori spoke again. "I agree with Mr. Lancaster. It's a bunch of junk."

Lucas raised his good hand and gestured to Tori. "There ya go. Smart girl."

Sloan and Bethany both laughed out loud. So did the teenagers. And it felt good. Nothing like some blunt honesty. With her pretty smile and long dark hair framing her face, Tori reminded

Bethany of Heather at the same age. Small in stature, but not in conviction. Not particularly inhibited either.

"Here's what I'm thinking." Sloan glanced down at Lucas. "And Dad, feel free to speak up. How about we jump into my SUV and take a trip to the party store in Landrum? We're moving into the holiday season. Let's think about what would dress up this place from now until the end of the year." He glanced at the table and then did an exaggerated eye roll at the kids whose smiles left no doubt that they enjoyed the performance.

Oh, brother. Sloan and Lucas weren't making this any easier. Bethany suppressed a laugh. Now Sloan was just shamelessly charming these kids.

"How about we start with a big banner that we could put up behind the reception desk," Sloan said. "Happy Halloween spelled out in bright colors."

"In orange and green, maybe a touch of black," Tori suggested, narrowing her eyes. "I'm seeing witches and ghosts on the counters."

"Or mobiles we could hang from the lights." Cooper pointed to the chandeliers over each side of the lobby.

"Whoa. I said a slush fund, not a bank account. Lower your sights to a banner and a few other items, like table decorations," Bethany said, not happy to be in this position where she'd have to impose limits like a boss.

"I've got an idea." Sloan reached into his pocket and pulled out some cash. Not a huge amount, but enough to show he had money and was willing to spend it. "Let's go spend this money on whatever you think will brighten the place. What do you think?"

No surprise, Bethany thought, when the kids responded with enthusiasm.

"Sounds like a good time to me." Lucas's expression was full of fun. "Can't go with you this time, though, but I'll supervise when you bring everything back."

"Uh-oh," Sloan responded in a dry voice.

"You really want to spend your pile of cash this way?" Bethany asked.

"Absolutely," Sloan said. "If the kids are free to go, we can leave right now."

Cooper held up his hand to get Sloan's attention. "Wait, wait, here's the thing. Our parents signed the form giving us permission to come to this place in my car." He gestured to Tori. "That means if we go to Landrum, we have to call our parents."

"That makes sense, Sloan." Bethany glanced at the kids. "Rules and regs, right?"

The kids nodded.

"Got it," Sloan said. "Sorry, I should have

thought of that myself. You go ahead and make your calls or send your texts. I'm happy to talk to parents, or Ms. Hoover can verify what we're up to."

"So much red tape," Tori said with a long-suffering sigh.

Bethany managed not to snicker. But not Lucas.

While the kids took a few steps away to text their parents, Sloan closed the distance between them. "The parents would probably like it if the director of Winding Creek came along. You have an impressive title, Ms. Hoover."

"And she's done a good job shaping up this place," Lucas said to Sloan, but then he turned to her. "Give yourself a little break. No telling what the Judge here and the kids might decide to buy. They might need a little supervision."

Bethany's first thought was to say a quick no, that she didn't have the time. On the other hand, she enjoyed these kids and expected to see a fair amount of them, and some of their classmates, as well, between now and the end of the year. Would she deny she enjoyed being around Sloan? No sense trying. Lucas was right, she did run the place, after all. As the person in charge, she could give herself permission. A lark, her mom called expeditions like this. "Okay, I'm in."

Sloan beamed. "Good. You can ride with me."

Bethany leaned closer to Sloan. "You'll put

a limit on how much you spend, right? These kids will see all sorts of irresistible, cute and fun items. Tori has a way with words and isn't afraid to use them."

Sloan guffawed. "Are you implying I might be a pushover?"

"Your word, not mine." She gave him a sidelong glance. "But I suppose you could take it that way."

Lucas, who'd been observing the kids, spoke up. "Hey, don't go off and leave me out here in the lobby. Andre will be coming around with my dinner in a while, and I don't want to miss it." With an eye roll, he added, "I never had my supper so early in my life as I do in this establishment."

While Sloan took him back to his room, she joined the kids. Neither had any trouble getting permission for the trip to Landrum. Tori might call it red tape, but Bethany depended on the school's community service program, so she'd follow the rules. Just because Cooper and his parents had been O'Malley Street neighbors, that didn't mean she could bypass the rules.

A few minutes later, Sloan reappeared and the kids and Sloan put their contact information in each other's phones. Bethany told Candace where she was going and what to pass on to Nell Roth, the evening receptionist, when she came in before Candace left for the day. "If you need me, call my cell. The Kingsleys and their visitors will be in and out all evening, so make sure Nell knows that the daughters, and maybe the pastor, might stay through the night."

Candace patted Bethany's shoulder. "I get it. You go. Have a good time doing something different."

"Thanks. I believe I will." Bethany smiled to herself, thinking that this was the kind of spur-of-the-moment mini adventure she used to cook up. She'd show up at Heather's house with ice skates and they'd take off to the skating pond in Landrum. Or, Heather dragged Bethany off to the trails on horseback at a moment's notice—even supplying the horse.

Bethany smiled to herself. Not being a horse girl like Heather, Bethany was good with the SUV—and Sloan.

CHAPTER FIVE

"Quincy might have said it couldn't be done," Sloan said, a note of solemnity in his voice.

"What is that?"

"Pulling you out of your office for a few hours," Sloan teased as they clicked their seat belts in place. "What tipped the scales and made you decide you could leave the center and come along?" It would be nice to think the prospect of spending time with him might have been a sufficient lure. That was his ego talking, though. Or maybe just a little wishful thinking.

"It's the kids' energy, Sloan. And the spirit these kids bring with them. As much as I enjoy working with older people, when it comes to energy, a double shot of youth is even better than a double shot of espresso."

"You're connected with many of the high school kids through their parents, aren't you?" Sloan asked.

"I suppose, especially all the kids the Lancasters and Stanhopes have accumulated along the way," Bethany said with a laugh in her voice.

"I, for one, am glad you came along, despite all that blasted red tape." He chuckled, realizing he hadn't had this kind of fun in a long time. Being with his legal colleagues all day long wasn't exactly a barrel of laughs, even if he enjoyed the work. Sometimes they'd banter about restaurants or sports or the latest series they streamed on their tablets late at night when they were too wound up to sleep. But whatever they talked about lacked a certain lighthearted quality.

He glanced sideways and saw Bethany's thoughtful expression reflected in the window. Were they just two adults having a good time with all that old teenage awkwardness gone? Maybe. But with time and experience, she was even smarter and more engaging now than she'd been twenty years ago. And she was incredibly beautiful. Those things might have a little something to do with how he felt about being with her.

"I'll let you in on my secret plan, Sloan." Her tone was more serious than expected. "I'm scheming to come up with ways our teen volunteers can interact more with the patients."

The intimate tone of voice made his heart skip a beat. For real. "Cooper and Tori provided my dad with an audience for the showman in him.

That's for sure. I get a kick out of seeing him like that."

Bethany smiled. "So I noticed."

"I'd forgotten that performer side of him." Sloan had been surprised when his dad's inner entertainer emerged. "Way back before Mom died, people used to describe him as a real character. And in a good way."

"I can see why," Bethany said. "And by the way, he might grouse and gripe a lot, but it's never about the staff."

"He's even stopped complaining about me." Sloan flashed a lopsided smile. "Speaking of performance, I never thought I'd look forward to being entertained by the shopping antics of a couple of teenagers."

Bethany flashed a cautionary look. "Fair warning. As soon as we're inside the store, they'll bring out their phones and start taking pictures. The next thing you know, they'll be posting the images everywhere and you'll wind up a social media star whether you like it or not."

"Oops. I never thought of that," Sloan said, turning onto the main road to Landrum, "but I've got nothing to hide. Besides, a photo record of the kids and their service hours is a good thing for Winding Creek. Right?"

"Exactly. Margaret, who does our in-house communication, also regularly adds updates to our website. We'll also send them on to the school for the community service section of the online student newspaper."

"I remember that, too." Sloan smiled. "Other than going from a print to digital school paper, some things don't change much."

"I remember helping out at the county health fair," Bethany said. "I always knew I wasn't interested in becoming the next Jen Hoover, you know, following in Mom's footsteps and raising sheep, selling wool, spinning and all that. But the health fair gave me the idea that I could be a nurse. It actually became my biggest ambition, my dream."

"And here you are," Sloan said.

"What about you? What was your dream?"

"In a nutshell, finding a life outside of Adelaide Creek," Sloan blurted without hesitation. "Once I was in college and saw possibilities, I thought more about what I didn't want. For starters, I was determined to find work that wouldn't bring me back to Adelaide Creek." Sloan was conscious of his voice rising on every word.

"Well, well, your tone leaves no room for doubt."

Sloan turned his head to see Bethany's eyebrows lifted in surprise. Or maybe she'd been shocked to know that going to college was a revelation to him. He'd been caught up in a sense of freedom, a profound realization that he wasn't required to follow the Lancaster path into ranching. And in his case, back to an indifferent dad.

"Like you, Bethany, I always knew I didn't want to take over the ranch, but I thought I was obligated to take that path." More precisely, he'd felt trapped in that ranching life. "What a relief to figure out that I had plenty of relatives only too happy to eventually manage Dad's acres and buy his cattle—and the horses."

"What a difference between you and me." Bethany spoke in a pensive tone. "I was happy to come home from college and make my life in Adelaide Creek. Even though Charlie was from northern Wyoming, he felt the same way about my hometown."

"It was less about the place and more about wanting to stop butting heads with my dad." Sloan paused. "You see how he is. Or, maybe I should say *was*. Time has mellowed him some." Wanting to shift the subject, he said, "You're a force in the community. I envy you in some ways."

"Because?"

Sloan took a few seconds to collect his thoughts. "It goes deeper than your roots. Your job puts you in touch with our generation's parents and grandparents, and the younger generation, too. It's like you see the full circle, somehow."

"That's exactly why I love it here. And Adelaide Creek has everything Charlie and I wanted for Heidi. Even with him gone now, she's still surrounded by love."

"And given the work you do, it appears you want the town to have what you might one day need for your parents— Winding Creek."

"Exactly." Bethany shrugged. "It's really pretty simple."

For you, Sloan thought, slowing for some road work ahead. He'd cut ties so completely that it never occurred to him to come back for his cousins' weddings or other milestones. It was as if limiting contact with his dad had meant more or less forgetting about his extended family. He could change that, though.

Bethany pointed out the passenger window. "The fields are flooded from the storms we've had. They've been worse than usual this year."

"Dad said so, too." Sloan glanced in the rearview mirror. "We're almost there and Cooper is still right behind us."

"I don't spend much of my free time at the mall, so it feels odd to be on a shopping trip," Bethany said. "Now and again, Mom and I drag each other out here." She chuckled. "Heather and I prefer to wander around in the shops in downtown Landrum, but only after we've treated ourselves to a leisurely lunch."

"I could have predicted that. I remember the

two of you. Joined at the hip. The tall blonde with the curly hair and the short girl with long dark hair. Funny, cute and smart." Looking back, though, maybe Bethany's air of independence intimidated him and that was why he'd been shy around her. Even then, she seemed to live by her own set of rules.

"Ever since I got here I've been taking odd trips down memory lane," Sloan said. "Some people look back on high school as a bad time, but I don't. I had my cousins and friends that kept me from being isolated with my dad." He sighed. "I suppose that sounded kind of dreary."

Bethany nodded to acknowledge his words, but didn't offer any other response. That was okay. It wasn't a good time to start another conversation about his dad, Sloan thought.

"Back to the present," Sloan said. "Once we're inside, I'll fade into the background. You and the kids know what's needed." He made the turn into the mall and found a parking place near the party store. Before cutting the engine, he turned to Bethany. "To be clear, I do intend to pay for everything. Consider it a donation. Hang on to your petty cash." He gave Bethany a mock frown to go with his bossy attorney's tone.

"You always carry around a wad of bills? You never know when someone might need some holiday decorations, huh?"

Sloan laughed. "That was for your benefit. I've also got a little showman in me. Get it from my dad, I guess."

"Okay, but they're still kids. You wait. I can hear the proposal now...a pumpkin in every room and a witch on every door."

Sloan laughed. "Good one, Bethany." Cooper pulled in next to him and the four of them headed for the door.

Once inside, Sloan hung back while Bethany freed two shopping carts from a long row. "Okay, kids, let's see what they have that's a little different."

"Ooh, you mean like those carved black crows and cats?" Tori pointed to a prominent display of pieces that looked like hand-carved wooden items.

"A girl after my own heart," Bethany said. "I like them—maybe they have ghosts and witches, too."

Off and running, Sloan thought. He wandered down the aisle that had racks of banners for Halloween and Thanksgiving. But in his mind he was back in the SUV still in an easy conversation with Bethany.

Cooper and Tori showed their playful mood when they started joking about loading the vehicles with giant inflatable pumpkins and ghosts for Winding Creek's lawn. Not on Bethany's watch, Sloan wagered. The two kids then headed straight for a long aisle that featured an extensive collection of witches, skeletons, carved cats and crows.

Still keeping his distance from the kids and Bethany, Sloan moved farther down the aisle and busied himself going through Halloween and Thanksgiving posters. He picked out the most colorful ones to brighten the dull walls in the lobby and common areas. The whole place needed a paint job. And Sloan could pay for it. Maybe he'd speak to Quincy about helping to brighten things up, while also remaining anonymous.

When he joined the others, Cooper was arranging boxes of Halloween items, almost filling the shopping cart. They also had turkeys and cornucopias and even a few carved Christmas trees.

"We struck gold with these," Bethany said. "Perfect for counters and the tables in the hub where the patients hang out and the lobby."

Sloan took a few shots of Cooper and Tori loading the boxes in the cart, while Bethany turned her attention to flameless candles.

With one cart fully loaded, the kids wandered into a section with mobiles and all kinds of signs and other odds and ends. Sloan followed with his phone positioned for more shots. Tori thrust out a hip and put one hand on the back of her head. "Hey, Cooper, strike a star pose for Sloan."

"Oh no...you're not talking me into that." Cooper backed away. "You know you're going to end up in the school paper, don't you?"

Bethany came back with boxes of flameless candles in a variety of sizes and piled them into the second cart.

"And we need some photos of you, Bethany," Sloan said, "so smile for the camera." He took a couple of shots and lowered his camera. When Cooper and Tori were distracted by a display of Christmas items, he showed Bethany the photos he'd just taken. "These could be part of a presentation to donors or for grant applications. Enlisting teens from the local high school to help out adds to the feel-good quality you've created at Winding Creek." With a quick shrug, he added, "I'd brag a little about giving students an opportunity to help make the center more cheerful for the residents and patients."

"We're already doing some of that, but we could make more of our community engagement theme. Especially with grants. Okay, go ahead and take whatever photos and videos you want," Bethany said. "We'll figure out how to use them later."

Bethany pointed to the candles. "They're safe, so they can be on all the time, and we control them with a remote."

"Good in the lobby," Cooper remarked as he

and Tori gathered around the two carts. They held a collection of large Halloween posters resembling old-fashioned, fairy-tale illustrations. "What do you think of these?"

"Definitely new and decidedly different." Bethany's expression brightened. "You watch, our patients and their visitors will comment on what you've done."

Sloan nodded, but if he believed that, between the carved items and artistic posters, the public spaces would take on a whole new look.

Tori waved her arm to encompass the two shopping carts. "See? Four heads really are better than one."

Sloan's eyes sparkled in amusement, but taking her seriously, Cooper nodded without breaking a smile. "Right, right."

Bethany came to Sloan's side. "Thanks to you, Winding Creek is going to look festive and bright."

"If you like, we'll come back for Christmas stuff another time—if you'll let me," Sloan said.

Bethany responded with a helpless shrug. "I guess if you show up with a pocketful of cash, I can't say no."

By the time he and the kids pushed the carts of items to the front, Sloan noted that Bethany wasn't with them.

"Where's Ms. Hoover?" he asked. "Did you see her leave?"

"Nope," the teens said in unison.

"Well, she can't have gone far." He smiled at the kids. "I'm her ride home."

They'd bought so much in bulk, so almost everything was already packaged, and checkout didn't take long. When Bethany appeared, she held tablecloths in her arms, two with a border of ghosts and witches and another with pumpkins and cranberries. "Just in time," she said, dropping them into the last cart. "For the tables we'll set up in the common areas," she explained.

The sky was turning violet and pink in the distance by the time they'd finished loading their purchases into the back of Sloan's SUV.

"Listen up, everyone," Sloan said. "We go right past the Burger Barn on our way home. I don't want to get anyone in trouble, but would your parents be okay with us stopping for a burger? It's my treat, so no one needs money."

Bethany put her hand on his arm. "Sloan, really. That's not necessary."

For a second, the look on Bethany's face gave him pause. Maybe he'd overstepped. A stab of regret confirmed that thought.

"Sounds like fun to me," Cooper said. "My mom and dad won't mind, but I'm Tori's ride." He turned to her. "What do you think?"

"I'll call my mom. She's probably still at work." She pointed to an office supply store at the opposite end of the mall. "That's where she works. Can't call my dad. He's stationed in South Carolina."

"Your dad is in the service?" Sloan asked.

Tori nodded. "The Marines. He's a colonel. Right now he's doing a lot of training." She took a few steps away to make her call, and less than a minute later, she rejoined the circle, smiling because her mom said yes.

Cooper made his call, and Bethany also made a couple of calls in quick succession. Meanwhile, Sloan wanted to know more about Tori's dad, who'd likely made his career in the service, but he could tell it wasn't the right time to ask questions. During his years in the army, he'd known so many men and women who had families. Separations, fear, injuries and putting lives back together—that was all part of the military life.

As Sloan pulled away from the mall and onto the road, he faced the reality that his motive for stopping at the Burger Barn was a chance to stretch out his time with Bethany. That thought took him back in a way he couldn't explain—or deny. From the moment he'd seen her, he'd been intrigued and drawn to her.

Alone, without the kids in earshot, he apologized for not consulting her first.

"That's okay. I'm enjoying this unexpected trip. But, yes, you should have consulted me."

She turned her head to look out the window. "While it's true that my parents almost never say no to watching Heidi, I still need to be careful not to take advantage of them. They have busy lives of their own."

"Uh, was Heidi upset?" Fearing the answer, he winced.

Bethany chuckled. "If you were three, well, almost four, and Grandpa was letting you help grill burgers and hot dogs and Grandma was frosting a chocolate cake, would you be upset?"

"Hey, next time, I'll invite this whole gang to your parents' house," Sloan teased. "Good times at the Hoovers'."

"And my mother would probably get all gushy and tell you what a good man you've turned into."

Sloan had no quick comeback, so he just shook his head. As they drove along, regret set in again, this time about the wisdom of spending so much time thinking about Bethany. But the more he saw of her, the more he wanted to be around her.

His first thoughts were about it being dangerous territory. But why? He wasn't going anywhere. At least for now. Deep down he'd known it all along. He had no intention of living in Denver ever again. He wouldn't drift back there. So, when the time came to move on, and he left Adelaide Creek, he would have a new plan in place.

CHAPTER SIX

BETHANY KEPT CROSSING off items on her daily to-do list, conscious how fast these October days were passing. She barely had time to take in the changes going on around her, including the layers of leaves covering Winding Creek's considerable grounds. As she'd hoped, the temporary repairs to the roof had held during the new round of storms that brought gusty winds and copious cold rain.

The subtle transformation of the center sometimes astonished her. The Saturday after their shopping excursion, while her mom baked cookies with Heidi, Bethany went into the office to catch up on paperwork. She planned to spend no more than an hour, two at most, but then Tori and Cooper had arrived to do their magic with the new decorations. They brought two more classmates with them, and in less than two hours the center was bright with a warm Halloween atmosphere. A good omen for the entire holiday season ahead.

As usual Sloan had brought Flash to see his dad and she watched from a distance as Sloan wheeled Lucas to the patient lounge to watch the kids put up banners and the new posters. As long as she was there, she decided to look in on some long-term patients, as well as recent arrivals in the rehab wing. Seeing patients take first steps after knee or hip replacements, consulting with the physical therapists about this or that patient put Bethany back into her old job in orthopedics. Her work as a nurse practitioner had been focused on post-surgical care, and emotional support often was as important as relieving their pain.

Bethany had deliberately hung back when Sloan, Lucas and some of the other residents gathered in the lobby with their pets and visited with the foursome of teens. She wasn't needed there, but she enjoyed watching Sloan interact with the teenagers as they went about hanging posters. He was the adult overseer, but in a laid-back manner that lacked even a hint of condescension. Impressive.

Whatever problems he and Lucas had weren't evident in their interactions during their visits, especially when Flash was around. Lucas was making the kind of progress with his recovery that boded well for him to return home—eventually—to his walks with Flash. Sloan had yet to talk about his plans when that happened. Curious. He was a partner in a law firm in Denver, but from what she could see, he was in no hurry to get back to his life there.

Now, a couple of days later, Bethany waited for Jen to show up with Heidi after school so they could head to Tall Tale for the kids' Halloween Party. She was not alone. She and the unit supervisors made an effort to staff the day to cover those with young children so they could bring them to this popular Halloween event. She'd planned her day to do the same.

When her mom texted to say she and Heidi had arrived, Bethany gathered her jacket and handbag and locked her office door behind her. When she rounded the corner to the residents' lobby, she spotted Heidi with Sloan and Lucas and some other residents. Her almost-four-year-old was chatting with Sloan like he—and Lucas— were family friends. Which was fast becoming the truth. Bethany had become used to seeing Sloan almost daily. He'd never missed even one day of visiting his dad. On Wednesday and Saturday, he brought Flash early and stayed as late as the policy allowed.

Even more significant to Bethany was the change in Lucas. Not nearly as dismissive as he'd been the first day of Sloan's visit, the older man was also less cantankerous. It seemed that father and son were warming up to each other.

When Bethany approached, Jen was admiring the table in the hub, where the candles were turned on, highlighting the Halloween carvings now arranged in groups. Bethany was particularly fond of the blue-black carved crows that sat between a cauldron and some witches and a couple of painted wooden turkeys in a brighter orange and deeper red than any seen in nature. The kitchen had put out a couple platters of Halloween cookies the high school kids had dropped off earlier.

The sight of her little family with Sloan and Lucas was a happy surprise, and yet ordinary in a pleasant sort of way.

Heidi was making Lucas and Sloan guess about her costume and who she was supposed to be.

"You're not exactly a princess, are you?" Lucas's expression was deliberately quizzical, as if lost in deep thought.

Heidi shook her head.

"Or, a queen," Sloan said, matching Lucas's expression.

"And not a witch, either," Lucas added.

"Are you going to tell them, Heidi?" Jen said.

Heidi shook her head again.

"What's this? You like our guessing game?" Sloan asked.

"They don't know who I am, Mommy," Heidi said as Bethany came closer. "They guessed wrong."

Bethany grinned at Sloan and Lucas. "Well, then, maybe you'll have to tell them before we leave for the party."

"Wait, wait. Can I get one more guess?" Lucas tapped his temple. "I think I've got it now."

Heidi took a second or two to consider her answer, but finally said, "Okay."

"Then I'll say you're a mermaid. I can tell by those fine silvery blue boots you're wearing."

Heidi's face lit up. "I'm Sylvie-the-mermaid. I live in a lake."

"Sylvie is a very fancy name. Did you make that up all by yourself?" Sloan asked.

Heidi tilted her head to the side and considered the question. "She's in a story. From the library."

"That's where we get lots of stories, huh?" Jen said.

Once the mermaid idea had taken hold, Bethany and her mom had cobbled together a costume. They'd even managed to find a remnant of shiny silver upholstery fabric to create the boots.

Watching Lucas's animated face, Bethany decided that he'd have made a good grandpa. Did he ever wonder, like Bethany did, why Sloan hadn't married and had a family? Would Sloan have mended fences with his dad if he'd had a child? Or would Lucas have softened toward Sloan?

Well, once again, Bethany had caught herself speculating about things that weren't any of her business. Not to mention irrelevant, anyway. On the flip side, she appreciated the sweet attention directed to her child.

"We should be on our way," Bethany said to Jen. She turned to Sloan and Lucas to add, "Cooper and Tori, along with a bunch of their classmates, are likely already there, including a girl named Mags, who puts on a great spooky ghost voice to greet all the kids when the lights are still low. She's become the assistant emcee who helps Dr. Tom host the kids' party. Most of the high school kids like to volunteer for the Halloween party. It gives them an excuse to hang out at the lodge."

"You should check out Tall Tale, Sloan," Jen said. "Bethany got us a family membership for the health club, so I have a place to swim laps in the winter. Don't have to go all the way to Landrum. Great breakfast bar, too."

"I'll have to do that soon," Sloan said, smiling at Bethany. "Everybody talks about the place."

A fond smile, Bethany thought. From the beginning, it seemed she and Sloan had fallen into their private style of communicating. It didn't necessarily require words. Still, she didn't always understand the way Sloan sometimes looked at her. Like now. Maybe it was as simple as enjoying himself with Jen and Heidi, while Lucas was in good spirits. A certain edge had disappeared from Sloan's demeanor. He'd been skeptical about Winding Creek, and seemed to put up with his dad more than enjoying him. If she were to put the changes into words, then the longer he was in Adelaide Creek, the more relaxed, and happier, he seemed.

"The Halloween parties are all Willow's doing, with some help from Tom," Jen said. "She's quite a woman, your cousin."

Interesting, Bethany thought. From the way Sloan snapped back into the conversation, it was obvious he'd been distracted. He nodded and mumbled something to Jen about hearing great things about Willow since he'd been back.

Bethany abruptly turned to leave without starting a new line of conversation. She'd been mulling over positive shifts in Sloan but now found herself suddenly annoyed that he had almost zero awareness of all that had gone on in his hometown, not even when his family was involved. She'd even seen his face go blank when patients mentioned the town hall fire. How could Sloan be unaware that his uncle Quincy had overseen the restoration of this historic gem of a building?

Willow herself had been a big part of turning the upscale Tall Tale Lodge & Spa into a local hot spot. For one thing, it had fast become the county's primary music venue.

On the way to the lodge, Bethany tried to keep her mind in the game, and off irrelevant things about Sloan. At the moment, the game involved deep conversations with Heidi about Sylvie-the-mermaid's ability to survive the winter in the lake. Heidi was certain that Sylvie had magical powers that would allow her to nestle among the plants and rocks and sleep all winter, same as grizzly bears.

"The way you explain that, Heidi, it makes a lot of sense," Bethany said when she'd turned off the engine. She stepped out of the car, suddenly hit with a wave of unwelcome nostalgia. She began the now familiar epic fight to stave off the grief that, like last year's Halloween party, threatened to put a damper on this annual event. By the time Heidi was out of the car, she was a ball of energy raring to go. When they got to the sidewalk, Bethany let Heidi run ahead to wait by the door.

Bethany started walking toward the entrance, but her mom put her hand on her arm to slow her down. "You aren't alone, honey. I remember Charlie having so much fun with Heidi on her first Halloween," Jen said, her tone loving and gentle. "She wasn't even walking yet."

"Since when are you a mind reader," Bethany said, giving her a warning look. "I haven't been thinking about it all day. Nothing like that. Or even during these last few days when we were putting Heidi's costume together. But when we pulled into the lot here?" Bethany swept both hands from one side of her body to the other. "Whoosh, the memories came over me like a tidal wave. Now I can't stop thinking about it."

"I understand." Jen nodded. "I'm sorry this has been one of those hard days."

"It wasn't. Not exactly." Bethany scoffed. "Uh, don't mind me. I've confused myself. Maybe it's just that Charlie, who wasn't from here, worked hard to become part of the community. But sometimes, talking to Sloan, I find myself irrationally mad at him. It's like he moved away and never gave us another thought, not even his slew of relatives." She swatted the air. "It's nothing. But it's the obvious contrast, I guess. But I know Sloan isn't a bad guy. I don't mean to imply he is."

"Yeah, well, maybe that apparent indifference comes back to his dad," Jen said.

"Well, that part I do understand, Mom. Even back in high school Lucas had those ridiculous nicknames for him." Bethany offered a weak smile. "I need to get this comparison out of my head. Charlie and Sloan, two different men. I was just bothered by his lack of awareness about what his relatives do for his hometown." She grimaced as she tried to wipe away these feelings. "I know, it's silly of me to think about any of that."

"Whatever happened in the past, from the looks of it, Sloan's made at least a degree of peace with his dad." Smiling wide, Jen added, "It's obvious he thinks the world of you."

Bethany jerked her head back. "Oh, I don't care about that, as long as he realizes I'm good at my job."

Jen's groan feigned disbelief. "You're fooling yourself, Bethany. Or you're missing how he looks at you."

Nonsense. Complete fantasy. Those words came to mind, but she chose not to blurt them. Instead, she said, "I don't think so, Mom. He knows I lost Charlie. I'm sure I give off a strong 'not available' vibe." She didn't have room for another man in her life. "My life is focused on Heidi."

Knowing her mother would try to dig deeper, Bethany hurried ahead and caught up to Heidi. She opened the door to the lobby and it was like entering a new world. Carved jack-o'-lanterns were stacked in a pyramid on a long table. The fireplace blazed, and teenagers stood by to help with the tables of cookies and candy.

Heidi tugged on her hand to move faster and join the growing crowd. "Okay, Sylvie-the-mermaid, this party is just getting started." Bethany took a deep breath and tried to sweep away the collage of memories that rushed back. Sloan was simply not relevant to her future any more than he was to her past.

SLOAN SPOTTED BRIDGET FIRST. He had to laugh at her getup. Between hair the color of plums, thanks to an outrageous wig, and the fringed skirt and jacket, plus the cowboy boots, his cousin carried off a country and western singer's costume with style. Likewise his cousin-in-law Clint, who sported an amazing amount of leather fringe himself.

Bethany had encouraged him to go to the lodge on Friday night for what she'd called the version of a Halloween bash for grown-ups. He'd been reluctant at first, but seeing Bridget's face light up when she saw him made him glad he came. His cousin made her way through the tables to greet him by the door. "We managed to pull you over here to have some fun after all." She stepped back to create more distance between them and gave him a head-to-toe once-over. She then raised her eyebrows and pursed her lips in disapproval. "Hmm…plain old jeans and a blazer. Not exactly a costume." An exaggerated sigh followed. "Since it's you, I guess we can overlook that."

"Really? I haven't thought about coming up with a costume since some frat house caper in college." Call him stuffy, but he'd never taken to the idea of adults dressing up in Halloween costumes. Too much bother to be fun. Looking at his cousins, he kept that opinion to himself.

"Don't be a crab. I'm just glad you're here." She pointed to Willow and Tom, both in 1940s getups. Sloan's childhood friend Jeff was in an old army uniform. Olivia, who Sloan knew little about apart from her being a doctor, wore all black, except for the elaborate blue-and-yellow butterfly wings hanging from her shoulders and down her arms.

He glanced around but didn't see Bethany. He assumed this would be an occasion to see her friends and enjoy a little music. She was the one who'd told him that the lodge hosted this Halloween party on the first Friday night after the actual holiday. Apparently, Bridget and Clint, whose kids were older teens now, rarely missed a performance of any band Tall Tale brought in. They also had a reputation as karaoke champions. But this particular night was special because it featured Grisham's Strummers, a home-grown band that included Tom's sister, Erin, as the lead singer and fiddler. Quincy had filled him in about

Erin and Tom discovering they were half siblings, and how Erin had become his uncle's chief wood restoration specialist. It had been a revelation to Quincy and the others, even Tom himself, that she also was an accomplished pianist, fiddler and a singer with a sweet clear voice.

"Quincy told me he's on grandpa duty this weekend," Sloan said, amused by how delighted his uncle had been to have an overnight with his granddaughter Naomi, not quite two years old. "I suppose that's true for Bethany's parents, too, huh?"

"Sometimes, but not tonight," Bridget said. "Bethany decided to skip this shindig. She claimed Heidi seemed sniffly, but I think she's avoiding the party. It's sort of a couples-night-out event. Well, at least among the couples in Bethany's circle."

"Really?" Disappointment slammed with a surprising level of strength and surprise. Well, maybe not. Who'd he been fooling? He'd told himself he'd drop by the Tall Tale Lodge to listen to the band and visit with his cousins and friends, maybe meet Erin and her boyfriend, Mack, one of the lodge's owners. A partial truth. Mostly, he'd looked forward to coming because he'd assumed seeing Bethany was part of the evening. Not an unreasonable expectation. She'd sold him on the event in the first place.

"Come, sit with us. We'll make it a cousins table."

Dutiful but disgruntled, Sloan followed Bridget to her table and was immediately captured in Willow's hug. "You're such a stranger. I haven't seen you since the harvest festival. I've visited Uncle Lucas on the way to work, but I've been too early to catch you. Uncle Lucas says you spend a lot of time with him there."

"Dad's coming along pretty well," Sloan said. "He likes it a lot when you and Bridget stop by."

When Willow introduced Tom Azar, the pediatrician took the opportunity to rave about her and the whole Lancaster clan. "Falling in love with Willow came with a big benefit, a lovely little baby girl. She's officially my daughter now." Tom's grin was mischievous. "And your enormous extended family."

Sloan grinned and nodded toward Willow and Bridget. "Your fine reputation really does precede you."

"Good to hear," Tom said with a laugh in his voice.

When the waiter came around, Sloan ordered a local beer and settled in.

"You came in just as Tom and I were telling Bridget that we've called the adoption agency where I got Naomi," Willow said, her face beaming. "We've put our names on the list for another baby."

"You look mighty happy about that." Sloan

smiled in response to Willow's glow as much as to her words. Sitting here with these two couples, he found himself perplexed by how seldom he'd thought about having a family, especially during these past few years when work defined everything. He'd dated women with kids, but not in a serious, family-focused kind of way. Even his dad assumed he had no interest in such things.

Hanging out with his cousins in a bar waiting for a band would be fine if this was simply one of his very rare visits home to help his dad, which always included the assumption he'd go back to his real life. But the longer he hung around Adelaide Creek, what was missing in his life increasingly weighed on his mind. Lack of connection summed it up. And he could only blame himself.

"Bethany has raved about Erin." Sloan directed his comment to Tom. "From what I've seen since I've been back, there's a lot of talent around here. And positive changes."

"You're just discovering that now," Bridget said flatly.

"It wasn't meant to be a slight," Sloan said.

"Yeah, well, it sounded like it came as a big surprise." Bridget's smile was tight and brief. "I'd have thought you'd miss a few things about the place where you were born and raised. I think most people call it home."

"C'mon, Bridget, my life took me elsewhere."

Was she trying to start something? "That's just how it turned out." He couldn't resist adding, "The world is bigger than Adelaide Creek."

Before Bridget had a chance to respond, Tom jumped in to ask about his dad's rehab. Sloan filled him in on the basics, realizing that he was painting a rosy picture of his dad. "I usually think of him as kind of a curmudgeon, but he's getting along with the staff at Winding Creek, and other patients, too. Near as I can tell."

"It's true. He's been living alone for so many years." Bridget's tone was pleasant again. "I know he loves his companion dog, but when I dropped in a couple of days ago, he was like a different man. Not the reclusive Lucas we've come to accept. Must be because you're here, Sloan. It's been so many years." She immediately tapped her mouth with her fingertips. "Oops, that didn't come out exactly the way I meant it."

"He was always like that, Bridget." Sloan sighed. "He loved my mother. She was his whole life, but when she was gone he lost interest in other people." Sloan could have added that he'd lost interest in his only child, but he wouldn't risk sounding bitter. Sloan wasn't interested in poisoning the well.

Bridget frowned. "I know you don't like hearing what seem like accusations, Sloan. But how would you know what your dad needs? You've ignored him for the last twenty years. Your whole adult life. Why is that?"

"You want to judge me, fine, Bridget. But is it so surprising that I've never had the feeling my dad cared to have me here?"

"Really, Sloan," Willow said in a quiet, subdued tone. "You think your father didn't want you to visit?"

"Not particularly, Willow. He didn't care one way or the other. He's had little to say to me over the years, even when I showed up for holiday breaks during college. Same with the phone calls." Wanting to make his case, but not seem resentful or whiny, he took the conversation in another direction. "Emails, and more recently texts, are a different story," Sloan said with a chuckle. "I'd send him photographs from Afghanistan or Germany. And he sent pictures of the border collie he rescued. He would tell me how far they'd walked in the woods. That was the high point of his life, and it was easy enough to communicate in emails. They replaced awkward phone calls." Sloan paused. "We don't fight, we don't argue, and the frozen silences so typical of my childhood are gone. Those worn-out nicknames for me aren't so bad in texts."

Bridget waved him off. "That's just your dad being himself. We all have to put up with our parents' quirks." She glanced at Clint. "Our kids will gripe about us."

Bridget didn't get it. Sloan doubted any of his cousins understood how different his father was from their parents, or the way the younger generation dealt with each other. "You all treat each other with respect—and love. You always have. My dad was different. But now I see him around other people and he's dropped some of his indifference. And I agree, that's a good thing. I can hardly believe it, but we seem to be enjoying each other's company."

He thought about telling Bridget and the others that he wasn't planning to go back to Denver. Yet something stopped him. Maybe because he didn't have an alternate plan. The cases he'd accepted had earned him a reputation as a gutsy attorney willing to take chances. That meant he was in a strong position to consider offers from firms in new and faraway locations. Or not. He liked practicing law, but maybe it was time to try something else. Whatever he decided, he'd never return to a life that drained every ounce of his energy. Still, he had no regrets. And being a partner meant he'd have to activate the slow process that allowed him to extricate himself from the firm. His years there had been lucrative and he'd put aside his share of settlement money, invested it, and that translated into having choices.

He almost laughed out loud. If he wanted to blow a few dollars on carved witches, cauldrons and crows, nothing stood in the way.

Sloan nodded to Willow and Bridget. "I have no regrets leaving town for college and then joining the military, or going to law school. Or, taking a risk and joining a new firm." They'd been a young, brash group that took a few chances that more staid law firms in Denver thought were misguided. But it wasn't important that his relatives understand that. "For now, I'll settle for our visits and I can't have too many pictures of Flash."

"The center of his life," Bridget said.

Sloan saw an opening and took it. "Hey, changing the subject. Bethany tells me this is a great place for food, as well as music."

"And here they come." Suddenly Tom got to his feet, the lapels of his too-big vintage suit flapping. He began clapping and in a matter of seconds the whole crowd was standing and applauding as Grisham's Strummers came on stage. Without a word they started playing a bluegrass tune that kept the audience on their feet. So, Sloan thought, this was Tom's sister, Erin, petite with long dark hair, wearing a tunic that sparkled, over jeans and boots. Watching her and seeing Tom's proud expression, Sloan couldn't help but envy the mark on the community these two newcomers had already made.

When Erin started singing an old revival song, solo at first, with the band joining in and building the tempo, Sloan immediately understood why this band had caught on. It made him want to move to the music, but at the same time, it touched something deep inside. Erin then sang an old, familiar ballad—"Maid of Constant Sorrow"—a cappella, in a powerful, clear voice. Love found, love lost—sometimes found again. But not often in those old Scottish or Irish ballads. He couldn't shake Bethany from his thoughts. She'd found love and lost it. Now he found himself wondering if she wanted to find it again. Not the kind of question he could pose, at least not yet.

His table companions were definitely couples in love, smiling at each other when they applauded, and exchanging affectionate smiles when the band played one of their favorite songs. Bethany stayed on his mind through the entire set, a mix of classic folk tunes and country and western and bluegrass, but he was relieved when it ended. When the final applause and cheers died down, Sloan decided it was time to leave. "I'm beat," he said, keeping his tone casual. "I'm going to slip out and head home." He looked around him and saw a few others heading toward the exits.

Bridget frowned at him. "You're not staying

for the second set? Uh-oh. It's because of me and what I said, isn't it?"

Sloan couldn't discern if she was teasing or not. Before he could figure that out or answer her question, she added, "I didn't mean to be so, so… blunt…but we've all been curious about what's been going on with you."

"Well, I'm here in town with no plans to head out for now, so that means I'll see you soon." Sloan got to his feet and affectionately squeezed Bridget's shoulder.

"I want you to come to our place for Sunday dinner soon. We try to do one big family dinner at the ranch every month." She stared at him. "Promise?"

"Promise."

Something had brought on the dizzying, rollercoaster ride of feelings. Even with his mind on Bethany, a part of him wanted to run away, forget Adelaide Creek and the people who were like strangers to him. But his next thought was about being drawn to a life in this town—alongside this large family he'd been born into. The challenges from Bridget about his dad were part of what churned inside of him. It had always seemed like the path of least resistance to ignore his dad as much as possible. Until now, he'd seen no reason to change. But seeing his dad every day, watching his determination to recover, made him think again. It was like watching and interacting with a different man now, a guy whose rough edges had been made smoother by time. Flash had done his part, too.

Sloan said his goodbyes to his tablemates, eager to be on his way. Maybe he was tired, or confused by his emotions, but an urge to be alone had become stronger. But before he walked away he turned to Willow and Tom. "This is my first time at the lodge, but it won't be my last. And Erin has a fabulous voice. I've got a friend, one of my law firm partners, coming for a visit over Veterans Day weekend, so we'll come here for a meal, probably more than once."

"I imagine Veterans Day has special meaning for you," Willow said in a low voice.

"Yes, it really does." Sloan didn't elaborate, but let those words be enough.

Sloan hadn't talked to anyone in Adelaide Creek about Lonnie, his colleague at the firm, and also his close friend. Because they were both veterans, and carried invisible wounds, they'd teamed up to do some pro bono work for vets over the years. Somehow, it never seemed like enough. Many years older than Sloan, Lonnie had served in the Army's JAG Corps in both Iraq and Afghanistan. Some of those cases haunted Lonnie, and Sloan had been an ear for her as much as she'd been for him.

Lonnie was still on his mind on the way to his vehicle, but his thoughts had come full circle by the time he was on the road toward home. He found himself annoyed with Bridget all over again. "She doesn't get it," Sloan muttered under his breath, aware he was being defensive. "Dad probably seems like Mr. Wonderful when my cousins and the rest of the clan see him." He hadn't thought to don protective armor to go out to a bar and listen to a popular band with his cousins.

Bethany popped into his mind. Again. His preoccupation with her had begun almost the minute he'd arrived and had only intensified since. So far, the trip to the party store and dinner with the teenagers at the Burger Barn were highlights in his visit home.

Sloan glanced at the clock on the dash. It wasn't so late...not even half past eight. Maybe he could call and ask if she was up for company. He could always use questions about his dad as an excuse for wanting to see her. Or, he could be completely honest and come right out and say that he'd expected to see her at the lodge. Then he could ask if he could stop by to say hello.

Bethany was still an enigma of sorts, to him, anyway. She was an open book when it came to her work, her bond with her family and friends, and, of course, her love for her child. As for what she wanted for herself, she was silent. From both pointed and casual remarks from her and others, Sloan surmised that Charlie Goodman had been one of the good guys. He and Bethany had tried to keep their lives as no-fuss as possible, and free of tending to four-legged critters or mowing acres of fields.

Sloan groaned. Enough with all the analysis. Go with the urge to see her. Instead of turning down the road leading home, he stopped at the scenic turnout ahead. Without thinking about it anymore, he called Bethany.

CHAPTER SEVEN

BETHANY RESPONDED TO the ring and looked at her screen. Hmm… Sloan? Odd that he would call her at home. "Hey, are you calling from the lodge? How's it going over there?" She was about to bring up Erin and the band when Sloan answered her question.

"No, no, I'm calling from my car. The band is great, but I left the lodge and was on my way home. I was wondering if I could drop by." Before she could respond, he added, "If it's inconvenient, just say so. I've got some things on my mind, you know, about my dad. If it's not too late, of course."

A puzzling request. But it wasn't like Sloan to ramble. A little confused by the call, she took a couple of seconds to respond. "Uh, I don't see why not. Heidi's already fast asleep."

"And probably dreaming about mermaids." Sloan's voice was soft and a little sweet.

Suddenly, she decided a visit from Sloan was exactly what she needed. "Sure, come on over."

"Good. Thanks. I'll see you in a few minutes."

Call ended. She rushed to her bedroom.

Ha! She was being ridiculous. Brushing her hair with one hand and rifling through a dresser drawer for her favorite sweater. But why? This was Sloan, after all. What difference did it make if she was in one of her old, shapeless sweatshirts, rather than her favorite scoop-neck sweater in a blue that matched her eyes? She glanced down at her skinny black jeans. They were fine for an unexpected visitor. She raised her head and looked at herself in the mirror. The pink flush on her cheeks had to be her imagination. Or maybe it was the lighting.

Why Sloan called was a whole different question to chew on. He'd expected to see her at the lodge that night. Not an unreasonable assumption. The rambling on about things on his mind sounded a little like an excuse. She could almost admire this spur-of-the moment call. She was adding the final touch, a bit of lipstick, when the doorbell rang.

When she opened the door and stood aside to let him in, she saw that he carried a paper bag shaped to package a bottle of wine. Seriously? Her stomach rolled with a touch of anxiety. For a couple of seconds she wished she was back in the old sweatshirt and had skipped the lipstick.

She led him to the open area that linked the kitchen and dining area to the family room–living room, where she'd had a fire going since late afternoon.

"Here, first things first." He handed her the paper bag. "A blast from the past, as they say."

"Oh yeah? Let's see, then." She had to be amused at her own relief when she saw the label on the bottle of Bubbling Creek Cider.

"I thought you might enjoy that," Sloan said. "We were practically raised on the stuff, huh?"

"So we were. Have a seat. I'll pour each of us a glass."

"Hmm... I like your place."

"For me, the views will always be the high point. Building this addition was one of the best decisions I ever made." She explained that after moving out of the bungalow in town, she had to face facts. Long-term, her old bunkhouse home was a little too small for her and Heidi.

Sloan had taken a seat on one end of the couch in front of the fire and she handed him a glass of the amber liquid before taking a seat at the other end. "A toast to our local cider," she said. "It never changes."

As soon as they touched glasses, Sloan pointed with his chin toward the two dollhouses sitting to one side of the hearth. "I see that your little mermaid is both a rancher and castle-dweller. Princess or queen?" He got to his feet and picked up one of the tiny sheep, purposely carved and painted to look like her mom's Icelandic and Shetland sheep with their full wool coats in place. "They're incredible. And they even have their pasture to graze."

"Charlie added the pebbles and bigger stones to look like a real Wyoming pasture, less than perfect by design."

Bethany saw Sloan's startled expression. Understandable, since Charlie had died when Heidi was a baby, much too young to play sheep rancher with her dollhouse and figures. Or with fairy-tale castles. "Uh, Charlie worked on that dollhouse when he was home and we stored it with Mom and Dad. I gave it to her about a year ago. Charlie started the castle. After he died, his dad finished it and gave it to her last Christmas."

"They're real heirlooms, aren't they?" Sloan said, coming back to the couch. "The workmanship and detail…it's amazing."

Bethany answered with a simple nod. "She's a fantasy kid. You saw the mermaid fascination. I like that she gets the magic of stories. There's the castle and all its trappings, alongside the sheep ranch that resembles what she sees every day." The thoughtful expression on Sloan's face as he gazed at the two dollhouses made Bethany a little self-conscious, as if Sloan could see into Charlie's heart and his delight in Heidi.

"Meanwhile, they're pieces of art in your living room," Sloan said. "Incredible."

"And she's old enough now to play make-believe and have the sheep carrying on conversations. Or, the princess and the prince. I love the way she raises and lowers her voice like I do when I read to her."

"Well, then, what do they talk about, this princess and the prince."

Before Bethany could think about it a giggle escaped. "The last conversation they had was about shearing sheep."

"Art imitates life, huh?"

"A little time travel, too, since she moved the sheep from the ranch to the castle one afternoon." Just thinking about it made Bethany laugh. "The young royals collaborate very nicely on things."

"How modern of them—and their parents."

"One day she'll be old enough to grasp that her dad made these special pieces for her. And her grandpa contributed. She's still a little too young to understand it."

"But you're right. It won't be long before she does."

Time to change the subject. "I'm glad you went to the lodge, Sloan, and heard Grisham's Strummers. Doesn't Erin have a great voice?"

Sloan nodded. "The band was terrific. And as Bridget and a lot of other people, particularly my relatives, are fond of reminding me, I've missed a lot of good things that have come to Adelaide Creek. Erin and Tom are certainly two special newcomers." Sloan scoffed. "Well, relative newcomers. It's nice to see it doesn't take at least two generations to be considered an Addie Creeker anymore."

"Yes," Bethany said with a laugh. "No more outsider talk, at least for now. Landrum also has a really great Children's Adventure Center. Young kids put on plays there. I'm thinking of asking them to perform at Winding Creek this coming winter. We have patients and their families or friends who'd enjoy that."

"That's one way to break the tedium of long stays in rehab, like my dad's." Sloan's expression turned thoughtful. "Odd, though—I'd have expected him to be restless by now, more crabby, not less." He scratched his head. "What does the director think about that?"

Bethany put her glass on the coffee table. "Serious question?"

"Uh, yes."

"Well, then, in my opinion Lucas was lonelier than he realized, or perhaps cared to admit. He's perked up having so many people around. You've seen that for yourself." She paused. "It's not an unusual development, and not that complicated."

He frowned. "Apparently, my family agrees.

They think…well, let's just say they blame me for some of my dad's reclusive ways."

Bethany didn't know what to say to that. "I get the feeling not many people understand the situation between you and your dad. I didn't, not until you said something about it."

Sloan nodded, but stared at the dollhouses when he said, "I'm not about to rewrite the past and turn it into a nicer story. But I don't want to continue to resent my dad for things that happened twenty or thirty years ago."

"But those things have a way of coloring everything else." She tilted her head and peered into Sloan's face. "Right?"

Sloan shrugged, a puzzling move, since at first he'd been eager to tell her about the way he and his dad clashed. She considered challenging him, but changed her mind.

"Well, will you look at this?" Sloan picked up the miniature rake for the Zen garden on the corner of the coffee table. "We have one of these in the staff lounge at the firm." He moved the piece of rose quartz through the sand, and then went back to reposition another piece he couldn't identify.

"That's blue jade, by the way," Bethany said. "I just put this Zen box on the table the other day. Heidi is old enough now not to eat the sand or put the stones in her mouth. I have one in the staff room, and we have them for the patients, too."

"Such fancy stones," Sloan observed, grinning. "The one in our lounge had whatever came in the box."

"Like the kind I bought for Winding Creek. Simple, but somehow lures people to play around with them. We sometimes use them in rehab before or after the PT sessions, and for patients who tend to be anxious."

"A worthy budget item." Sloan pushed the rake back and angled another stone forward by making curvy lines in the empty sand left behind.

"Oh, I bought them myself," Bethany said. "We can get people to donate their old jigsaw puzzles and some board games, but Zen gardens aren't so common. But we had them at the hospital for patients in rehab. I saw how people were drawn to them."

The fire was burning down, but it was getting late and she wasn't inclined to add logs. Despite the seriousness of the conversation, and the bittersweet memories that always danced in her mind when Charlie came up, she enjoyed having Sloan in her house appreciating Heidi's dollhouses and raking sand and moving stones.

There was something different about him, rippling beneath the surface, as he made a couple of more moves in the Zen box. For sure, wanting to come by to talk about his dad's recovery was a ruse. But why?

In the almost two years since Charlie died, single men around town hadn't shown much interest in her. That was fine since she had no intention of dating. Why bother when she couldn't imagine falling in love again? It wouldn't make sense. She hadn't counted on Sloan's attention, which set off a new and different reaction. But, she reasoned, his real life was busy, demanded his full attention and was anchored in a city a day's drive away. Reminding herself of those facts, she could find no risk in simply enjoying a glass of cider in front of a fire with an old friend.

Besides, those dollhouses sent a clear enough message to any single man who'd consider showing interest in her. She and Heidi were a package deal. Raising her daughter would always come first in whatever decision she made about a job, a home, and most certainly a man.

Sloan put the rake back in the sand next to a chunk of polished rose quartz. Glancing at him, she realized he was looking pretty comfortable on her couch staring into the fire. Maybe a little too comfortable. No more than a second or two after she had that thought, he frowned as he leaned forward and drained his glass. "It may be too early to ask, but do you think my dad will actually be capable of taking care of himself? Alone, at home?"

Bethany had a ready answer, happily an optimistic one. "Based on what I see with my own eyes and the reports from his team, Lucas is expected to make a full recovery, more or less. That means yes, he can live on his own. Maybe he'll want someone to clean his house for him, or perhaps he'll hire someone to fix meals he can stash in his freezer. If that's the case, I can provide referrals."

"What a relief." Sloan's heavy sigh reflected that feeling. "Dad always seemed so much older than other fathers. And I was in my twenties before it hit me how many years older than Quincy my dad is. But then my mom and dad had me so much later in life. I recall a couple of teachers who didn't know us thought they were my grandparents."

"Lucas mentioned their age difference the other day," Bethany said. "He jokingly referred to Quincy as his baby brother. Seriously, though, Lucas is in pretty good shape for a man in his late seventies. All that physical work paid off, plus his long treks with his canine friends."

Sloan nodded, but then he looked at her with a quizzical expression. "A couple of times now, he makes a point of saying that my mom was, in his words, real happy when I came along." Sloan shook his head. "It came out of the blue."

"Does he talk that way often? Is he asking you about the past and what you remember and things like that?" Bethany asked, her interest piqued.

"Maybe talking about holidays or mentioning little things your mom did."

"As a matter of fact, he is." Sloan gave her a tender smile. "It's important to him that I tell him memories about my mom. It was almost like he was pressuring me."

"You don't talk about your special memories very often, do you?"

"No, it's true. Besides, who knows why certain things stay forever in the brain's memory files? But when he was probing I told him about how she smelled like pine cones when she made holiday wreaths. Lots of my memories include how the house smelled—or Mom herself."

Bethany smiled. "That's true for most of us. Scents have great power to bring on bouts of nostalgia."

"Mom did ranch work and never had an outside job, but looking back, she put so much into our home, and into making life good for me and my dad." Sloan gestured to the fire and the dollhouses, and a bright red-and-blue toy box. "Like you do here for Heidi."

Bethany could blush thinking about Sloan's exaggeration. "No, no...sure I like a comfy home and healthy food for Heidi and me, but I don't spend much time at it. I buy a lot of that comfort."

"You're a little busy. What you do is both important and ambitious." Sloan paused. "I'm wondering if Dad is thinking about his mortality now. Other than assuring me that he has a will, he's never said much about dying before. Maybe this stroke has him going through his life and his memories."

Bethany nodded. "When they've survived a crisis, many older people tend to be philosophical. Some treat it like a second chance to resolve old conflicts from earlier times." Bethany allowed that she might be wrong about Lucas, but her observations over the years held true. "I believe your dad is opening his eyes and seeing his grown-up son. Maybe for the first time."

Sloan stood and went to the fireplace, taking the poker and stirring the chunks of wood. Then he rested his elbow on the oak mantel and turned to face Bethany. "I see it, too." He looked like he had more to say. He kept his gaze on her during a long pause. "He could have died, Bethany, and I'd have missed seeing his softer, more affectionate side."

"And he's aware of that."

Sloan shook his head. "Some things have been truly eye-opening. He knows so little about me. He was worried I'd get fired for taking this time off. He even offered me a loan."

Bethany was silent while Sloan glanced around the room, his eyebrows knit in thought. "Well, like I told Bridget, Dad and I have communicated through emails and texts—and pictures of the dog."

"But Sloan, what did you expect? Your last visit was five years ago."

Sloan put up his hands as if warding off a blow he knew was coming. "You sound like Bridget now." He shifted his weight from one foot to the other, finally making his way back to the couch.

"Are you concerned about going back to Denver?"

"Not anymore." He offered a faint, almost secretive smile. "I haven't talked to anyone about this yet, not even my dad or Quincy, but what I do next and where I move is yet to be determined. And with Dad's situation, I won't make big decisions for a while. But I'm certain I'm not going back to Denver."

Surprisingly good—and scary—news, as her rapid heartbeat demonstrated. It shouldn't matter, but it did. Lucas would need some support from Sloan for a while. She cleared her throat before speaking. "So that's why you keep insisting that you can stay for as long as he needs you."

"Exactly. Besides…" He stopped talking and stared down into the fire.

"Besides what?" Bethany was too curious to hold back.

"Oh, nothing. I'll tell you about my decision another time. Complicated reasons."

Bethany couldn't help but wonder if a woman

was one of the complications. But she wouldn't go near that topic. "What will you do here—or anywhere else?"

Sloan chuckled as he lifted his shoulders and extended his hands to the side. "I don't know. It's up for grabs."

"Really?" That sounded odd.

"I'm not trying to be coy, but being in healthcare you understand burnout. In the case of my firm and my colleagues, our success can come at a big price. My team has worked together on the last three significant and complex cases for five straight years." Sloan laid out the facts of their foolish and punishing schedule. "To one degree or another, we've all paid. When I got the call about Dad, there was no question in my mind what to do. I negotiated a leave of absence. Dad was the catalyst, but I would have done it eventually, anyway."

Not expecting this look into Sloan's life, Bethany could see this wasn't the same man who showed up in Winding Creek's lobby, a guy with the decided air of cool confidence typical of successful people. Bethany took her time responding. She would have bought a little more time by refilling their glasses, but the bottle was empty now. "Wow. I didn't see any of this coming."

He waved her off as he came back to the couch and checked the screen on his phone. "I knew it had gotten late, but not this late."

"Who cares? I'm enjoying our conversation." She smiled. "Matter of fact, I always like running into you at the center."

Sloan's face brightened at her words. Without thinking about it, or weighing all the pros and cons, she blurted, "Did you ever roller-skate?"

A curious frown greeted that question. "Uh, well, a few times. A bunch of us used to go now and then. Why do you ask?"

"Well, you may not have heard the news, but the Children's Adventure Center and the city of Landrum teamed up and tomorrow is the grand opening of a brand-new roller skating rink. I'm planning to take Heidi for the little kids' skating time in the morning." She cocked her head. "Want to come along? Downtown Landrum is a lot different than it used to be. You'll see. And I can promise you a hot dog lunch." The words were coming out of her mouth before she could stop to consider them. But once she put them out there, she couldn't change her mind.

"Sunday morning, you say?" He flashed a broad smile.

"Uh-huh."

"I'm in," he said. "Sounds like fun." He narrowed his eyes as if assessing her. "Are you sure your little girl won't mind an extra person?"

Bethany laughed. "Are you kidding? Heidi loves an audience. Seriously." The bigger question was what Sloan could possibly find interesting about a bunch of little kids learning to roller-skate. But she'd plunged in.

"Well, count me in," Sloan said, adding a quick apology about staying too long. "I should go. I imagine Heidi is up at the crack of dawn."

Adjusting to Sloan's abrupt departure, Bethany stood and picked up the empty glasses from the coffee table. "I'm glad you stopped by. And you're right. Sleeping in on weekends isn't a concept Heidi understands."

Bethany was both sorry to see him go and relieved, too. She needed to watch herself with this incredibly attractive man, especially since her assumption was wrong. This wasn't going to be a here-today, gone-tomorrow situation. He probably wasn't likely to stay in Adelaide Creek for good, though.

When they got to her door, she put her hand on his arm. "Thanks for the cider. My favorite."

"You're welcome," Sloan said, and then as if it was the most natural thing in the world, he leaned in and kissed her cheek.

Hmm...it was quick and short...but as sweet if not more than the cider they'd just had.

"So, I'll see you tomorrow," Bethany said. She flipped on the outside lights and watched him walk to his SUV. Or maybe it was more of a saunter. He wasn't exactly hurrying away.

CHAPTER EIGHT

CHANGE CAME SLOWLY to his hometown, and to Landrum. As kids they'd called it "the big town," the county seat. Back when he was a teenager on the cusp of leaving Adelaide Creek, Sloan wouldn't have thought much about the slow rhythm of his homeplace. But being in the heart of Landrum on the occasion of the grand opening of the roller skating rink, he had to rethink his assumptions. And that was only the latest addition that was important on this chilly early November day. In the five years since his last visit, Landrum had doubled the size of the gallery, added the Children's Adventure Center, and in the same cluster of the older downtown buildings, opened the roller skating rink. More restaurants and Western-themed shops attracted tourists and locals alike. Sloan could feel the vitality of both towns, Landrum and Adelaide Creek.

When Sloan stepped inside the building, his first instinct was to put his hands over his ears to block the tinny music and the shouts and squeals of small children. But above the cacophony he heard a familiar child's voice shout, "Mommy, there's Sloan." When he followed the voice, he spotted Heidi pointing at him. Bethany looked up and waved.

He bypassed the main rink, where a few young kids were already skating, and joined Bethany and Heidi on a bench adjacent to a mini rink. From the look and size of it, it was reserved for the little kids to get their skating legs under them. A few kids around Heidi's age and their parents, presumably, were stumbling through the first stage of turning these preschoolers into skaters. Bethany was securing the brightly colored straps on Heidi's skates.

"Are blue and yellow your favorite colors, Heidi?" Sloan asked when he arrived.

Heidi tilted her head and frowned in thought before she shook her head. "I like red better."

"But these blue and yellow skates are especially for kids like you, first-timers," Bethany said, giving Sloan a pointed look. "And they're perfect."

Sloan grinned at Heidi. "I agree. You look very grown-up."

"The skate lady says I look like a girl who learns fast."

"Well, you did tell me you're almost four, so that sounds right to me." Sloan had fuzzy flashes of being around four or so and learning to ice skate on the pond at the ranch. He had vague memories of his wobbly ankles, and falling and sliding on the ice, but not for long. His mom had quickly got him up on his feet to try again.

"I didn't roller-skate for the first time until I was in college," Bethany said, "and Heather dragged me off to a rink near campus where a lot of kids from our dorm hung out. We had so much fun trying to stay upright." She chuckled as if recalling that mini adventure from the past.

"The two rinks are a clever idea." Sloan watched nearby kids Heidi's age as they managed to glide along, even if for only a couple of seconds as they struggled to put one foot in front of the other. "It'll be easier to get her moving in this smaller space."

"Good for me, too," Bethany said, already on skates and pulling Heidi up off the bench.

"Look at you, Heidi. Standing tall already," Sloan said. "If I'm going to keep up with you, I better get some skates." As he walked to the rental window, it hit Sloan that he'd spent very little time around kids of any age. But that didn't prevent him from enjoying Heidi now.

He picked up skates in his size and got back to the bench about the time Heidi caught on to the one-foot-in-front-of-the-other idea. "Like walking," Bethany said, "only gliding."

Once he had his skates on, the tottering legs of childhood made a return appearance, and he grabbed the high railing to balance himself. Ooh, the last thing he wanted was to embarrass himself and spend time sprawled on the floor. His muscle memory was fixed on ice skating, and when he let go of the railing, one foot went out from under him and he fell on his backside at the very moment a man guiding a boy no older than five passed him by.

"Look, Mommy!" the now familiar voice shouted from across the rink. "Sloan fell down."

Laughing at himself, he waved and said he was fine. It didn't take long to get to his feet and on the move again. The guy with the little boy offered good-natured reassuring words as they skated by him a second time. Determined to catch up with Bethany and Heidi, he ventured out again, this time finding his footing and establishing a workable rhythm.

"You are a fast learner, Heidi." Heidi had let go of her mom's hands and was moving forward upright, if a little awkwardly. Sloan chuckled. "Hey, you can give me a few tips."

"You look none the worse..." Bethany grinned, looking away from Heidi just long enough to miss her go down on her side.

"Oops." Sloan stopped in place. "Time to get right up."

He spoke at the same instant Bethany noted the fall and in one quick motion put her hands under

Heidi's arms and lifted her up. She took Heidi's hand and gently pulled her forward. "Can't stop. Gotta keep going."

Easier said than done, Sloan thought. But Bethany had acted so quickly Heidi didn't have time to be self-conscious or even embarrassed. Sloan found his skating legs and took some turns around the rink with Bethany and Heidi, who found her sweet spot of speed and footwork on the third and fourth turns, although she still hung on to the two fingers Bethany extended.

Some of the other kids who had been in the mini rink had now made their way to the main rink, which was reserved for the youngest children during the early morning hours. Heidi noticed. "Can we go inside the big rink now?"

"I think we can," Bethany said, "and you can hang on to my fingers for as long as you like."

They had plenty of room in the larger rink, and Bethany skated next to Heidi on one side and Sloan fell in step next to Heidi on the other side.

"She's catching on, huh?"

Bethany nodded. "I'm just now feeling a little more comfortable myself and moving without fear that I'll crash to the floor."

"You're ahead of me," Sloan said.

"You didn't hurt yourself, did you?" Bethany asked.

"Nah. Only my pride." He gave her a hangdog look over Heidi's head.

When a couple of skaters only a little older than Heidi sped past, she wobbled, but then grabbed hold of Sloan's index finger to catch her balance. Even Heidi was silent as they skated down the long rink, with the carnival music and noisy crowd as background. As his muscles remembered what he'd learned as a young boy, Sloan stopped thinking about every move, and he and Bethany synced their steps with Heidi's.

"This is amazing," Bethany said over the noise.

She didn't need to explain. Their thoughts were aligned as well as their movements.

"I can do it," Heidi said, first dropping Sloan's finger and then Bethany's. "I'm in the big rink."

"Yes, you are," Bethany said, smiling at Heidi, and then exchanged a quick glance with Sloan. "Such a big girl now."

Without being able to pinpoint why, or even describe what he was experiencing, he felt something shift inside. He knew for sure this was an important day. Looking at Bethany, Sloan saw pleasure and affection for her child written on her face, but he was sure she regretted not being able to share this everyday kind of milestone with Charlie. Although aware he couldn't fill those big dad-shoes, he had the sense of being in the right place on this particular day. The way Heidi trusted him to help her keep her balance touched his heart. Such a minor thing, but he liked the feeling.

"How about one more turn?" Bethany asked Heidi as they rounded the curve at the top of the rink. "It's almost time for the bigger kids to have their hour in the rink to skate."

"Can we come here again?" Heidi asked.

"I think we will definitely arrange to roller-skate another day."

"And you can come, too, Sloan." Heidi looked happy with herself and the day. "Please."

"Aren't you sweet," Sloan said, walking a line that acknowledged her invitation without committing to coming along. Not that he'd mind, but it wasn't up to him. Or Heidi.

Heidi grinned, but then her mind took off for the next thing. Lunch, specifically hot dogs. When they went back to the bench to change from skates back to street shoes, Heidi's mind was already across the street at The Dive, which had got its name when it opened in the 1960s. It specialized in hot dogs and burgers, along with salty fries and hot chili topping. "I like The Dive," Sloan said, "and I don't mind admitting I spent a lot of time there when I was a kid."

"Me, too, especially as a teenager." Bethany teased. "You remember when a bunch of us would come here after basketball games. We'd push the old wooden picnic tables together and share baskets of fries."

"And soft-serve ice cream," Sloan added.

"The picnic tables are inside. But why?" Heidi asked.

"Hmm...maybe because they're strong and take a lot of hard use," Bethany said.

"And can be dragged around." Sloan had to laugh at how much the name of the place fit.

Heidi slipped into her shoes and put her hands on her hips. "Okay. I'm ready."

As they headed for the door, Sloan took a detour and returned their three pairs of skates to the rental window. He rejoined Bethany and Heidi on the sidewalk, discussing what they'd have for lunch. Before they'd finished crossing the street, Heidi settled on her order, with an emphasis on dessert. The Dive was crowded now, with kids and adults coming in and out.

"Why don't you find us a table and I'll get in line and order for us," Sloan said.

Bethany nodded but reached into her fanny pack. "Here, I've got cash. I'll pay for lunch."

Sloan jumped in and waved her off. "You can treat another time. Let me take care of lunch today." He raised his voice to be sure she heard him over the noise.

"Really?" Bethany looked at him skeptically. "Are you sure?"

"Positive, but hurry, the tables are filling up fast."

"Okay." Bethany pointed to the sea of people and tables and waitstaff zipping back and forth as they bussed tables. The staff all wore the same outfit of black jeans and red T-shirts printed with the image of a diver midair above the water. "Wish us luck."

Sloan slipped into the back of the line, repeating the order in his mind while he watched Bethany guide her daughter around the tables to one in the corner, where a teenager was replacing old newsprint to cover it with a new batch. Some things really didn't change. In an instant he was pulled back into his high school years when he and his buddies devoured hot dog or burger baskets after basketball practice as a snack, and then went home for dinner with their families. A couple of his friends then started their evening shifts behind the counter. It was a prized part-time job for teens. But like Bethany and many of their friends, Sloan was a ranch kid and his part-time job was at home. Sloan's head was so steeped in his teenage past he was surprised when it was his turn at the counter. He put the order in and was given a number.

"Shouldn't be long, sir." The teen, who looked barely old enough to have a job, shifted his attention to the next person in line.

As Sloan approached the table in the back, he

noted Bethany's pensive expression as she stared out the window. Next to her, Heidi's eyes were focused the other way and on the people of all ages in motion. When Heidi spotted him, she smiled as if excited to see him. She waved and nudged her mom. Bethany seemed startled to be pulled out of her reverie. It struck Sloan that he'd happily watch Bethany's changing expressions all day.

He'd barely settled across from the two and put the plastic number, 15, in the stand on the table when a young woman arrived with the tray of baskets. "Wow, that was fast."

"We aim to please. Raise your hand high if you need anything else." The server pointed to a counter, where they'd find soft-service ice cream and bins of toppings. "And when you're ready, help yourself."

"A blast from the past?" Sloan said, nodding at Heidi. "Ha! Isn't that the truth. What's really changed?" Bethany asked. "They added a few new items and doubled their size when they expanded into what used to be the gift shop next door. I think that's it."

"Looking at the staff reminds me of how young we were when we hung out here." Even to his own ears, he sounded nostalgic.

"It hits me, too. We're only in our thirties, but high school seems long ago."

Heidi took a bite of a french fry. "How old are you when you're old?"

"Hmm, that's hard to say exactly," Bethany said.

"Grandpa Dan said he was getting old," Heidi said. "Then Grandma Jen said he wasn't seventy yet. Not old."

Along with Heidi, Sloan was curious how Bethany would field that question. Jen and Dan seemed young in their sixties, as opposed to his dad, who was closer to eighty, but had seemed old for a long time.

"Oh, that's just the way people talk, sweetie. Grandma was teasing Grandpa Dan a little." Bethany sent Sloan an amused smile. "Sloan and I were saying that it seemed so long ago that we used to come to The Dive after school. But we're not old, not at all."

"A girl in my class told me that you don't die until you're really, really old." Heidi took a huge bite of her hot dog. So big she wouldn't be able to talk and chew.

Bethany's expression darkened, but not for long. She limited her response to teasing Heidi about her mouthful of food, while at the same time, drowning her fries in ketchup.

Sensing this was a tricky topic, and probably not the first time it came up, Sloan allowed his thoughts to drift to his own past. Not only his mother dying when he was nine, but the times he'd witnessed young soldiers die. And civilians. Bethany knew the sadness and pain of loss. So did he.

He was lost in his own unwelcome memories when Heidi tugged on Bethany's sleeve. "I told Sophie she was wrong. My daddy wasn't old when he died."

Sloan wasn't surprised that Bethany didn't seem to be taken aback by Heidi's words. "That's true, sweetie. But still, you always know one thing for sure. Your daddy loved you so much."

Heidi nodded. "Yep." She picked up a fry. "More ketchup, please."

On to the next thing, Sloan thought, as Bethany picked up the squeeze bottle of ketchup and made squiggly lines with the ketchup on the fries. The upside of a child's curious and busy mind.

"You'll come to the Veterans Day commemoration next weekend, won't you?" Bethany asked.

"For sure. I'm bringing a friend from Denver. Her name is Lonnie Richardson. The trip was planned around that weekend."

"Uh, Veterans Day? Your friend is coming specifically for that day?"

"That might seem odd," Sloan said, "but Lonnie and I are the only two veterans in our firm. She was a JAG Corps officer, you know, the Judge Advocate General. She spent her whole career as an army attorney. We've done a little pro bono advocacy work for veterans on the side."

"Wow. I wouldn't have thought you'd have had the time for that."

Sloan shrugged. "We didn't. But we worked together and made the time, especially when we realized so many veterans' issues keep popping up. She served in Afghanistan, too," Sloan explained, "so we understand each other in a way other people don't, maybe can't."

Bethany gave him a firm nod. "Well, I understand, if only because of Charlie. He went into contract intelligence work after having the same kind of specialty in the military. I always knew he was part of a wonderful band of brothers and sisters." She smiled. "Like you...and your friend."

"You'll meet Lonnie. You'll like her a lot. I'm sure of it."

"Well, I'll, uh, look forward to it." She cleared her throat. "I'm having one of my buffet dinners that night. At my house. I invite most everyone I know to drop by. Including you, and your friend."

"You amaze me," Sloan said. "You have more energy than anyone I know. And now, throwing a big dinner."

Bethany scoffed. "I'll burst that bubble right away, Sloan. When I entertain, and I do like having people over, I use a really great caterer, Donna Kay. Her crew takes care of all the details, including the china and silverware, and then they show up and whisk it all away afterward."

"Smart," he said, admiring the way she managed her life. "Speaking of whisking things away, I've polished off everything but the paper lining and the basket."

Heidi giggled. "You can't eat paper."

"You don't miss a thing, Miss Heidi, do you?"

"You're done, too," Bethany said to Heidi, "and so am I. We should get our dessert and be on our way. I think Sloan needs to visit his dad."

Unlike him and Bethany, Heidi had room for soft serve with caramel syrup. Amused, Sloan watched Bethany follow Heidi's directions down to a final spoonful of sprinkles. As soon as she'd polished off her sundae, they stood, and in a flash one of the kids in a red T-shirt was at the table and stacking the empty baskets.

"I do need to get to Winding Creek," Sloan said. "My dad's expecting me."

"You look happy about that." Her tone was low and warm.

Something had changed over the last few weeks. Instead of dutifully visiting his dad, Sloan looked forward to seeing him. He nodded. "You're right. I am."

THE PINCH OF jealousy in Bethany's gut threw her off her game. Jealous of a woman she didn't know. A friend. No mention of a romance. But she couldn't get the visit off her mind. So ridiculous. If Sloan had a girlfriend, he wouldn't have left the lodge early to visit an old school chum, now would he? *Okay, admit it.* Maybe she enjoyed Sloan's company a little too much. One minute he'd confided that he wasn't going back to Denver, and the next minute she'd invited him to go roller skating.

Now it was Monday and she couldn't shake the odd preoccupation with Sloan's woman friend. As a diversion, she'd even roped her mom into a shopping trip yesterday afternoon. Grandpa Dan had immediately agreed to entertain Heidi for a few hours while her mom and Grandma Jen took off for the mall. It was fun, too, especially because they came back with shopping bags loaded with new clothes, including shirts for Dad and a winter jacket for Heidi. Bethany chatted with her mom about everything from roller skates to roof repairs, but studiously avoided bringing up Sloan.

Ignoring the paperwork on her desk, she picked up her tablet and started down the hallway designated for patients likely to become permanent residents of Winding Creek. First stop, a patient transferred from the hospital on Friday. She'd been alone, with no family members with her. When Bethany entered the room, a nurse was adjusting the IV of the sleeping patient. A woman stood next to the bed.

Bethany nodded to the nurse and approached the woman, who was close to her own age, and introduced herself. She quickly learned the visitor was Emily, the woman's granddaughter, the patient's only living family.

"It's been just me and Grandma Lynn for a few years now," Emily said, explaining that she was an only child and so was her mom. "I got here as soon as I could. I was coming to visit next month for Gram's ninetieth birthday. It wasn't going to be a big party, but still…"

Bethany glanced at the tablet and perused the summary of this patient's medical history. Indeed, the new patient, Lynn Paulson, would turn ninety in December. "She's been living on her own, I see, and doing well." Mrs. Paulson was sleeping, so Bethany coaxed Emily into the hall while the nursing assistant did all the little things to make sure Mrs. Paulson was comfortable.

For a few minutes the stress in Emily's face disappeared, replaced by a calm demeanor as she told an abbreviated story of Grandma Lynn's previous ability to age on her own terms. And that meant remaining independent. "I arranged for a cleaning service and for someone to run errands and drive her to appointments," Emily said. Mrs. Paulson lived in a house on a block off Merchant Street that was lined with mostly large, stately homes.

Emily let out a heavy sigh. "Grandma had been content and hadn't shown many obvious signs of decline, but now the doctor told me her heart has weakened." With a helpless shrug, she added, "She's dying of old age."

Bethany responded to Emily's confusion. "Your grandmother has lived fully and well for almost ninety years. And stayed in her home. That's exactly what we all hope for our parents." She paused. "Looking at her chart, I can see that she never had a fall, a stroke, or even elevated blood pressure until a couple of years ago. Remarkable."

Emily let out a light laugh. "You forgot something. She was, as the doctor said, 'sharp as a tack.'"

"Another piece of good luck, huh?" Bethany lightly rested her hand on Emily's shoulder. "It sounds stark, but sometimes, a decline is rapid, and I can't promise she'll get better. I can promise we'll do our best to keep her comfortable. All of us together."

For that minute, Bethany's doubts about taking on the job of breathing new life into Winding Creek vanished, as if blown away in a gust of wind. At this moment, this facility was exactly what Lynn and her granddaughter needed.

"How long are you staying in Adelaide Creek?" she asked.

"Not sure. Grandma is my only family, so I'm taking family leave from my job. I'm an accountant at a firm in Salt Lake City. If she's not able to go back home, I'll need time to deal with the house. Later, I suppose I'll sell it." A secretive smile took over Emily's face. "Then again, maybe not. I like Adelaide Creek."

"I'm glad you don't have the pressure to get back to work," Bethany said. "We're here for you, too. If you need anything, all you have to do is ask. By the way, we're proud of our cafeteria fare."

Emily thanked her and went back inside the room. The nursing assistant had pulled the lounge chair closer to her grandmother's bed. The medical staff would take care of Mrs. Paulson, but Bethany made a mental note to check on Emily at the end of the day.

Bethany moved on to the newest patient admitted to the rehab unit. She had just enough time to introduce herself before relatives converged on the room. As long as she was close by, she popped into Lucas's room to say hello. He was in his chair watching the morning news, but clicked the TV off as soon as she appeared in the doorway.

"Hey, look who's here," Lucas said. "The busiest woman in Adelaide Creek."

"You're in good spirits on this Monday morning," Bethany said, responding to Lucas's cheerful mood.

"I'm okay. My grown-up boy told me about the roller skating rink opening up downtown." Lucas snickered. "Said he only landed on his bottom once."

Bethany laughed. "Yes, you're definitely in good humor today." Lucas really had come a long way from the crotchety old man she'd first met.

"Sloan brought Flash around on Saturday. A dose of that dog makes me feel real good. I'll see him again on Wednesday, looking forward to that." Lucas frowned. "Not sure about next weekend, though."

"I don't think the Veterans Day ceremony will interfere with your visit with Flash. It's held in the morning, so he can—"

"But he's got that lady friend coming to town," Lucas interrupted. "Did he tell you about that?"

"Uh, yes, I believe he did mention that. Her name is Lonnie, I recall." Bethany struggled to keep a breezy tone.

"Didn't tell me much about her," Lucas said, "except to say she was a partner at the firm."

"And a veteran." Bethany added that detail because it was important to Sloan.

"And not long ago I teased Sloan about not being a one-woman man like Quincy and me."

Lucas gave the arm of the chair a whack. "Oh, boy, he didn't like that. Told me not to give up on him yet. Could be that Lonnie is the one."

Bethany shrugged, in a quick casual sort of way. "Guess we'll see."

"Sloan's bringing me down to that memorial at the cemetery. Taking the wheelchair for me once we get there," Lucas said. "My first time out."

"Good for you. You've made a lot of progress in such a short time." Bethany was grateful for the change of subject. "And if I'm going to make any progress today, I need to get back to my office."

"Kidding aside, you work hard here," Lucas said, "and you're raising your little girl by yourself, too. Can't be easy."

Since that came out of the blue, Bethany was self-conscious about Lucas's words. "Fortunately, I love my work here at Winding Creek, and Heidi has two sets of grandparents who are over the moon for her."

"Well, maybe one day another good man will come along…uh, you know what I mean."

Bethany forced a smile. "Hmm… Seems I'm a one-man woman. I'm a lot like you and Quincy." She immediately regretted her defensive tone. She should have written off Lucas's words as meaningless small talk, but too late now. Needing to go, she pivoted fast. "Wow, I'm going to be late for a meeting." Already in motion, she gave Lucas a quick wave. "See you soon."

On the way back to her office a text came in from Quincy, as she expected on Monday mornings, their typical check-in time. Only this time he said: nd u to call bk soon as u can

It sounded ominous, not typical for Quincy, a serious guy, but not by any stretch an alarmist.

Bethany looked at the notes in front of her and stared at her computer. She'd planned to catch up with reports and review staff evaluations. But she looked at her phone, then reached for it and returned the call.

Quincy answered on the first ring, and given the level of noise, Bethany surmised he was outside. "One sec…" The line went quiet for what seemed like a long few seconds before he came back. "I'm inside the construction trailer now. I'll get to the point. Can you meet with the board this afternoon? Uh, online."

She couldn't ignore the lurch in her gut. "Of course, but what's the rush? I was about to finish up the board report. I've got the census numbers, and some details about the improvements we put in place."

"This is more about strategy, Bethany. It seems the guys from that group in Seattle have been making the rounds."

Good ol' Todd Webber. "The Ashley Group. Who's he lobbying?"

"Oh, they've sent some special mailings to the mayor and the town council, and the business owners on Merchant Street. Even the health department in Landrum. They've hit key people around the county."

"Why Landrum? Their city officials haven't taken a position on local control of Winding Creek." As individuals, though, most in the small business community supported the center staying in public hands. When it came down to it, for decades, Quincy had been a powerful voice of experience in town. People respected his success as a businessman and his public service, which made him a more persuasive advocate than Bethany.

"I got one of Ashley's glossy sales packets at the shop, too. I'll show it to you. We have to pay attention to the hard sell going on in the county, especially with the hospital and Department of Health, and senior citizen advocates. And we can't forget nurses."

"You can tell the board I'll adjust my schedule." Bethany had a lot riding on every meeting with the board. "What are they questioning? I send them regular email updates and they've signed off on the patient satisfaction survey we're launching in January."

"We don't need to be defensive, Bethany," Quincy said. "They want assurances. Let's face it, our finances are a little shaky. Another grant application was turned down by that foundation in Jackson."

She couldn't dwell on that now. "An idea is forming in my head. Nothing huge, but a way to increase our contact with people in town, the real stakeholders. Something we should have been doing all along. Text me the time. We'll be ready on my end."

When she ended the call with Quincy, she hurried across the hall to Margaret, Bethany's first hire when she took over last January. Her title was part-time administrative assistant, but she handled many things, including internal communications. Bethany couldn't think of a solid reason she couldn't assemble a formal newsletter for external use. Something to augment the bulletins Margaret already handled.

"I'm interrupting," Bethany said, "but can you take a quick break from whatever you're doing?"

"Of course." Margaret turned away from the screen. "Perfect timing. I was spell-checking the report you asked for."

"Good. I'll need it forwarded to the board as soon as possible. We're having an impromptu board meeting."

"Today?"

"Uh-huh. This afternoon." Bethany gave Margaret a quick rundown on her conversation with Quincy. "I had an idea I thought we'd develop next year, but I want to jumpstart it."

"A newsletter? Right?"

"You're reading my mind again."

"Nope. I read your memos—every one of them. You mentioned this a few months ago, at the same time we were breathing life into our website."

Amused, Bethany recalled the exact memo directed to Margaret in which she brainstormed ideas to make Winding Creek a more vital part of the community. The connection to the high school was good, and participating in markets and fairs, but they needed greater visibility. "Okay. Item number whatever was about an online newsletter targeted to Adelaide Creek folks first, and adding key players in the small towns around us and Landrum."

"I thought that was a great idea," Margaret said. "Occasional bulletins and mentions in the newspaper aren't enough. What do you need to get started?"

"A mockup of a newsletter—let's start with two pages, with some photos. If this works out, we'll add more and go from there."

"Good, keep it simple. Do you have a headline? How about the high school kids and decorations—you sent photos for the file." Margaret hesitated. "Sloan with the kids at the party store, too. We can publicly thank him for lending a hand."

"I'm not sure. He keeps insisting it's no big deal, that he's here for his dad." Bethany paused. "But I'll ask him. This is just a design. We're not writing the copy today."

"And let's reserve a block for an update of our fundraising and the roof repairs," Margaret said. "We have before and after photos. And for that section, we can thank the *anonymous* donor."

Bethany filled in the blank. Quincy. At some point he was bound to finally admit he'd paid for the repairs himself. This wasn't the first time Quincy had dug deep into his own pockets to fund a project.

"We'll have it posted on the Adelaide Creek website, of course," Margaret said, "but I'll print a few copies to put in the library and at the reception desk."

First things first. Without the mockup, Bethany had nothing tangible to sell to the board. "I shouldn't have waited so long. But we had so many other things to do to keep this place open."

"Why don't you leave me to it," Margaret said, her voice soft and reassuring. "I'll do it right now, before I work on the other reports."

Bethany nodded gratefully.

The rest of the day she was in and out of her office, first to chat with two patients released from the rehab unit to continue their recovery at home. She liked adding the personal touch in wishing them well, usually meeting them in the lobby on their way out of the center. All those years of nursing had convinced her that personal contact was even more important in the age of cyber-communication. In between those visits and a series of phone calls, she got a text setting up the online meeting for late that afternoon.

Before she had a chance for a break, the hour for the meeting arrived. She entered the conference room a little bedraggled. Quincy and her old friend Alice Buckley were already online when she took her seat and joined the meeting. Good news, the board liked Margaret's newsletter mockup. Important work, keeping the center in the public eye. But that mattered little next to the bigger issue.

Throughout the meeting, Bethany found herself steering two different trains of thought. One train was all about the upbeat sense of making progress. Another demanded a deeper understanding that not everybody in town or the county thought her efforts, or the board of directors' commitments, were worth it. The stark truth was, some in town were of the view that they should take the easy way out and sell Winding Creek to the Ashley Group. Let the staff, including Bethany, become employees of this national chain.

As she was pondering that dreary thought, Quincy spoke up and reminded the board that much of the administrative staff, including Bethany, would likely be replaced by individuals handpicked by the Ashley Group. And not necessarily hired from a pool of county residents.

"That's a nonstarter," Alice Buckley said. "If it came to that, we'd make it a strong negotiating point. I'm not signing off on a deal that replaces the staff that Bethany and the department heads have put together. No way."

"Wait, Alice. This isn't a plan. No one is proposing this yet," Quincy said. "Ashley can send out its PR, but that doesn't mean they'll succeed."

"Meanwhile, we need to sell *our* idea." Alice picked up Bethany's report, and the mockup of the newsletter. "Over the long run, it's much better for Adelaide Creek. That's why I'm here. So, let's increase visibility and keep selling what we're doing."

Bethany understood Alice on many levels, and had been impressed that she'd spent her term as mayor as more than a manager. She was a booster. Long-term, she advocated for creating a public park and nature center on the acres surrounding Winding Creek.

Quincy grinned. "Thanks, Alice. That's the spirit. Let's remember, we negotiated a two-year contract with the town council. We've got a little over a year to turn around Winding Creek." Quincy paused. "Frankly, we're doing more than holding our own. We've made significant, measurable progress."

Bethany didn't need to add anything here. These individuals might be supporters, but when agreeing to serve on the board, they'd been clear that their support wasn't unconditional. Winding Creek had to deliver.

No pressure, huh?

Bethany had to swallow back her other idea. At some point, she would talk with Quincy about the next step in their vision. She'd use that sports motto he liked to persuade him to accelerate the pace of their vision...go big or go home. It was all she could do not to blurt it out. For some reason, Sloan came to mind. Without even hearing his opinion, Bethany knew for certain what he would say. Like Quincy, he'd tell her timing was everything. And this wasn't the time.

CHAPTER NINE

AT LOOSE ENDS on the days before Lonnie was due to arrive, Sloan kept up with his dad and prepared to have a guest in a house that hadn't seen one in many years. Bethany was a constant presence in his thoughts in all kinds of ways, mostly irrational. For one thing, he wondered how Lonnie would take to Bethany, speculation that didn't make much sense. But the question rolled around in his head anyway. He'd only involved Lonnie in his pathetic love life once. That was when Teresa had indicted him for lack of attention, and cited a series of canceled dates as items she entered for evidence. Lonnie had tried to be kind about it, but she'd more or less told him that she'd have found him guilty, too. In other words, it served him right.

Sloan also saw Bethany at Winding Creek almost daily. He felt more and more drawn to her, even recalling the spicy scent of her hair when he'd kissed her cheek at her door when he left her house the other night. He'd often thought about how good she looked, but now he couldn't forget that heady smell, or the softness of her sweater. She must have known that it was the same shade of blue as her eyes.

These images would float around in his mind as he spent a couple of mornings fixing up the room Sloan's mother had kept ready for guests, even if they'd been few and far between. Nothing had changed in twenty years, except for the added layers of dust. Sloan cleaned with the windows open to coax fresh air into the room. It was the largest of two bedrooms on the second floor and it was an en suite. After his mother died, Sloan and his dad rarely had occasion to go upstairs, because the three first-floor bedrooms more than met their needs.

Sloan stared at a painting on the wall and recalled coming home from school one day to find his mother on a ladder rolling pale gray paint on the walls of this room. Two days later, he'd helped his mom hang the oil painting she'd bought from Heather's mom, Noreen Stanhope. A prominent local artist, Noreen had been known for her work showing Wyoming's iconic sheep ranches and horses grazing on pastures. Her depiction of the mountains, often rendered in deep purples and pinks, also were prominent in the collection of her work at the county gallery, and the subject of the painting Sloan stared at now. After Lonnie left, he'd move that painting to a wall in his room downstairs.

His dad, notoriously thrifty, had a linen closet full of drab, worn-out towels and sheets, but Sloan dug deep into the piles and eventually pulled out a set of good enough white sheets with a yellow floral pattern. He'd given Lonnie fair warning that the farmhouse was no upscale B and B or quaint country inn. Her response was typical of her. "Must I remind you that I'm used to both military housing and tent camping in the mountains. Fancy isn't my style."

Sloan smiled to himself. He'd never had a friend quite like Lonnie. Not long after he joined the firm as a young associate, Lonnie had come aboard, too, after retiring from active duty. Sloan had welcomed having another vet as part of the firm, where interest in veterans issues ran occasionally hot but mostly cold, among the partners. Or, as Lonnie had observed, a classic case of "out of sight, out of mind." She'd barely settled in when her JAG reserve unit had been called up for duty in Afghanistan.

Before Lonnie left, Sloan had taken her out to a steakhouse to celebrate her fiftieth birthday. Their conversation drifted to her twenty-year career as a military attorney. That dinner was a few years ago, but he remembered coming away with a sense that he had more in common with her than with any other colleague.

They'd exchanged regular emails over the next

six months, at which point, her special deployment was over and she came home and returned to the firm. The two of them had joined forces to do some pro bono work for vets. It started when he became a listening ear for Lonnie, the one person she could count on to understand stories of soldiers in trouble of one kind or another. More than anything, she'd committed herself to searching for help for brain-injured soldiers, retired or still on active duty. She took offense at the underreporting of the long-term effects of these injuries. Her anger was a tool that helped to build trust with vets.

When she asked him to come to support group meetings, he'd watched her gently coax men and women to open up about their symptoms and their lives. Sloan had tried to put his four years of military experience behind him, taking the attitude of: *Move on. If you can't forget, then try to ignore what you remember.* A fool's errand, as he'd learned from Lonnie. Sloan had never known what it was like to have an older sister, but over time, he and Lonnie had declared themselves each other's family.

Sloan snapped back to the present when Flash wandered into the room and sat at his feet. The dog was smart. It was as if he could count the days on the calendar and needed to remind Sloan that Wednesday had rolled around again. "I got it buddy, it's time to see Lucas. Then later, I'll introduce you to a good friend of mine. You'll like her, I promise."

With that, he picked up his travel pack for Flash. Treats, leash and a couple of chew toys. Sloan was ready to hit the road, and Lonnie was on the road, too, and would join him at Winding Creek later that afternoon. They planned it that way so she could meet Lucas, and most likely, Bethany.

"We're right on time, Flash, thanks to you," Sloan said after pulling into the lot. He walked inside Winding Creek with a couple of other people on the same mission, bringing a dog to visit their owner-patient. Like Flash, these other dogs were setting a fast pace to get to their owners. He and his dad would hang out with some of these people and pets in the residents' lounge later.

When he got to the door of his dad's room, Lucas was already in his wheelchair ready for Flash. Before they'd go for a walk, though, there'd be a good ten minutes of affectionate hugs and pats and the dog's tail going wild with glee.

As always, Sloan hung back and watched the reunion unfold. Wednesday and Saturday, his dad's best days of the week. Same as Flash. "Flash is going to be so happy when you're back where you belong."

"I suppose so," Lucas said.

A little lukewarm. "You don't sound all that excited."

"There's nothing I want more than to have Flash with me all the time." Lucas bobbed his head from side to side. "I guess I can manage okay in that big ol' house. Don't need much more than three rooms anyway."

"You have a while to think about that, Dad. By the time you get home you'll be walking on your own, maybe with a cane. And I've got some leads on a couple of cleaning services we can use," Sloan said, wanting his dad to be clear that he wouldn't be entirely on his own. "Bethany tells me the caterer in town has people working for her who also prepare and deliver meals. And I'm not going anywhere. At least not anytime soon."

"Still don't get how a man your age isn't going off to work every day. But speaking of Bethany, I told her you had a lady friend coming to visit. She's eager to meet her."

"Lady friend?" Sloan groaned. "That sounds... well, wrong. She's a friend and a colleague. Calling her that makes it sound like a woman I date."

Lucas's eyes opened wide in surprise. "She's not? 'Course I thought so. Why didn't you say something? And why isn't she a lady friend?"

"Because she's like a sister, that's why." No need to mention a sister almost twenty years older. "It's my fault. I should have explained.

Lonnie and I don't go out on dates. We work together on cases, and we understand the challenges a lot of vets face when they come back from their deployment." That explanation was apparently enough, because his dad didn't ask more questions, but focused on the dog.

"Say, Flash, shall we go out to see if any of your new friends are here today?" The dog stood and put his head in Lucas's lap. "Aw, he wants me to give the top of his head some attention." He began stroking the dog's head with his good hand, and waved to the door with the other.

"Okay, Dad, off we go. Looks like you're gaining strength in that hand. That's good."

Flash trotted along next to the wheelchair with Lucas keeping a grip on the leash. It wasn't long before one of the smaller dogs already in the hub began barking. "There's Ripple," Sloan said, "as usual, barking when he sees Flash."

When Lucas maneuvered the chair closer, Flash sniffed Ripple's head and that satisfied the much smaller dog. He stretched out next to his owner, looking sweet again.

Sloan stayed back as Lucas began chatting with the other patients in the lounge, most of whom were in the rehab unit and, like him, expected to return home. A few patients were permanent residents, and frail in a way that Lucas was not.

Sloan looked around the lobby, pleased by

its festive look. The high school kids had come back and changed the decorations, so ghosts and witches had made their exit and turkeys and gourds and cornucopias had taken their place.

An incoming text let him know Lonnie had taken the exit off the highway and was on the road into town. With his dad chatting with the others, Sloan went to the reception desk and asked Candace if Bethany was in her office and was it okay to knock on her door.

"Sorry, Sloan, Bethany is at the hospital in Landrum. There's a management seminar going on for the next couple of days. She'll be out of the office until next week."

Disappointed, way out of proportion to what had happened, Sloan hoped he'd covered himself with his artificially cheerful response. "Well, then, I'll catch her another time."

Lucas was curiously quiet when Sloan wheeled Lucas back to his room.

"I'll be glad to meet this lawyer lady," Lucas said. "On Veterans Day, will you take me to the war memorial? I'll do okay in the wheelchair."

"Sure, Dad. I planned to take you if you want to go," Sloan said, clearing his throat to hide the crack in his voice. "We'll stash the chair in the back seat."

"I guess if she's not a, you know, lady friend,

she still must be pretty special. You know, serving the country and all."

"She is, Dad. She went through a lot in the two wars."

Lucas was scratching Flash's back. He stopped abruptly. "Tell me, what was it like to fly those 'copters in Afghanistan?"

Before now, his dad had almost never asked about his time in the service, so Sloan welcomed the questions. He picked through some memories and told his dad about the time he'd evacuated a military dog along with two wounded soldiers. "The guys were awake and frantic about us getting to the field hospital in time to save Bordon."

"I guess the handlers get pretty attached."

"They do, and people like me, who try to evacuate wounded soldiers, also get caught up in the urgency." Because it had a good outcome, Sloan chose another story to tell, this one about rescuing an injured child, a little girl. Talking about the war often brought up memories Sloan didn't welcome, but he persevered because he appreciated that his dad had asked about it. From the way his expressions changed with the details, Sloan was certain his dad was interested. Better late than not at all, Sloan thought.

Sloan didn't recount the tedium of war, the hurry-up-and-wait pace, the underlying anxiety that intensified at odd times, or the way impatience and fear could erupt into what looked and sounded like anger. Instead, he talked about the relationships with others in his unit and how he enjoyed the flying itself.

Lucas moved his hand like a roller coaster in motion. "Sounds like a lot of ups and downs."

"Like that roller coaster you're imitating." Some details were stark and didn't fade. He wasn't sure what to say next when Lonnie's text came in. He looked up and smiled at his dad. "And she's arrived and is parking as we speak." He got to his feet. "I'll meet her at the door and bring her back here. Maybe she'll be ready for some coffee."

Lucas tapped the arm of the wheelchair. "And I wouldn't mind a cup myself. We can go to the cafeteria, huh?"

Sloan nodded and went out to the lobby and out through the revolving door and there was Lonnie walking toward him, a big smile on her face. It seemed every time he saw Lonnie he was surprised by how diminutive she was. Barely five feet tall. He leaned down and caught his friend in a big warm hug.

"I do like your longer hair," Lonnie said. "And the jeans. Bet you haven't put on a gray suit in a while." She stepped back and gave him a once-over. "You're looking good all around."

"So are you. And now Dad is itching to meet

you. By the way, he's likely to tell you he thought you were my *lady* friend." Sloan ran his hand down the back of his head, noting that it might be time for a haircut. He hadn't thought about it before.

Lonnie rolled her eyes. "Oh, well, I'll tell him I never had a brother and you never had a sister, so we adopted each other."

"I think he gets that now. So, we have a plan. Coffee in the cafeteria."

"Lead the way, soldier."

Sloan scoffed, but before he could respond, Lonnie reacted to the lounge full of patients, families and dogs. "Will you look at that? How fun."

"And beneficial. It really is therapy. Being able to spend time with Flash has made all the difference in Dad's rehab."

He led Lonnie down the hall to his dad's room. When Flash saw Sloan coming toward him, he got up on all fours. "Standing at attention," Sloan said, "as he always does when a new person is around."

"Well, well, you must be Flash." Lonnie approached the dog, and then extended her hand to Lucas. "And you must be Mr. Lancaster."

"Call me Lucas. Everybody does." He gave Lonnie's hand a quick shake. "I've heard a lot about you. I figured you had to be a lot older if you spent so many years in the military."

Lonnie patted the top of her head. "Hey, just

because I've got white hair like you doesn't make me old. Got it?"

Lucas laughed. "Okay, okay, I got it."

"Come on, you two, let's get some coffee," Sloan said. "You can debate who has the best white hair later."

"What about Bethany? Can she join us?" Lonnie asked.

"Unfortunately, no." He explained why she wouldn't be around for a couple of days.

"I see. Too bad. I was looking forward to meeting her."

"She's quite a gal," Lucas said. "Runs a tight ship here, and has a little girl. Widow, too."

"Yes, Sloan told me a lot about her," Lonnie said. She crouched down and patted Flash's neck. "I can see we're going to be fast friends. I hear we can go for long walks every morning."

Sloan turned the wheelchair and Lucas took hold of the leash to keep Flash close to his side as they made their way to the cafeteria.

Lucas glanced up at Lonnie. "Turned out to be a good day, Lonnie."

Sloan smiled at Lonnie. It was good to see his dad so lively. All that was missing was Bethany.

ALONG WITH HER parents and Heidi at her side, Bethany arrived at the cemetery with plenty of time to spare. No matter how she tried to spin it, being at the memorial was hard. And that had nothing to do with Charlie's death. As long as Bethany could remember, it had been a difficult day for her mother. Although decades ago, Jen had never completely reconciled herself to her much older brother's death in Vietnam. Bethany took a deep breath and scanned the crowd. Presumably, the woman with Sloan was his friend, Lonnie Richardson, a petite woman with a cloud of white curly hair. And now Sloan and Lonnie were heading her way, and moving fast.

As Sloan made the introductions, Bethany's wave of relief over her obvious misreading of the situation left her a little shaky. Sure, Lonnie could have been Sloan's girlfriend. But from the way Lonnie responded to Sloan's introductions, she could see how wrong she'd been. The little stabs of jealousy that had stung her ever since hearing Lonnie's name seemed so ridiculous now. Lonnie herself was the surprise. Her fashionably large black eyeglass frames were a perfect contrast to her smooth, fair skin and gray irises. Her jeans and red jacket fit like they'd been hand-tailored.

"Sloan has told me so much about you, Bethany," Lonnie said, taking her hand in both of hers, "and your family." She nodded to the picnic bench where Heidi stood with her Grandpa Dan close by. "I bet that's your little girl. Sloan's so fond of her. He's had a lot to say about Heidi."

"Yes, that's my girl. And my dad. I'll introduce you to him and my mom." Bethany scanned the area. "I don't see Mom now, but she was just here." Without considering if it was a good idea to reveal this much or not, Bethany blurted, "This is a hard day for my mom. She was a little girl when the older brother she loved so much was killed in Vietnam. It left a hole in her heart. I don't see it ever fully healing."

"Sloan also explained that your late husband served." She leaned in closer to Bethany and spoke in a near whisper. "My best pal thinks the world of you."

Bethany took in a breath, surprised not only by the words but the intimate tone coming from the woman she'd just met. "That's nice to hear. I doubt it comes as a surprise that he's been talking nonstop about your visit."

Lonnie pointed to Sloan who had left the area to position his dad's wheelchair on the concrete semicircle around the memorial. Quincy had joined them and the three were chatting. "I'm guessing that's Quincy, Sloan's uncle?"

"Yep, Quincy is my partner in reviving Winding Creek. More to the point, he's an important person in our community. Economically, of course, because he's a builder and employs lots of people. But he also does an amazing amount of volunteer work."

"An imposing figure, too, huh?" Lonnie glanced at Bethany, eyebrows raised.

Amused at the way Lonnie stared at Quincy, Bethany said, "Ah, you noticed. Yes, he's quite a presence." Changing the subject, Bethany nodded toward Lucas. "While my dad is watching Heidi, I need to say hello to Lucas. Come with me. I'll introduce you to Quincy."

Quincy looked up when Bethany led Lonnie to Lucas's side. Bethany almost laughed out loud. He was staring at Lonnie with the same intensity she'd been watching him.

"No introduction needed to this woman," Quincy said, moving around Sloan to get closer to Lonnie and extend his hand. "I'm so glad you're here, Lonnie. Based on everything Sloan has said, we like you already."

Lonnie's fair complexion turned a little pink now. "Yes, we purposely chose this weekend as the right time for a visit. And to meet you and Lucas, and Bethany, of course, and more of Sloan's family." Lonnie smiled at Quincy. "Besides, I've missed your nephew."

Since the two had eyes only for each other, Bethany stepped away and went to greet Lucas and Sloan. Lucas had on a jacket and scarf, with a hat and gloves in his lap. Bethany put her hand on Lucas's arm. "I see you're prepared for a chilly day."

"I wouldn't have bothered," Lucas said, waving the gloves, "but Sloan insisted, you know, just in case."

"Good for him." She glanced at Sloan, who was staring at Lonnie and Quincy. "Earth to Sloan," she teased, waving her hand in front of his face.

He startled but recovered quickly. "Looks like my uncle and my guest will get along just fine?"

Bethany smiled. "So I noticed." In the distance, she also noted her mom had joined her dad and Heidi. "They're going to start soon, so I'll go join my folks now." The tone of her voice had changed from light to somber.

"We'll see you later, maybe at the refreshment table." Sloan looked at her with empathy clear in his expression.

Of course, he'd understand her feelings on a day like this. Charlie had left the active military behind and was a civilian employee when he'd died in the explosion. Bethany had received only abbreviated and vague information on purpose. Details about the event were classified. She'd always regret that what she could pass on to Charlie's parents was short on specifics.

When Bethany reached her family, she linked her arm through her mother's, with Heidi still standing on the bench with Dad. Silently, they watched the area around the memorial fill in, mostly with some older vets taking seats in the semicircle of folding chairs. A few were in wheelchairs and Bethany noted a couple of young vets using canes to walk, but standing nonetheless.

"The older ones are being replaced now, aren't they?" A rhetorical question from her dad.

Bethany agreed. "More young families, too, so many who are much younger than me."

The stone war memorial had been placed in front of the veterans section of Adelaide Creek's cemetery, which was an extension of the grounds around the now-restored town hall. As usual, she savored a surge of gratitude over this charming and historic town. Like her, Adelaide Creek had seen tough times, but it had reinvented itself enough over time to keep thriving. She'd managed to do that for herself, but it remained to be seen if her efforts would be enough to meet the challenge to make sure Winding Creek could thrive, too.

Her grandparents and great-grandparents had gravestones in the town cemetery, but the uncle she'd never met was buried with others killed in war. In the oldest section of the cemetery, one particular stone marked the place where Adelaide Stanhope was buried. The town had been named for her, one of the first residents. As kids Heather and Jeff claimed bragging rights about that connection. On the other hand, the Lancasters had their own sprawling cemetery on the ranch where Quincy and Lucas had grown up.

The memorial listed all who served in the various wars, including the lone veteran of the Spanish American War. Those who hadn't come home had the year of their death etched in the plaque next to their birth date. The list of names was shorter for WWI than for World War II, and a considerable number of names appeared for vets of Korea and Vietnam. Until recently, every year more of those serving in Iraq and Afghanistan were added.

Bethany focused on the chairperson of this year's ceremony, an older man and a patient of hers in the orthopedic unit a few years back. As they sang the national anthem to open the ceremony, the day turned blustery, with a quickly darkening sky. She glanced at Lucas, who was pulling the wool hat down over his ears. Using both hands, she noted. The dexterity in his affected hand was returning faster than his ability to walk.

After the anthem, two younger veterans of the recent wars, both of them women, came forward and began reading the names of those in town who'd served in the two wars of the twenty-first century. When one of the women read Sloan's name, he jerked his head back in surprise, as if he hadn't expected his name to be included. No one else was surprised, though, not Lucas or Quincy.

Bethany took pride in the fairly big gathering, considering the size of the town. She gauged the crowd as close to one hundred. At other town events, too, Bethany found pleasure in looking into a group like this and seeing people she knew, even casually. This morning, though cold, was no different, and she returned the waves from a couple of women who bought wool from her mom, and two nurses she'd worked with at the hospital. A couple of Winding Creek employees had slipped into the outer circle of the gathering.

Out of the corner of her eye, Bethany saw her mom lower her head when one of the Vietnam vets spoke about why he kept coming back year after year. He never wanted the most recent veterans to be isolated or forgotten, and being present was the best way to show that commitment. At some point during this annual commemoration, her mother's eyes always turned misty. Perhaps her mom thought it was even more important to recognize her brother's service because Jen was the only family left to remember his death in 1970. As if the loss had been hers too, Bethany found her own eyes pooling with tears.

When the speeches were over, a hush came over the crowd. A young woman stepped forward and sang "My Country, 'tis of Thee" to close the ceremony. The quiet lasted for a few seconds before the din of voices started again.

Bethany offered to get her parents coffee to help them stay warm while they mingled with people they knew. When she got to the table, Sloan and Quincy were already in line at the coffee urn, running the same errand for Lonnie and Lucas. When the way cleared, Sloan stepped up and filled two cups and then handed them to her. "That'll save you some time."

When she turned around, her mother was with Lonnie, who was holding one of Jen's hands in hers. "Look at that, Sloan. Lonnie is with my mom."

"She saw Jen's emotional reaction and asked me if I thought it would be okay for her to approach. I encouraged her." Sloan looked in Bethany's eyes. "Lonnie understands what it's like to have a hard time handling these ceremonies, but like your mom, she shows up."

"Did she lose someone?" Bethany asked.

Sloan shook his head. "No, no. But maybe because she was in the JAG Corps, it often hit her that those she prosecuted and defended were in some way casualties of the war, too." Sloan took in a deep breath and puffed out his cheeks, as if frustrated by his thoughts. "She's really sensitive. Helping vets is her outlet. It's almost like it's how she blows off steam."

"How was the ceremony for you today?" Bethany was trying to rise above her own emotions.

She imagined Sloan was doing the same, although for different reasons.

"I'm okay," Sloan said. "Lonnie and I used to go to events to mark the day in Denver, once at a union hall, but usually at a church across the street from our office downtown. We went no matter what else was going on with one of our cases." His expression grew more thoughtful. "Lonnie especially found it odd that no one else in the firm was interested in coming with us. Granted, we're a small firm, but still…"

"Good thing you have each other." She lowered her voice when she asked about Lonnie's plans. "Will she move on, like you're doing?"

Sloan smiled. "She hasn't said anything yet, but between you and me, I wouldn't be surprised if she brings that up at some point while she's here."

Out of the corner of her eye, she saw Heather and Matt and the twins coming toward them. The twins were subdued. They were nine now and understood that their mother had died in Afghanistan. Luckily, they'd had their uncle Matt, and then Heather, once they met and married.

"One of your mom's paintings is in the room where Lonnie is staying," Sloan said to Heather. "I have a memory of Mom buying it when you and I were pretty young."

"I'm glad you have it," Heather said. "I tend

to see my mom's paintings wherever I go, or at least the prints the gallery sells."

When Sloan turned back to the refreshment table, he and Matt started talking about the commemoration. Bethany led Heather away from the cluster of people to deliver the coffee to her parents. "Compliments of Sloan," she said, before moving away with Heather and answering all her best friend's questions about Lucas and Lonnie, and what was going on with Sloan.

Heather pointed at Matt and Sloan talking. "It seems odd that I didn't know Sloan had been in the army," Heather said. "We didn't get a chance to do more than wave at each other at the lodge on Halloween, but I hope to see more of him."

"He and Lonnie are coming to my buffet dinner tonight," Bethany said. "You'll have a chance to talk to him then."

"The twins are looking forward to playing with Heidi and Naomi." Heather smiled, but it vanished quickly. "Every year their mom's death seems to become more real." As if reading Bethany's mind, Heather added, "I know it's still hard for Jen."

Looking past Heather, Bethany spotted Sloan delivering coffee to Lucas and Quincy, while Lonnie was still talking to Jen. The two women, essentially contemporaries, had their heads together in conversation. "They're becoming thick as thieves."

"I see that," Heather remarked. "Here comes Matt now. Sloan is on his way over, too. Matt and I need to retrieve Nick and Lucy from the playground and head home."

The two made a quick exit, leaving Sloan at Bethany's side. Sloan quickly picked up on what Bethany had seen passing between Lonnie and Jen. As he watched them, his smile was faint, but it revealed the tenderness of his feelings for Lonnie.

"Nice, huh?" Bethany whispered.

"I know one thing for sure. Lonnie makes friends easily." He sent Bethany a pointed smile. "Watching Quincy talking to her made that clear enough." Suddenly, Sloan grinned. "Well, speak of the devil."

Quincy came closer and wasted no time addressing Sloan. "Are you and Lonnie going to the buffet dinner tonight?" He turned to Bethany. "Oops, they're invited, right?"

"Seriously?" Bethany laughed. "Like I'd invite half the town and forget Sloan and Lonnie."

"We wouldn't miss it, Quincy." Sloan checked his watch. "We need to get going soon, though. I need to deliver Dad to the center and bring Flash for his Saturday visit."

"Well, then, I'll see you both later. The buffet will officially open at six o'clock." Bethany turned to leave and join her parents. "Don't be late."

After they'd said their goodbyes, Bethany jumped on Jen's suggestion that the four of them lighten up their sober mood by having brunch at the Tall Tale Lodge.

Less than an hour later, they were sharing a table in the corner of the lodge's cozy serving area. Over made-to-order omelets, French toast, and warm, cinnamon-spiced apples, Jen shifted the conversation in the direction of Bethany's annual buffet that night.

As much as Bethany tried to listen, she had trouble keeping her mind off Sloan and her speculation about his time in the service. Lonnie's openhearted manner and her visible reaction to Quincy also intrigued her, not to mention her kindness to Jen. She smiled to herself. She was really looking forward to her houseful of company.

When she and Heidi arrived home she had the satisfaction of knowing she had very little to do. Donna Kay, Adelaide Creek's one and only caterer, would handle most everything, from main dishes, salads and desserts, down to the last plate, bowl and fork. Bethany had been one of Donna Kay's first customers—Donna had catered Bethany's tiny wedding shower. It had gone over so well that later she and Charlie decided to throw annual preholiday buffet get-togethers for friends and colleagues, and all it took to make those dinners happen was a phone call to Donna. Bethany couldn't help but claim a little credit for helping the catering company grow quickly and attract business from all over the county. She had two full-time employees now, and at least a dozen people to call on for help with a host of one-off gigs.

As long as Bethany had Donna Kay around, she'd decided to continue this November buffet dinner when she moved into the bunkhouse and built the addition.

Exchanging her jeans and sweater for a festive red tunic and wide-legged, silk pants, plus her dressy black flats, she was ready to go. And so was Heidi, in her favorite dress, the color of peaches. Bethany was moving a child-size table into place next to her windows when her dad pulled up in his truck.

Heidi ran to the window. "Grandpa's here."

"He's bringing the extra chairs for us, honey."

"And Grandma's cakes?"

"They'll be here soon, sweetie. Don't you worry."

"Here comes another truck," Heidi said.

"And it's full of food," Bethany said, happy to see Donna Kay's van. While her dad arranged the chairs, Bethany helped Donna and her assistant bring in the food and arrange the chafing dishes on the table and the side dishes and plates and tableware on the counters.

"You're all set," Donna said, smiling. "You know what to do. We'll be back to whisk it all away."

Bethany inhaled the aromas of glazed ham and baked apples. Following her lead, Heidi looked up to the ceiling and sniffed the air. "Our house smells nice."

When her dad and Donna left, Bethany lit the candles on the mantel and scanned the room. All set.

"Okay, Heidi, what time is it?"

Heidi lifted her arms over her head and threw her head back. "It's showtime, Mommy!"

Bethany put her hand to her ear. "And I think I hear the sound of someone driving up to our house."

She took one last look around before going to the door. By the time she opened it and stepped onto the porch, a second vehicle had turned off the road and was headed her way. Showtime, indeed.

CHAPTER TEN

SLOAN MIGHT TRY to call himself a loner, but that wasn't really true. Being with other people at the war memorial that morning punctuated that reality. As if being in Adelaide Creek awakened something in him, the need for a sense of belonging involved more than identifying with other vets. It extended to the community he'd left behind. That morning's ceremony would have been an entirely different experience if he'd gone alone and tried to slip in and out unnoticed. Even more, he and his dad had talked very little about Afghanistan and his deployment, but for the first time, he'd shared this Veterans Day event with his father.

Then there was Quincy. Had he ever seen the normally smooth, poised Quincy get a little tongue-tied? Not that he could remember. Yet Sloan couldn't think of any other word for his uncle's awkwardness around Lonnie. Kind of like a besotted seventeen-year-old. Apparently, Bethany had noticed it, too. Well, maybe everybody saw it. Especially Lonnie, who had pumped him for more specifics about Quincy on the drive to Bethany's buffet.

Sloan turned into the Hoover ranch and made the quarter-mile drive to Bethany's bunkhouse, finding a parking place among the half a dozen or so vehicles already there. A thin slice of purple and pink sunset sky remained behind the mountains, reminding him of Noreen Stanhope's paintings, but it wouldn't be long before a dark evening set in. Too bad the cloud cover that had been with them all day would block the sky full of stars.

"What a location," Lonnie said, following him toward the bunkhouse, "and a charming little house."

"Deceptively small from the outside. You'll see." Sloan opened the door. "No need to knock. I'm not sure anyone would hear it anyway."

"It's pretty noisy, all right." Lonnie stepped inside. "I don't see Bethany, but there's Quincy. He's by that gorgeous fireplace." She waved at him. "Wow, two fireplaces. You're right. It's a lot bigger once you get inside."

Well, well, look at Quincy's face, all lit up. Lonnie headed right for him. Sloan understood. He felt the same way around Bethany, although he tried to hide it. Sometimes, he thought Bethany was doing the same. But if Lonnie and

Quincy were trying to pretend they weren't like magnets pulled to each other, they were doing a poor job.

Lonnie had a few obstacles on the winding trip around furniture and kids to cross the room and end up at the large fireplace at the far end of the addition. He intended to follow so he could introduce Lonnie to Bridget and Willow, but he hung back. Quincy could make the introductions. Besides, Sloan didn't know everyone. Tom was with Jeff and a couple of men Sloan didn't recognize, and Bridget's older girls were entertaining some little kids in a section of the family room reserved for the toy box and the dollhouses. He also recognized Candace and Margaret, and some others from Winding Creek.

Standing alone now, he heard someone calling his name and recognized it as Jen's.

"Want to help?" Jen asked, from her place at the kitchen table.

"Sure. What do you need?"

"You arrived just in time to help me rearrange the chafing dishes the caterer left on the dining table. The food's hot, so it's time to start filling our plates."

"Full-service catering, I see." Sloan looked at the spread of food and a serving stand holding white plates and bowls. "Right down to the salad forks."

"Pretty clever of me, don't you think?" Bethany said, emerging from the hallway into the kitchen, carrying two folding chairs. "I love entertaining, but who has time to cook?"

Sloan took the chairs from her hands and added them to a seating area along the wide windows. At the moment, what looked like a children's table filled part of the space.

"Where's Lonnie?" Bethany asked, scanning the family room. "Oh, there she is." She glanced at Sloan, her eyes wide with amusement. "With Quincy."

"Yes, it must be quite a conversation."

Quincy had lowered his head to hear Lonnie over the din of the crowd. He was smiling, and then said something that made Lonnie burst out laughing. Quincy looked pleased by her response.

Sloan exchanged a quick glance with Bethany, whose cheeks had turned pink. She quickly turned away and started removing the cover from the salads on the kitchen counter.

"Since my houseguest doesn't need help becoming acquainted, consider me your hired hand." Sloan included both Bethany and Jen. "Go ahead, boss me around."

Between the three of them they quickly uncovered the chafing dishes and rearranged the salads and hot rolls on the counters. They added extra serving spoons and forks.

"Very impressive spread," Sloan said.

"I'm so glad you and Lonnie are here for this." Bethany smiled. "Come to think of it, quite a few of your relatives are already milling about. They're regulars in my home."

Before he could respond, Jen got their attention. "Hey, you two, let's ring the dinner bell. If we count the floor around the coffee table, we have enough nooks and crannies for everyone."

"Hey, I'm fine with the floor," Sloan said, nodding at Bridget's girls, who were entertaining Heather and Matt Burton's twins, Lucy and Nick, along with Heidi. "I can help my nieces entertain the kids."

"We'll figure it out. We always do." Jen tilted her head toward the guests. "No one ever complains to the manager."

Sloan could see why Bethany had a full house. From what he could tell, the guests were a mix of old and new friends, and people from her professional life. He recognized the head of the PT department at Winding Creek in conversation with the former mayor, Alice, who Quincy had told him was on the care center's board. Their childhood friends mingled with newcomers.

Bethany had made use of every inch of space. Heather and Matt had positioned themselves to pour wine into glasses from bottles of red and white lined up on the mantel. Cold beer and sparkling water were on ice in an old-fashioned washtub in the kitchen. The scents of hot bread and buttery rosemary potatoes, and many more enticing smells, added to the warmth created by the two small fires.

Bethany picked up a fork and tapped it against a glass. It worked to quiet the room and get her guests' attention. "Grab a plate, everyone, and eat while it's hot." She smiled at her mom. "But save room for Jen Hoover's famous cakes."

Sloan positioned chairs near the kids' table. Then he headed toward Quincy and Lonnie, who hadn't moved. Quincy was listening intensely, as if he didn't want to miss a word of what Lonnie had had to say. Before Sloan reached them, they shifted their focus when Naomi toddled over to Quincy and wrapped her arms around his leg to make sure she had his attention.

"I see you." Quincy reached down and picked her up to rest on his hip.

Sloan then joined them. "She's adorable," Lonnie said, "isn't she, Sloan?"

Lonnie, who had an animated demeanor on a run-of-the-mill day, exuded even more energy as she smiled at Naomi and gave her sneakered foot a little shake. They didn't run into many small children in their line of work, so he'd never heard his friend gush over a baby.

"Very cute, and Naomi knows her own mind

already. She's my cousin's child, so that makes her my second cousin or something like that. Right, Quincy?" Sloan had to think that over.

Quincy made a face at the baby. "Beats me. All I know is she's my first grandchild. Lucky me."

"Why don't you two go to the buffet?" Sloan said, although a long line was forming. "You can claim a couple of empty chairs by the window in the other room."

"This is such a lovely house," Lonnie said with a sigh. "And here comes one of its occupants, Heidi herself."

Dan Hoover approached them holding Heidi's hand and joked with Quincy about being on grandpa duty. While they chatted, Lonnie stepped to the side and took Sloan's arm and drew him away.

"I'm so glad I came to see you," Lonnie said. "True, this morning's commemoration was a little sad. I know it was for you, too, but I've met a bunch of interesting people. It's not hard to see why you're drawn to Bethany." She gestured around the room. "Look at this gathering."

Drawn to Bethany? Of course, Lonnie would notice. Time to change the subject. "In your conversations with Quincy, I assume he told you he'll help us set up a meeting next week for some veterans. It's short notice, but Quincy has a huge network."

Lonnie nodded. "I told him that based on the work you and I have done in Denver..." She stared out the window next to the fireplace. "I think..." She sighed. "Given the kind of lingering disabilities we see, our advocacy work is becoming even more in demand."

"I agree. That's why I want to make time for a meeting while you're here. Since Quincy used to be on the town council, people still come to him with their concerns." Not to mention that his opinions carried a lot of weight in Adelaide Creek.

Lonnie drew her head back and looked up into his face. "Your decision not to come back to the firm is final, isn't it? No second thoughts?"

"Definitely final, Lonnie. I'm done with that pace. I told Bethany about it the other day, but I haven't mentioned it to anyone else. So, please, don't pass it on. I don't know what's ahead, but I'm sure of what I want to leave behind." Sloan spoke in a whisper, but when he looked around, no one was paying attention to them talking in the corner. "It's time to do something else. I'd like to put some of that money to good use. I don't know how or where, but I don't need to figure that out while my dad needs me around."

"I can't say I blame you. My mind is running off this way and that." Lonnie took his arm and steered them back to Quincy. "Enough of this.

We've got days to hash this over. I'm hungry. Let's eat."

The next couple of hours passed quickly. When he'd sampled some of everything on the buffet, including slices of ham and rare roast beef, Sloan mingled with people he hadn't seen in a long time. He also stopped to chat with Andre and Candace and some other staff from Winding Creek. The day he arrived, Sloan would never have predicted the positive things he'd hear about his father from these very people. Lucas had nothing but compliments for the cooks, and as long as he could see Flash two days a week, nothing else mattered. As Sloan chatted with different guests, he found himself watching Bethany moving around the room, talking with everyone and making sure all her guests had what they needed.

Heather came up to him just when he'd polished off his glass of red wine and was about to get a cup of coffee. "Seeing you here with all of us is like old times—as teenagers." She squeezed his hand. "I'll bet Bethany has filled you in on what the rest of our crowd has been up to."

"She has, but speaking of that, how are you feeling?" Sloan asked. "And when is your baby due?"

"Not until late January, so I have a ways to go." Heather gestured toward Bethany, who was with her mom cutting pieces of the two cakes and putting them on serving plates. Then she looked up at him through amused eyes. "If I said you're fast becoming one of Bethany's biggest fans, would I be wrong?"

Saw right through him. Heather had always been that kind of person. Sharp-eyed, observant. "You're incorrigible, Heather."

"Funny thing, Bethany has used those same words for me from time to time."

Sloan shrugged. "Then it must be true."

"To be serious about it, from what I've seen, you're good for Bethany. After Charlie died, she was entirely focused on making sure Heidi was okay. Then the Winding Creek project with Quincy took over her life. We still spend time together and all that, but now she seems more…" Heather made circles with her hands "…more open to life. Her life, not just Heidi's."

Sloan smiled, thinking that what Heather said was true for him. From the day he came upon her directing her staff during a flood in the lobby, Sloan had noted changes in himself. For one thing, he'd come to town waffling about what to do next, or where to do it. It wasn't just about the firm and the huge cases, or Denver itself. He liked the law, but he'd never again allow his life to be dominated by work and more work.

As if reading his mind, Heather cocked her

head and appeared to study him. "Maybe it will turn out that she's good for you, too."

"I get the feeling that Bethany hasn't been all that isolated from the world." He gestured around the room. "Look at all these people here in her beautiful home. Seems to me she's done a remarkable job of getting on with her life."

"Right you are. But except for Heidi and Winding Creek, she's done all this without much enthusiasm. Last year, she had this dinner. She put up a good front, but it was like going through the motions." Heather's face brightened. "But I see her tonight and she's got some of her old radiance back."

At the moment, Bethany was carrying two slices of cake for Heather's twins and leading them to the kids' table. From a distance he played the silent observer. So did Heather.

"I bet you're like aunts to each other's kids," Sloan said.

"That we are."

"You may be incorrigible, Heather, but you're a great best friend."

Heather flashed a smug look. "It's a lifelong title. Lucky for me, the feeling is mutual." She patted his arm. "I need to say hello to a couple of people before I find Matt and we get on the road. See you soon. Hope your dad keeps getting better."

When Heather left, Sloan crossed the room and sat on the floor at the coffee table with Lonnie and Quincy.

"The departures have started," Lonnie said.

Quincy had his eye on Willow and Tom, who were heading to the door with Naomi, whose protests against leaving were loud and tearful. "I said my goodbyes, so I'm not going to get involved." Quincy smiled. "The little cutie is tired. She's had a big day."

"Spoken like an understanding granddad," Lonnie teased.

"Speaking of kids," Sloan said, getting to his feet, "I see Heidi is by herself. I guess her favorite adults are occupied. I'll go say hello to her before we leave."

As he looked around, Bethany was pouring coffee for some Winding Creek employees, while Jen hurried to gather the empty serving bowls. "You like your grandma's chocolate cake, don't you?" Sloan said, pulling up an empty chair next to Heidi.

Heidi nodded. "I like her cookies, too, but she didn't bring them today."

"Tell me about them."

Sloan's heart grew softer by the minute as he learned more about the way this little girl's grandparents were part of her life. From baking cookies after school to visiting the sheep shelters with Jen to playing word games with Dan. The more she talked, the more clearly the picture of a family with routines and traditions formed. Perhaps an impenetrable group of four. Would they invite anyone else to join them? Or the more pointed question: Was there room for him?

He was mulling that question when he felt a hand on his shoulder. "Is my daughter talking your ear off? Maybe she's spilling family secrets?"

"If learning your dad is a wizard with board games is a secret, then she's guilty as charged." Sloan got to his feet.

Bethany snickered. "It's the way his fierce inner competitor shows up."

"Your dinner is a big hit. And you make it look easy."

"Barely a crumb left on Mom's cake plates." Bethany moved a little closer to him. "Speaking of big hits, have you noticed that Lonnie and Quincy have spent most the evening joined at the hip?" Bethany's eyes sparkled and she spoke barely above a whisper. "And I understand why. Lonnie is really interesting."

Sloan couldn't resist teasing just a little. "I see this development amuses you? Now, why is that?"

"I just think they look kind of…you know… cozy, that's all."

Yep, Sloan thought, his uncle and his friend had eyes only for each other.

"Is Lonnie currently unattached?"

"She's been unattached for as long as I've known her. She was married and divorced in her twenties, but she rarely talks about it. She threw herself into her military career and volunteer work for various causes."

They abruptly stopped talking when Quincy approached. Saying she needed to help her mom, Bethany backed away, leaving him alone with Quincy. His uncle didn't waste a second before speaking up. "Lonnie's a fascinating woman, Sloan. She thinks you're the best." He wagged his finger at Sloan. "You've been modest about what you've been up to all these years, the kinds of cases you've handled. Lonnie had a lot to say about that."

Sloan waved off the praise. "Apparently, Lonnie thinks you're pretty fascinating, too."

Quincy smiled faintly, but changed the subject to the upcoming meeting, scheduled now for Thursday. "We've got a couple people we think will join us on short notice."

"Thursday's fine." Sloan grinned. "You're good at making things happen, and fast."

"Well, I had a chance to chat with Tom earlier. The mother of one of his patients is a vet with some issues. Tom contacted her while we were talking, and she's eager to meet you and Lonnie. She'll reach out to two other vets in her network in Landrum."

"And you arranged all that in the last couple of hours? In between roast beef, potatoes and coconut cake?"

"We can't waste time, Sloan," Quincy said with conviction. "Lonnie has to get back to Denver...soon."

Sloan resisted the urge to tease Quincy, maybe because his uncle might tease him back. Bethany was now at the door saying goodbye to a group of guests, so it was time to make his exit with Lonnie.

When Sloan went to join Lonnie, she was already talking with Bethany and admiring the bunkhouse and its views from every window. And the whimsical dollhouses. "I've only been in Adelaide Creek for a few days, but I'm so taken with the town and impressed with every person I've met." Lonnie's eyes cut away to Quincy.

Lonnie reached up to give Bethany a quick hug. "I envy you. Your daughter is a dream. I suppose I should say, I envy your parents. They have such a wonderful granddaughter. What an imagination. A sheep rancher one minute, and a queen in her castle the next."

"Thanks for that," Bethany said, her expression showing how touched she was by Lonnie's words.

Lonnie jabbed the air sideways with her thumb aimed at Sloan. "I think Sloan has been a little modest about the kind of work he's done at our firm."

"It's been hard to get him to talk about specifics, that's for sure," Quincy said. "I think we'll have to demand a deposition."

When Quincy walked Lonnie out to the porch, Sloan gave Bethany a quick hug and kissed her cheek. "I can't think of a better way to spend an evening. I've spent far too many weekends in front of my computer preparing for Monday." Sloan looked into Bethany's pretty blue eyes. "I'll see you soon."

"Monday," she whispered.

It was as if they were sharing a secret, Sloan thought.

When he and Lonnie settled into his SUV, they were barely underway down the long drive to the road when Lonnie said, "You're half in love with her already, aren't you?"

Sloan groaned. "Is it that obvious?"

Lonnie shrugged. "Pretty much. But maybe the others don't know what you look like when you're interested in a woman. It's been so long, I almost forgot you have it in you."

"Guess I could say the same about you. My uncle is not easily charmed."

"Want to know the truth?"

"Always," Sloan said.

"I can't wait to see your uncle again." Lonnie sighed. "I bet you think that sounds dumb."

"Not for one second, Lonnie." He understood more than he liked to admit. It was possible that half in love was only half the truth.

CHAPTER ELEVEN

BETHANY KNOCKED ON the half-open door and stuck her head into the room. "Mind if I come in?"

"'Course not," Lucas said, waving her inside. "We're telling your old friend here about Veterans Day. A real nice event."

"You remember Gary Vaughn?" Sloan asked.

Bethany nodded at Gary, grateful to Sloan for asking the question. As familiar as the man was, she'd been racking her brain to remember his name. "Sure I do. But he was an upperclassman, a couple of years ahead of me." She spoke as if that had made him someone to admire from afar. She also remembered Gary as one of the smartest kids in the school, a perpetual member of the honor society. "Welcome, Gary. I saw Amy Vaughn on my list of new patients to visit today. Is she your mother?"

"Yes, and Mom finally agreed to a knee replacement. They did the surgery a few days ago. She was transferred here for rehab. I just got here a few minutes ago from Santa Fe." Gary nodded at Sloan. "His mother and my mom were really good friends. Mom still brings her up now and again."

Bethany smiled. "How long are you staying in town? Maybe we can grab a cup of coffee while you're here." She was curious about Gary and what he'd been doing all these years.

"Sounds good," Gary said.

"Those ladies grew up together," Lucas said. "Their daddies worked in the mine outside Landrum. Back when there was a mine." When he finished the sentence, Lucas put his head back and closed his eyes.

Maybe it was the mention of his mom, but it was clear Lucas was worn out from the visit. Sloan exchanged a glance with Bethany. "Speaking of coffee, want to take a break and head to the cafeteria now?" he asked.

Gary nodded. "Sure."

"I can take a break," Bethany said without hesitation. She needed a diversion to get her mind off more bad news about grants.

"While you're gone, I'll take a little nap here in my comfy chair." Lucas pointed to the sunlight slanting through the blinds on the window. "Don't like being in bed until it's dark."

"We're alike in that way, Dad," Sloan said, getting to his feet. "We won't be long." They filed out and started down the hall.

"For the first time, Dad asked me serious questions about flying medevacs," Sloan said. "Being with us on Veterans Day and hearing Lonnie talk about her JAG Corps work aroused his interest in hearing more about my time in the war."

"Not so surprising, I guess," Gary said. "Lots of people didn't want to hear another word about those two long wars."

"No kidding," Sloan said, a little sarcastically, "I've noticed. But I'm his kid, Gary."

Bethany was on Sloan's side with that. She understood that Lucas showing interest in his son's life, even going back to his army days, was another sign of improvement. Bethany crossed the room to claim an empty table by the window while Sloan and Gary went to the counter.

"At least the coffee is great here," Gary said when he came back. He raised his cup and did a little eye roll. "But this place has seen better days. What's with the closed-off rooms? Must be so run-down they can't use them." He caught Bethany's eye. "Oops... I suppose I shouldn't have put it quite that way."

Bethany scoffed. "Oh, that's okay. Speak your mind. Better days are right around the corner, anyway."

"You always were an outspoken sort, Gary," Sloan said, his voice bordering on stern. "If it weren't for Bethany, this place would be boarded up, or torn down, or in a bidding war with national chains of care centers. You'd be heading miles and miles across the county to see your mom."

"Feel free to register your complaints with me, Gary." Bethany tapped her chest. "You can't offend me. I'm working hard here, along with a dedicated board. We're determined to turn Winding Creek around."

"Okay, I stand corrected," Gary said. "But what's the story? How did this place end up like this?"

"Quincy and Bethany want to keep it locally owned and run." Sloan explained what kind of work was needed.

"Some people in town like our plan, a lot," Bethany said with a sigh. "But others think we should sell to whoever offers the most money."

Bethany gave Gary credit for listening, but their old friend also had other things on his mind, namely what he and his wife could do with their eight-year-old daughter while they were in town.

"Check out the Children's Adventure Center," Bethany said. "Oh, and the new public roller skating rink is open this weekend." She nodded to Sloan. "We took my almost four-year-old on the day of its grand opening. Lots of fun."

Gary looked from Sloan to Bethany. "Hey, thanks. My little girl loves to roller-skate." He stared down at his cup. "You know, Lucas was talking a lot about the Vets Day ceremony, but

I don't recall ever marking that here in town," Gary said. "My grandfather was in the Marines. Served in Korea, but no one ever mentioned it. Not even my Mom."

"That's too bad," Sloan said.

"Like Sloan, my late husband was in the army, too," Bethany said.

"Oh, I'm sorry. I didn't know...your, uh, situation," Gary said. "What did he do?"

Bethany briefly explained the circumstances of Charlie's service and his death, but she sensed Gary's attention was waning. As soon as she was done, Gary asked Sloan what he was up to.

Sloan took a sip of his coffee before answering. "I'm an attorney in a small firm in Denver."

Gary's eyebrows rose in interest. "Successful?"

Like Sloan had once remarked, most people preferred career talk to war talk. Bethany could see that in this conversation.

"Mostly." Sloan stopped talking but kept his gaze on Gary. "One of my partners and I do some veterans advocacy, too."

"Oh, speaking of that, where's Lonnie?" Bethany asked. "She decided not to visit today?"

"She's with Quincy over in Landrum. He wants to show her the county gallery." A smile tugged at the corners of his mouth when he looked at Bethany.

She acknowledged his amused smile with one

of her own. She was enjoying what seemed like a secret, like a couple of teenagers catching two single teachers out on a date.

"I feel a lot better about my mom being here after talking to the two of you," Gary said, smiling at Bethany. "I remember you as a confident girl. You always seemed to know what you wanted and were determined to get it."

"I couldn't have said it better," Sloan declared.

In a low voice, Gary said, "But Bethany, I'm really sorry about your husband."

"Thanks, Gary. But I've got Heidi and she's a blessing."

"A great kid." Sloan spoke in a hearty tone. "Full of fun and very outspoken."

"But here's my dilemma," Gary said. "We don't think my mom can go back to her big, rambling house. She wants to move to a place, you know, like independent living. But her friends are here, and her church, not in Santa Fe where we live. But if we can't find an alternative..." Gary shrugged. "She may have to. The waiting lists for places in Landrum are long."

Bethany winced at the familiar story, but she wouldn't miss an opportunity. "Offering that kind of housing is part of my—our—long-term vision. Right now, we have a severe shortage of housing designed for someone like your mother."

Gary's expression turned grim. "Sounds okay,

but how fast can your nonprofit make that happen? We're going to need this in a matter of weeks, not years."

Sloan nodded. "The board is appearing at a town meeting in December to defend what they've done so far."

Bethany groaned. "Where's the trust?" She paused before adding, "It's true, though, our full vision is more complicated. I wish we could offer your mom the living arrangement she needs right now. I'm sorry, Gary."

Bethany's phone pinged an incoming text. She got to her feet and picked up her coffee. "I've ignored some texts and emails. And I've got an online meetup with Quincy late this afternoon, so I better be on my way." She lifted her to-go cup still half-full of coffee. "Thanks, Sloan."

She patted Gary's shoulder as she walked past him. "If you need anything, let me know."

When she was on the other side of the double doors, she checked her phone right away. The news wasn't good. Quincy wouldn't be happy either. Another grant application denied. This was the third one. And Bethany thought she knew why.

SLOAN UNCLIPPED THE leash on Flash and added more water to his bowl. "I'll be back later. You won't be alone for long." That might be true, but it still bothered Sloan to leave the dog behind.

Poor dog. No matter how long Sloan kept Flash outside tramping through the fields, it couldn't make up for what the dog was missing with Lucas.

"Such a cold morning," Lonnie said, appearing at his side. "But my puffy coat ought to be enough to ward off the chill." She leaned down to pat the dog's head. "You had a good walk, huh? Lucky me, Flash, I got to stay warm under the covers."

"The things we do for love, eh, Flash?" Sloan pulled on his gloves as they headed to the door and stepped outside.

He'd done an informal inventory of his father's cold weather gear and added several items to his Christmas list. His dad wouldn't like it if Sloan bought him new things just because. "It's odd the way my dad will skimp on clothes—his all-weather coat is practically threadbare. But he has three pairs of the best walking boots money can buy. And they cover all the bases, regular, extra-warm and waterproof."

"You're surprised?"

"I shouldn't be." Sloan pulled the door closed behind him. "But seeing some of his worn-out things reminds me of how he's managed, or not, on his own."

"But the boots tell you a lot about his priorities. Obviously, he was capable of getting what he needed for what's most important to him." Lonnie pointed to an overgrown path that went past the barn. "Where does that go?"

"Into the woods," Sloan said. "I followed it with Flash on his walk this morning. It's not easy to navigate, but the dog seems to know it well. Dad won't like that it'll have to be off-limits for him now." He let out a heavy sigh.

Lonnie playfully smacked his arm. "Hey, counselor," she said softly, "let's get on with it. It's time to make good on your promise to take me to Tall Tale for waffles."

Sloan welcomed the distraction. As they walked to his SUV, he pointed to a couple of giant cottonwood trees a stone's throw from the second barn, where they'd kept their four horses and more stored hay. "Over by that barn is where I saw my first bear, well, plural—a mama and two cubs."

"What did you do?"

"I stood like a statue, and so did she, but then she turned and ran across that field and the cubs followed." Sloan tsked and shook his head. "I was about six, but I didn't tell anyone because I wasn't supposed to wander alone all the way to the two barns. Somehow, Mom knew, though. At dinner she told Dad she'd seen the three bears running across the field. She'd throw a look my way now and again while she talked, and in that knowing way only mothers can do."

Sloan hadn't thought about that story in years. But the memory was vivid, like it happened yesterday. Being around his dad triggered thoughts of his mom and incidents from his childhood in Adelaide Creek.

"As the youngest, and the only girl in a family of five kids, I saw that kind of pointed expression a lot. I had to break a few rules to keep up with my brothers," Lonnie reminisced.

They rode to the lodge in a comfortable silence broken only when Lonnie's phone chimed and she slipped it out of her pocket. When she smiled at the screen, he knew it was Quincy.

"Uh, that was Quincy, confirming that he'd see us soon."

Confirming again? As if they'd forget. Judging from the way texts had been flying back and forth, the lunch and the gallery trip with Quincy a couple of days ago were a great success.

Lonnie tried to respond but they'd hit a dead spot. She gave up and lowered the phone, but then she blurted, "I wish I didn't have to go home on Sunday. I like watching you reinvent yourself. Now I need to decide if I'm ready for the same makeover."

Sloan grinned. "Is that what you think I'm doing? But it's not about giving up the law. It comes down to the drive to do something useful with my money." He stopped talking when they rounded the curve that opened up a new view of the mountains in the distance. "I miss these peaks that seem to go on forever."

"You've shared so little about this town and your family," Lonnie said, "so I didn't know what to expect. But I like hearing your stories."

"I've spent so many years avoiding my dad that I've missed out on spending time with the slew of cousins in my huge Lancaster clan."

"It doesn't have to be that way, Sloan."

Sloan admitted to himself that was true. "Bethany thinks Dad's been lonelier than he'd realized. But being around patients and staff has perked him up. That's why I'm thinking he needs a permanent change. But it's not up to me. An independent-living, studio-type apartment would suit him fine. As long as he can have Flash and a place to walk him, Dad doesn't care about having a lot of space."

His dad's future was still on his mind when he parked and claimed an empty table in the Tall Tale Lodge's lobby. While they waited for their waffle order, they filled their plates with fresh fruit and slices of breakfast ham.

Lonnie scanned the lobby as they went back to their table. "Such an elegant place."

"And fancier than any other spot in Adelaide Creek. I'm told the population is over five hundred now." Sloan used his fork to cut off a piece of the waffle. "Another positive sign for the future."

"You sound like Bethany talking about her vision."

Was that a teasing tone he heard in Lonnie's voice?

Lonnie leaned back in her chair. "Here's a question for you, Sloan. Are you the anonymous donor who paid for the roof repairs?"

Sloan let out a frustrated grunt. He looked around, hoping no one had overheard her. "Did Quincy tell you that?"

"No, no. I asked Quincy. I thought he'd probably put up the money, but he insisted that wasn't the case. He was quite adamant about that." Giving him a sidelong glance, Lonnie added, "That made me think of you." She peered into his face. "You're awfully quiet."

Sloan dragged his palm down his cheek and across his jaw in frustration. "It started with an urgent need and a stopgap roof repair. I could write a check and solve the problem. But I insisted on anonymity." He gave her a warning look. "Got it?"

"Why?"

Sloan asked himself that now. It had seemed like such a simple thing to do. "At the time, I'd been in town for all of a day, my first visit in five years. I suppose I didn't want to look like

I'd crashed into town and started to throw my money around. Like some big shot. It was a snap decision."

"You wanna know what I think?"

Sloan laughed. "I almost always want to know what you think. But this time, I'm not so sure."

"I'll blunder in, anyway. You could see Bethany had a lot to deal with. You gave her one less thing to worry about."

"True enough," Sloan said, "but now I don't want anyone to think I'm trying to show off."

Lonnie folded her arms across her chest. "I know you, Sloan. You don't want Bethany to see you that way. But why are you trying not to feel what you feel?"

Sloan didn't try to deny he knew what she meant. He wanted to brush off the question. Instead, he stumbled around to find an answer he hoped would satisfy Lonnie. Finally, he found words for his fears. "It comes down to Heidi. It's so clear that Bethany wants to keep Charlie alive for her child. Bethany and her parents have given the little girl a secure, complete life." He shook his head. "That means sending the message that she's not available. I got her message, okay?"

Lonnie's expression showed skepticism, but she said nothing, leaving Sloan to wonder if she really understood. Looking around, he saw the breakfast bar in the lobby had thinned, and yet, some couples and groups had taken their coffee closer to the fireplace. The sun had broken through the earlier cloud cover and streamed through the large windows, revealing a brilliant blue sky. Lonnie's silence was typical of her. The more important the issue at hand, professional or personal, the longer she took to consider her words.

"You're probably right." Lonnie spoke more slowly than was typical for her. "She's decided against inviting another man into her life. That doesn't mean she can't be taken by surprise and change her mind. After all, Bethany didn't know you'd suddenly show up." Lonnie paused. "Just sayin'. I see the way she looks at you. Not so different from the way you look at her."

Sloan had hoped that some of those expressions he'd seen on Bethany's face were real and not a figment of his imagination or mere wishful thinking. Maybe Lonnie was right. He chuckled. "Heidi seems to like me. At least there's that."

"That's a very big deal."

Sloan smiled at Lonnie and then pointed to the giant brass clock on the wall behind the chef's station. "We need to go. We can't be late, especially since Quincy is meeting us at O'Connor Mansion to open the room for us."

Lonnie waved her phone. She didn't waste a second getting to her feet. "I like it here." She glanced up at the chandelier above them and at the fireplace nearby. "And that was an excellent waffle."

"Maybe we'll come here again before you have to head home."

Lonnie frowned as she offered only a faint smile. "Yes, home. I don't know, Sloan. I've got commitments at the firm I intend to fulfill, of course, but..."

"But?" Sloan studied Lonnie's expression as he pulled cash out of his pocket and left it with the check on the table.

"I'm like you, thinking about what I want to do next. That's all."

Lonnie made it clear she wasn't ready to elaborate, and since Sloan couldn't get his mind off Bethany, they left the lodge in silence.

"Whatever happens with Lucas," Lonnie said when they were on the road in the direction of town, "your house would make a great B and B. You have five bedrooms, and you could probably convert the barns into studios or larger apartments."

"Are you percolating an idea?" Sloan asked.

"Nah...just an observation. That kind of work isn't for me."

"And here I think of it as a kind of shabby old farmhouse." Sloan understood that his old homestead had value, but he imagined one of the next generation of cousins raising a large family in it.

"It only needs some work, my friend. It's a gold mine. Mark my words."

What to do with his old house wasn't uppermost in his mind when a few minutes later, Quincy greeted them at the mansion. First up, he gave them a quick tour of what had once been an estate owned by a several-generations-old family in Adelaide Creek. The gleaming oak staircase and woodwork, plus crystal chandeliers and elaborate bronze sconces, were like remnants of an earlier time.

"When I was a kid this place was an eyesore," Sloan said, "with dirty windows and grounds full of weeds. Now thanks to Quincy, Bethany tells me it's a community center that hosts parties and weddings, but has conference rooms for corporate meetings, too."

"Perfect for meetings like the one you've got planned," Quincy said, standing by the door, ready to leave them and go to his shop and tend to his own business.

"I thought you were staying," Lonnie said.

"I'll come back a little later," Quincy said. "I'll support what comes of this, but these folks won't open up unless they're sure it's private." Quincy held up a handwritten sign directing visitors upstairs. "I'll post this on my way out."

Sloan was curiously nervous about what he and Lonnie were doing, but when the two men and a woman walked into the conference room, he relaxed. He was exactly where he was supposed to be, doing the work he was meant to do. Lonnie, rising from her chair and extending her hand, exuded competence.

"Thanks for coming today," Sloan said, explaining a little about his army service and the reason he was in Adelaide Creek. Lonnie told them about her background and her role in advocating for veterans in their Denver law firm.

"While I'm here with my dad and Lonnie is visiting, we wanted to reach out and see if we can be of any help to local vets. We're curious about what kind of a network you have here, and how you support each other."

"Why don't you start by telling us a little bit about your situation and go from there," Lonnie suggested. She gestured to a pitcher of ice water and glasses sitting on a credenza at one end of the room. "Help yourself. We're here to listen."

Later, Sloan realized how quickly he was brought back to those first months he was home from the military. Regardless of starting law school, he'd had episodes of feeling disconnected, even alienated, among otherwise likable classmates. That, and coping with sleepless nights followed by disturbing dreams. He hadn't been wounded, but he'd been in the thick of the action. Even all these years later, loud noises startled him. The smell of gasoline or diesel fuel triggered anxiety.

"My complaint? It takes too long to get anything done." Josh, a former marine with a leg injury that hadn't healed well, flopped back in the chair and folded his arms across his chest. "I don't want to be declared disabled, man. What I need is the treatment the doctor tells me can make it right. And I can't be moving my family across the state to get it."

Vivian, an army nurse, had ongoing health problems related to an injury, but she deflected attention from herself to Alex, the youngest vet, probably still in his midtwenties. He had such severe PTSD he couldn't hold a job. He was still searching for effective treatment and the right healthcare resources.

Sloan exchanged a glance with Lonnie. They'd dealt with the same problems in Denver, ultimately representing a couple of young men in situations like Alex's. They'd won in both cases. They defined winning as securing treatment, along with housing and ongoing support.

Lonnie, who had more experience handling these kinds of concerns, didn't hold back. "We'll look at each case and come up with a plan. I'm leaving for Denver soon, but Sloan is here. We'll gather more details, but you're not alone."

Sloan described the cases he and Lonnie had insisted on taking at their firm. Their partners' responses to their effort weren't enthusiastic. But he and Lonnie argued that being uniquely qualified to understand the needs of the veterans made these specific pro bono cases good matches for the firm. "It hadn't taken long for word to spread about the work we were doing. Now we want to do what we can here."

Before the meeting broke up, Sloan asked for more information about the network of veterans in the county. Unfortunately, the connections were haphazard, with long distances working against them. Sloan committed to attending the next group meeting and Lonnie also agreed to hold online Q&A sessions.

"We cross generations," Vivian said, "so it can be hard to find each other and offer support. Alex's family and mine happen to go to the same church."

Despite those months of sleeplessness and, at times, his awkward adjustment to civilian life, coming back from the war zone had been relatively easy for Sloan. He'd known that at the time, which was why he hadn't confided in anyone about his issues. But looking at Alex, Josh and Vivian, he told himself that however he shaped his work life going forward, he'd stay involved with vets.

"Veterans are welcome to meet here in person. We can hash out our issues and see how we can support each other. I don't know where I'll be located a few months from now, but I'm here now and I will show up."

Lonnie looked up from her computer and nodded. "I'll join you when I visit." She smiled at Sloan. "I've come to like this town."

And she already had some fans, Sloan thought.

The meeting broke up, but not without Lonnie collecting phone numbers and emails and promising to get more facts together on what each of the three needed. Vivian added a couple of her contacts to Lonnie's list. "No single story is exactly like another, but they're all worth hearing."

Lonnie texted Quincy and he responded right away with an offer to take them both to lunch at the Merchant Street Diner. "I told him we accept."

Sloan made a quick decision. "You two have fun without me. I need to see my dad." And Bethany. Something was pushing at him. Call it an impulse.

Lonnie frowned. "Are you sure?"

"Absolutely. You can ask Quincy to drop you off at Winding Creek and we'll go home together from there."

Her expression quizzical, Lonnie responded with a quick "Sounds like a plan."

Sloan and Lonnie put the room back the way they found it and took the pitcher and glasses down to the kitchen. By the time Quincy arrived, they were ready to lock up.

"I'll see you two later," Sloan said. He got into his SUV and drove away as Quincy and Lonnie started down the block toward the diner. It was difficult not to stare at his friend and his uncle. They were falling in love in front of his eyes.

When he arrived at Winding Creek, he asked Candace if Bethany was in. He thought he'd say hello before visiting with his dad.

"She's in her office. But she's with someone, though. One of your high school friends."

Assuming it was Heather, Sloan said, "Probably Heather. I'll go say hello to my dad and come back."

"Actually, Sloan, it's a guy... Gary something."

"Oh, sure, Gary. His mom is here."

"I'll tell her you're here." Candace rang her office before Sloan could tell her he was fine waiting.

He was walking away when Bethany responded to Candace.

"She says you should join them."

Sloan grinned and started toward Bethany's office. "Well, then, the woman in charge has spoken."

The office door was open when Sloan arrived. "Hey, you two." He nodded at Gary. "How's your mom?"

"Coming along." Gary stood. "I was just leaving to go check in on her now." He nodded at Bethany. "Thanks."

Bethany waved to the empty chair. "Have a seat. Before Gary popped in, I was preparing reports for the December meeting. You know, getting my ducks in a row."

Sloan remained standing in front of the desk. "That meeting is still a ways off. You've got lots of time to shore up all your facts and figures."

"I suppose you're right." She flashed a quizzical look. "Uh, where's Lonnie?"

Sloan's mouth curled up in a sly, closed-mouth smile. "I begged off lunch at the diner, so my uncle and Lonnie could go alone. I have a strong feeling they were just as happy to be a twosome."

"So we weren't wrong about what we saw."

"Nope. I've noticed Lonnie finds a way to bring Quincy into many conversations." He paused. "I've got a better idea about how to spend an afternoon."

"Oh?" She flashed a teasing smile and waved at her computer screen. "Better than plowing through grant applications?"

"Much better. I've got a proposition for you." Sloan folded his arms across his chest. "Do you want to know what it is?"

Bethany leaned forward. "I do. But I warn you, it better be good."

Amused by the sparkle in her eyes, he said, "Okay, here it is. I was thinking we'd kick off the afternoon with lunch downtown, maybe at that brand-new place, The Mountain Café."

"I haven't been there yet." Bethany let out a light laugh. "Good start."

"Uh-oh. The next part of my plan involves me asking you for help."

Her quick frown communicated curiosity. "With what?"

"A little early Christmas shopping for my dad."

"Ah, you have my attention." Bethany closed the files on her desk and after a couple of clicks, she shut her laptop. "This isn't the first time you've reminded me that I can take a few hours off now and again."

"You more than make up for it," Sloan said. "Most days you're here early and stay late."

"So I could use a little shopping fun." She tilted her head flirtatiously. "But you had me at the café lunch."

Sloan smiled. "Good. Let's go."

CHAPTER TWELVE

BETHANY STOOD NEXT TO Sloan at the long rack of men's all-weather jackets and barn coats. He gave each coat a careful look before sliding the hanger down the rack. "What brought this on? Whether it's Christmas shopping, or just because, why are you buying Lucas new, well, new everything?"

"I'm tired of looking at all his threadbare stuff. Even his gloves are worn-out. I remember his old coat from two visits ago—that would make it at least a decade old." Sloan lifted a coat with a lined hood off the rack and held it up to get a better look. "If...when...I move on I'd like to leave him with some new clothes and outdoor gear. Lonnie noticed his walking shoes and boots are the only newer items he has. Dad isn't exactly penniless, you know. Far from it. But he's always prided himself on being a thrifty man. Sometimes to a fault."

Bethany nodded, understanding Sloan's motivation. "I like his spirit. He's determined to get back outside with Flash. He feels like he can't let the dog down." She nodded at the fleece-lined jacket in dark green with big practical pockets. "Looks good. Warm hood, too." Bethany shrugged. "Just my opinion, but…"

"It's not too different from the old one."

"Probably a good thing," Bethany offered. "He's gone through enough change lately."

"Right. You're really helping me out here. I'm getting a better sense of my dad these days, but I've never bought him clothes."

"Don't be so modest. The other day Lucas told me that a couple of Christmases ago, you gave him a new cell phone and arranged for the bill to be sent to you."

Sloan turned a little pink as he searched for a response. "I didn't realize he'd mentioned that." Then he scoffed. "If it weren't for that cell, I wouldn't have a phone filled with photos of Flash."

It seemed Sloan really didn't know the extent to which Lucas remembered the things his son had done for him. The two had walled off their feelings for each other. At least until recently. Bethany had seen that shift for herself.

"What do you say, next stop, gloves and hats?" Sloan folded the coat over his arm and led the way to a different department.

"And then you can splurge on sweaters and shirts," Bethany teased. "Might as well do it now."

Sloan laughed. "Are you sure you don't mind?"

"Not a bit." The truth was, she enjoyed it. She hadn't been weighed down by thoughts of Winding Creek and her decision to go all in on what she proposed. She'd already convinced Quincy that they'd been thinking too small. When the time was right, she'd tell Sloan.

Bethany stood aside while Sloan paid for the items they bought—three shopping bags full of new clothes for Lucas. Watching him pleasantly interacting with the saleswoman, it struck her again that he was such an attractive guy. Confident, too, making it easy to picture him in command in a courtroom, yet without a hint of self-importance.

When she was away from Sloan, she could tell herself that nothing had changed. He was an old school friend, who'd be on his way out of town again soon. She was simply enjoying his company. Her emotions told a different story when she was with him, though. Even this simple shopping trip. Not a grand date, but as she walked alongside him as they left the store, the afternoon felt special—and fun.

"This was great," Sloan said, "but I've kept you away too long. I'll run you back to Winding Creek."

"Sure. That's good." Reluctantly, she added, "I suppose it's time."

"I WAS DISAPPOINTED that Lonnie wouldn't be coming back for Winding Creek's Thanksgiving dinner," Quincy said, "but now I'm relieved."

Sloan stood with his uncle at the glass wall of the lobby of Winding Creek, staring at the snow piling up. The vehicles in the lot had become snow-covered mounds on a flat, all-white field. Earlier that morning, Quincy had picked up Sloan in his truck with a snowplow attached. Bethany had started out while it was still dark and made it here before conditions had turned ugly. Now they were stuck at the center until the snow stopped and the county's fleet of plows could begin to clear the roads.

"That's true, but she only had the one day off, anyway." Sloan couldn't resist teasing Quincy a little. "Besides, she didn't want to break tradition." For all the years he'd known Lonnie, she spent Thanksgiving with a couple of women friends and their families for a potluck dinner. But it was the Black Friday shopping frenzy that had taken Sloan by surprise.

"She told me about that." Quincy chuckled. "I never took Lonnie for one of those people who rushed out at dawn on Black Friday to chase a bargain."

Sloan didn't bother to ask Quincy how he knew about Lonnie's plans. It was clear they were in touch regularly, but his uncle limited how much he'd say about it, and so did Lonnie.

Sloan spun around at the sound of Bethany's voice. "Are you two going to stand there all day staring at the snow?"

"We just might. What's it to ya?" Quincy teased.

"For one thing, we're serving Thanksgiving dinner, even if we won't have the crowd we expected. We have patients and essential staff," Bethany said. "I'm going to check to see which patients would like to join us in the cafeteria. But we've got employees to help serve meals in the rooms, too."

A gust of wind interrupted the relative quiet of the lobby and blasted snow against the glass wall next to the revolving doors where they stood. "Good thing we've got nurses and aides to cover the next shift. I've sent messages out. I don't want people trying to get here."

"What's the status of the generators?" Sloan asked.

"No worries. We're covered."

"We have periodic inspections," Quincy added. "We've also got double backup systems. But we're on an automatic usage cut if we lose power."

The three of them jumped when another blast of wind and horizontal snow obscured the parking lot. Bam, the lobby went dark. Sloan held his breath, but in seconds, he heard the click as the lights powered on fully in the hub, but at only half strength in the front lobby and corridors. A few patients had been in the hub chatting and watching news of the storm on the TV mounted in the corner. They had lights, and that TV was powered on, too.

Bethany started to walk away. "I'll check the kitchen."

Quincy followed. "I'll go check in with the maintenance crew about the generators and the heating system."

Sloan took off in the other direction. "I'll look in on some patients and let them know everything is okay."

Given the brutal weather forecast early this morning, Sloan had doubted he'd be able to get home that day, so he'd brought Flash and some dog food with him to the center. He'd left it up to Bethany to decide where his help was most needed. He guessed he'd be wheeling the cart and delivering dinner trays to patients who couldn't get to the cafeteria.

He put himself in Bethany's shoes, and Quincy's. This was supposed to be a big day for Winding Creek, perhaps the launch of a tradition. But Willow and Tom were staying home with the baby, and so were the other Lancasters and Stanhopes. Jen and Dan had agreed to keep Heidi for the day.

A few family members came early, but most

abandoned their plans to be part of the Thanksgiving dinner and left to get home or back to their hotels while the roads were still passable. Sloan continued making rounds, like he'd seen Bethany do every day for several weeks now. He carried his tablet to take notes and keep track of who wanted to join the gathering in the cafeteria for dinner. This was admittedly an easy job, but by the time Sloan slipped into his dad's room, he was full of admiration for the focus Bethany brought to every patient in the center—and their families. His feelings for her had steadily deepened, and now he held out some hope that she might change her mind about her future.

He found his dad sleeping, an open magazine in his lap, and Flash snoozing at his feet. The snow was piled against the window, with more falling. Not wanting to wake either, Sloan quietly backed out of the room. He left the door about a third of the way open, the way his dad liked it. Then he headed for the cafeteria, where both Bethany and Quincy were conferring with the head of food service.

"We're going to start serving in a little while," Bethany said as soon as he joined them.

"My dad dozed off, but he'll want to join us."

Between the staff on duty extending their shifts and some family members pitching in, the day went on as an abbreviated version of the plan, thanks to the efficient backup power. When the time came, Sloan teamed up with Quincy to help the aides transport patients to and from the cafeteria. They'd managed to achieve a family atmosphere—many of the patients were familiar with each other, and to regular visitors like Sloan.

Sloan watched his dad cut off a piece of pumpkin pie with a fork, and without thinking use his other hand to steady the plate. A visible sign of progress. When he looked away, he saw that Bethany had been noting his dad's movements, too. As if realizing she was being watched, she glanced at him. Maybe it was his imagination, but when they held each other's gaze, it was as if they were the only people in the room.

After dinner, while Sloan sat with his dad and some other patients and visitors in the hub, Quincy checked the weather forecasts. "It's not all bad news," he said. "But for the first time Friday's Christmas Market and Santa Claus was canceled, and rescheduled for next Saturday. Wise decision."

Later in the evening, the power cycled on, but the storm was still going. No one was going anywhere. The highway was closed and the secondary, side roads wouldn't get attention until morning.

The patients were settled in their rooms and staff had set up some cots in the cafeteria and arranged among themselves how they'd rotate their hours through the night and early morning, until the plows cleared the roads. Bethany had a folding cot in her office closet. She'd brought it from home, along with extra blankets after a freakish early spring storm the previous March had made travel impossible. Sloan said he'd be fine dozing in his dad's lounge chair. Quincy took one of the empty hospice rooms and an elderly visitor took the other.

Sloan looked for Bethany to see if she was up for conversation or if not, to say good-night, but didn't see her and her office door was closed. But sleep didn't come easily, and after a couple of restless, uncomfortable hours, Sloan quietly slipped out of the room and headed to the hub. He was on his way to one of the couches when a shaft of light at the end of one of the corridors caught his eye. His dad had told him that the rooms at the end of that corridor had been closed up after being damaged in an unusually bad storm years before. The previous owners had done only enough to stop the leaks but never made them fit for patients again. He headed that way knowing exactly what, or rather who, he'd find.

Sloan knocked on the door before he went in and saw Bethany pulling on a loose piece of the window frame. Unsure what she was up to, he said, "Want a hand?"

"Oh, hi. I saw this strip of wood dangling, and I started yanking at it." She stood aside to make room for him.

Sloan took hold of the cracked wooden piece and gave it a pull with such force he had to step back to keep his balance. Then he triumphantly held it up. "Any other jobs that require my manly strength?" He flexed his biceps, which earned a laugh from Bethany.

"Well, let me think." She tapped her index finger over her mouth. "I've made an executive decision. I'm done for today," she said. "But why are you wandering the halls after midnight?"

"Couldn't sleep." He gestured toward the open door. "Unlike my dad and Flash. Even with their long naps, they're both fast asleep. This is one of the closed-up rooms, right?" Sloan snorted. "Were you going to start renovating it yourself? With your bare hands?"

"Ha ha. Make fun of me if you will." Bethany walked away from the window. "I couldn't seem to settle down. I had my mind on a grant Quincy and I are going after. I was actually thinking about your dad when I wandered in here. And Gary's mom, too. Quincy and I haven't discussed all this in detail yet, not with anyone. We will, soon, though."

Sloan didn't probe any further and was silent as Bethany led the way out of the room. "Do you want to take a walk, maybe find some leftover pie?" he asked. "We can probably manage in the kitchen without waking the people sleeping in the cafeteria."

"Such a good idea, Sloan. I happen to know where the staff stores the leftover baked goods. We can have our pick."

He offered his arm, and he noticed her smile when she took it. "Considering everything, it turned into a good day at Winding Creek, after all."

"Yes." Her smile grew.

They whispered and tiptoed around the kitchen, turning on only enough light to see what they were doing. As they raided the leftover cookies, breads, cakes and pies, made especially for thanksgiving, Bethany spotted two slices of blueberry pie already on plates. She smiled flirtatiously. "Are those okay?"

"Oh, yeah."

"Let's take our spoils back to my office. We can watch the storm from my window. And we won't have to talk so quietly."

"Sounds good." He lifted a tray from the top of the stack and loaded it with their plates and forks. Bethany added two bottles of sparkling water and they left the kitchen and went around the corner to her office. She didn't flip on the light but moved to the picture window. Sloan put the tray on the desk and joined her.

The streetlights illuminated the snow falling nearly horizontally in the strong wind. The lawn and trees outside Bethany's office were covered, and cars and trucks were white bumps rising from a bed of snow.

"See? Don't I have a great view? The storm might have washed out our plans for our Thanksgiving shindig," Bethany said, "but the snow is lovely to look at."

Sloan turned and leaned his shoulder against the window. Bethany mirrored him, so they stood face-to-face. He reached out and brushed his fingertips across her cheek. "You made the day work, you know. You wouldn't let Thanksgiving go down in defeat."

She responded with a shy smile and lowered her gaze. "C'mon, it took all of us."

"Maybe, but you set the tone. I won't let you deny it."

Bethany grinned. "Oh, okay. I won't protest."

Sloan took a deep breath and cupped the side of her face in his palm. She didn't move or turn away, but her eyes closed for a second or two. "You know, you're pretty sweet to look at, too." He lowered his mouth and kissed her. A light kiss, but when she responded, he took it as a positive sign and kissed her again.

"Now you're making me blush, Sloan."

"I hope so." When he stepped back, her shy smile appeared again. Before this special moment turned awkward, he said, "I think we have just enough light to see the slices of pie." He rolled her office chair to the window and then pulled up one of the guest chairs next to it.

As they polished off their middle-of-the-night snack, Sloan let his mind form a picture of what his life would be if he didn't take off and head for a new job far away from Adelaide Creek. When he'd first arrived it had seemed logical, almost inevitable. But things changed. He'd changed. Could be Bethany was allowing herself to change a little, too.

CHAPTER THIRTEEN

"EVERY YEAR THE Christmas Market attracts more people," Bethany said, "and the changed date hasn't hurt us at all." Behind the counter in her mom's booth, Bethany turned the heater up to its highest setting. "I know I say this every year, but it's a good thing these booths have heaters."

"Now, who would be waving at us from across the square?" Jen asked. "I think a friend of yours is trying to get your attention."

Bethany followed her mom's gaze, and sure enough, Quincy and Sloan were waving. Bethany waved back, but Jen gestured for them to come over.

"Can we get you something from the food tent?" Sloan asked when they'd reached the booth. "Hot chocolate or coffee? It's really cold today. Too cold for me to bring my dad."

"All the better for selling mom's famous wool and herbs and her top-selling stocking stuffer item, lavender sachets." Her mom's booth was one in a row that lined Merchant Street. Bethany inhaled the holiday scent coming from Maxine's Wreaths, the booth next door. "Mom and I take breaks. We can get something later."

"Speak for yourself," Jen said. "If the nice man is buying, I'll have a hot chocolate." She glanced at Bethany. "Go ahead, Sloan, make that two."

Bethany cast an incredulous look at her mom. "What's gotten into you?"

"Whatever it is, it's good," Sloan said, stepping away. "Two hot chocolates, coming right up."

"As cold and raw as it is, the crowd waiting to see Santa is bigger than last year," Quincy said.

"The kids are really bundled up, including Heidi." Bethany had dressed her in thick fleece pants and a matching jacket. At the moment Heidi stood with Grandpa Dan, who was adjusting the scarf wrapped around her neck and then covering her nose and mouth. As soon as he was done, Heidi hopped on one foot to make a circle around Dan. Then she switched feet and went back the other way. "I guess as long as she's in motion, she'll be okay."

"They'll have a long wait. I'll take over in a few minutes," Bethany said. "I don't want Dad to get too cold. To him, the best thing about the Christmas Market is drinking coffee with his friends in the heated food tent."

Dad usually helped her mom with the booth setup, and then sought out his group of buddies who gathered where there were strategically located heaters.

Snow was swirling in the air as Bethany watched her dad and her daughter from a distance. They had their heads thrown back and their tongues out to catch snowflakes. Her mom came to her side. "It's fun to see them together, isn't it?"

"Willow brought Naomi earlier and after a little conference with Santa, she took the cutie home," Quincy said.

Bethany's heart always melted when from a distance she had a chance to watch her parents with Heidi. These kinds of occasions had been hard at first. Bethany couldn't stop herself from thinking about Charlie—she'd begun accepting his absence as her new normal.

When Sloan came back with the cups of hot chocolate, they barely got two sips in before Jen hurried away to help a customer choose some wool. Bethany took care of a couple of big sales and sent the customers off with their purchases in Cold Country Wool's shopping bags. When she looked up, Sloan had wandered over to Dan and Heidi.

She focused on replenishing the basket of lavender sachets, when she heard a familiar voice and turned to say hello.

"Looking gorgeous, as always," Heather said, reaching across the counter to give Bethany a quick hug. "I see a trip to Santa is in the works."

She turned to draw Bethany's attention to Heidi with both Sloan and her grandpa Dan. Sloan gave Bethany and Heather a quick wave from their place in line. Quincy had left and was standing with the mayor in Adelaide Creek's booth.

"Heidi has been in constant motion all morning."

Heather offered a smug smile. "One of my favorite pastimes is watching him watching you."

Bethany was about to innocently ask who she was talking about, but even in the cold her cheeks warmed. "Oh, C'mon. What are you talking about?" She regretted the words the minute they came out of her mouth because Heather would consider it a serious question.

"Sloan enjoys being around you. You fascinate him. Even when he's with Quincy and the others, he has his eye on you working in the booth. You must notice that at Winding Creek. You said he visits Lucas every day."

True enough. And she'd become used to visiting Lucas's room and chatting with the two of them, maybe taking a coffee break in the cafeteria with Sloan, or sometimes with Lucas, too.

Heather aimed a pointed look at Bethany. "The man is obviously smitten. Are you playing hard to get?"

"I'm not playing anything. You know that. I'm not *hard* to get, I'm impossible." Or that was what she kept insisting, even to herself. "Nothing's changed."

Heather threw her head back and groaned. "Oh, Bethany. A good man is falling in love with you. Are you really going to shut him down?" She lowered her voice. "You said almost those exact words to me years ago about Matt. Now it's my chance to return the favor."

Bethany looked away and sighed. It was difficult to hide things from the maid of honor at her wedding and the person who she'd leaned on the most when Charlie died. Standing there, with people coming and going, the snow swirling, holiday music coming from the loudspeakers, she knew fooling her friend was out of the question. She gestured toward him. Sloan was listening intently to something Heidi was telling him. "I mean, what's not to like?"

Heather cocked her head. "Good question, my friend."

A wave of girlish fun washed over Bethany. "Okay, okay, you're right. The more I see of him, the more I look forward to seeing him again. As it is, we chat almost every day."

"Something feels right about this scenario. The three of you. A family, with your parents and Lucas."

"Getting way ahead of yourself," Bethany warned in a singsong tone. "And here comes my dad now. Quick change of subject, Heather. The big town meeting that seemed so far off is finally almost here. Next week, in fact. You know I have so much at stake."

"Okay, but think about what I said. The way I see it, your heart is at stake." Heather greeted Dan but quickly left.

"Was it something I said?" Dan joked. "I hope I didn't interrupt you and Heather. But Sloan offered to wait in line with Heidi. She's toasty warm, but I'm not. I'm going to take a break in the tent."

"No, not at all. We were chatting about the meeting I've been fretting about."

"Oh, that. I'm sure it's going to work out fine." Dan gave the counter a quick pat and backed away. "I'll see you in a bit." He nodded toward Sloan and Heidi. "Good to have a backup on a day like this. Your little girl seems to like the guy, too. A lot."

A lull in the foot traffic left Bethany free to watch Sloan twirl Heidi under his arm as she did a little dance to move a space up in the line. Bethany would have liked to hear what they were saying, but Sloan seemed to have no trouble interacting with a three-year-old. And Heidi wasn't a bit shy around him. Bethany couldn't take her eyes off the two, but as much as she enjoyed seeing Sloan so good with Heidi, it made her anxious, too. She'd declared her heart closed at least in part because she didn't want to watch Heidi struggle to adjust to a stepdad. Bethany had been definitive about it, too, brushing off her parents, and Heather, who'd tried to point out how rigid she was being. Now the easy way Heidi acted with Sloan poked holes in that stance.

When her mom finished with two of her regular customers, she came to the front of the booth. "Dad went to the food tent to warm up," Bethany explained.

"Heidi seems happy enough—and warm," Jen said, smiling. "Good thing Sloan was around."

Bethany nodded, but didn't comment. If she encouraged more conversation, her mom would sound exactly like Heather.

Dan rejoined Heidi when she was going to be the next child in line. Sloan didn't back away, and after she gave Santa—the well-disguised high school principal—her list, Sloan and Dan took her to the hot chocolate table together. Nice, Bethany thought.

Later, when Bethany was back home and fixing dinner, Quincy called. She greeted him with "Have you warmed up yet from the Christmas Market visit?"

"Barely. But it was fun. I'm not complaining. But I called because I wanted to tell you that we have a source for the seed money we need."

Bethany's stomach jumped in surprise. "For

converting those rooms to studios? Are you serious? Who's putting up the money?"

"Well, uh, good ol' anonymous." Quincy paused. "The funds can be delivered in a matter of days."

As if she hadn't been aware of the tension she was holding in her body, her shoulders slumped in relief and elation set in. "Wow, wow. This opens up sources of matching funds. We're on our way, Quincy."

She wouldn't waste her breath asking who this Mr. or Ms. Anonymous was, but at some point, Quincy would have to confide in her.

"This is exciting, Bethany. But it doesn't mean the naysayers will jump on board with us. Remember that at the meeting."

"You're right. It's hard not to leap way ahead of myself. It sure adds some punch to our argument, though." In between stirring the spaghetti sauce and chatting with Heidi about elves and gnomes and Christmas trees, Bethany mentally rewrote portions of her answers to questions she expected to be asked at the meeting. They'd knocked on doors to find a game changer and the door had finally opened.

WHEN BETHANY TOOK her place at the table next to Quincy and Alice, she held the image of Lucas and Gary's mom, Amy, in her head. Miraculously, in the last few days, her focus had been less on this town meeting and her long to-do list, and more on the end result. She'd finally absorbed what both Sloan and Quincy had been saying. This wasn't a personal win or loss for her. The fact that some pieces were coming together couldn't either puff up or diminish her. This whole process reminded Bethany that she still had a lot to learn.

These things were going through her mind while she listened to Alice Buckley finish up the summary of Winding Creek's statistics and finances. And their progress. "We've made impressive progress in all areas, from external communications, community involvement, and so on."

"A quick question before we move on," the current mayor, Zoe Lerner, interjected. "What is the status of the offer to buy Winding Creek?"

"Nothing has changed," Alice said. "One corporation is quite active in trying to persuade the major players in public health to see the advantages of selling. A few other companies have made inquiries."

"Are you asking us to consider any of these offers?" Zoe asked.

Quincy spoke up quickly. "Not at all." He glanced at Bethany. "We have expansion plans in place, and given all that's happened, we see no reason to even think about selling."

More than at any other town meeting she'd attended since she'd started working at Winding

Creek, Bethany was excited rather than nervous. That bubble burst when a voice boomed from the back.

"Still don't understand why we didn't sell it when we first took it over. We're wasting our time."

Bethany knew that voice. A rancher named Hayes. He'd been against the plan for the center from the beginning. His comments came as no surprise.

Hayes took long strides to the mic, but instead of speaking into it, he turned to face the panel. "If you're making so much progress, why does the place still look like a dump?"

A few people in the audience laughed lightly at the question, but Bethany always had a ready answer to those observations.

"I'm happy to clarify that." She smiled broadly. "Our rehab department has state-of-the-art equipment. The previous owners had not kept up with the most important mission of Winding Creek. As the newly hired director, I addressed that on the first day." Bethany tapped her index finger on the desk for emphasis. Maybe a little too hard. But win or lose, she wouldn't put up with judgments about the medical equipment. "We chose equipment updates over repaving the parking lot or painting the building inside and out. What good is a nice paint job without the ability to deliver the highest quality care?"

Bethany looked around the room. A few people in the audience shook their heads, but the people who nodded apparently approved.

"If we sell to a corporation, we'd also lose the spirit of what we're doing with Winding Creek in the first place, which is to keep it a community-owned facility." She took a deep breath.

Hayes groaned and swatted the air in frustration. "Yeah, maybe so. If we were talking about funding a playground or adding to the town's parking capacity or something doable." He waved a brochure. "But this chain has a lot to offer. For one thing, they'll keep the place updated, and they claim they'll have most of the current staff stay. You won't need a donation jar to fund a new roof."

"So far, the facility is almost self-sustaining. It relies on fundraising projects to make up the difference, Hayes," Zoe said. "And they've been successful."

"When it comes to who takes care of my mom and dad, I don't think it matters that the town owns the place," Hayes said. "This company has a reputation. Let's leave it to the experts."

"And you have a vested interest, Bethany," a woman called out from the audience. "If we sell, you might lose your job."

Bethany was ready to pounce at that implication, but Quincy spoke first.

"That's not fair to Ms. Hoover," Quincy quickly

interjected. "She's had a long career as an orthopedic nurse practitioner, and earned a master's in public health. A woman with her qualifications would not be unemployed for long."

Smiling at Quincy, Bethany added, "This is about my belief in community ownership and maintaining our ability to meet the needs of our growing aging population." Now was as good a time as any. She glanced at Quincy and then Alice. Both gave her a subtle nod. "The reason we're applying for several grants is to help us expand our services, which will allow us to add a much-needed residential living component."

"And for those of you worrying about selling the facility or the land, what we propose adds to the value," Quincy said.

"Why do you care, Quincy?" Hayes asked. "You're a developer, so why not sell the land?"

"Well, Hayes, we need services and independent-living housing for the elderly more than we need another new mansion, that's why."

Good answer. Quincy wasn't known as a snarky kind of guy, but he'd revealed a touch of impatience.

Murmurs of approval rippled through the room. Once restored, the O'Connor Mansion had quickly become a popular venue for weddings, conferences and other events. The sound of a gavel brought silence to the room.

"We need to wrap this up," Zoe said, "so Bethany, can you describe the grants in a sentence or two?"

Bethany nodded. She finally had the chance to describe her vision. "We've secured seed money to convert a few currently out-of-service rooms to independent-living studios, which we can then leverage to qualify for matching grants. All the info is included in the reports I submitted."

"Wait a second," Hayes said. "Where did the seed money come from? Another anonymous donor?"

"No, the same anonymous donor," Quincy said.

"How do we know it's a trustworthy person? Can you guarantee it's not shady money?" Hayes demanded.

Bethany frowned. Shady money? Where had that idea come from? Eventually, though, Quincy would have to come forward and out himself as the donor. That would put those questions to rest. Assuming that another person wasn't really Mr. or Ms. Anonymous.

"Yes, I certainly can." Quincy's loud voice resonated through the room. "In the board report, I verified that. I had to guarantee anonymity, but I'm familiar with the individual."

Bethany decided to rescue Quincy from more questions. "Take a look at our website and newsletter. Everything we do is a matter of public record. And stop by, visit, take a look at what we're doing. My door is always open."

Hayes shook his head but went back to his seat. Within minutes the meeting was over. Bethany noted the audience, who appeared to be getting into their jackets and coats and quickly heading toward the door. "Onward, or so it seems," she said, looking at Alice and Quincy. Alice patted her shoulder. "You fielded questions very well."

"Thanks. I guess I'm beginning to understand this kind of role a little more."

"I'll say," Quincy said.

Bethany turned to the sound of Sloan's voice.

"I was hanging out in the back. Nice job." He nodded to Quincy and Alice.

Quincy took out his phone and studied his screen. "Gotta run." He hurried off. Alice quickly followed.

"I'm glad I don't have to autopsy the meeting," Bethany said. "Somehow, the new part of the plan sort of slid by. It's all true, of course. And I think Hayes distracted people." She raised her hands in surrender. "But I'm not criticizing him. He has a right to his opinion."

"Changing the subject," Sloan said, "if you're free, how about you and Heidi coming out to my house for breakfast. This Saturday morning? Flash is good with kids. You two can join us on a walk around the old place."

Without hesitating, Bethany agreed. "Sounds good. And what can I bring?"

"Other than Heidi, not a thing."

"If you say so." Bethany picked up her coat and Sloan held it for her to slip into. He gave her shoulders a little extra squeeze before he dropped his hands.

On the way to her car, Sloan said, "Does Quincy seem a little preoccupied lately? I went into his office the other day. He was texting on his phone and nearly jumped out of his chair when he saw me."

"Now that you mention it, he does seem different," Bethany said. "A little secretive. He rushed off after the meeting. Usually, he hangs around a little while."

A smile lit up Sloan's face. "Are you thinking what I'm thinking?"

Bethany laughed. "I'm thinking you might see your old friend again soon. Thanksgiving didn't work out, but maybe she'll be here for Christmas."

Sloan lowered his head in a firm nod. "Exactly. And from what I can tell, no one else knows. Not even Willow. Not yet." Sloan kissed her cheek. "I'll see you at my house, say around nine o'clock?"

"Sure." Pulling out onto the street, Bethany smiled to herself. She'd changed. It hadn't even occurred to her to say no.

CHAPTER FOURTEEN

"No barking, Flash. Heidi is your friend, just like Bethany." With that warning, Sloan stood on the porch as Bethany made her way down the winding drive to the house. At some point during this visit, Sloan was determined to tell Bethany about the source of the seed money, namely the foundation he'd set up a few days ago. He'd have eventually told her he was the donor for the roof repairs, but in the scheme of things that was minor. He didn't imagine her getting too upset. But the cost of converting rooms and changing the profile of Winding Creek? Well, that was something else altogether.

When he greeted Bethany and Heidi, Sloan couldn't hold Flash back any longer. Excited by unexpected company, the dog could hardly contain himself. His tail wildly wagging, he pulled against Sloan, who now had a firm grasp on his collar. "Flash, Flash, don't make a liar out of me, buddy."

Heidi moved halfway behind Bethany. "I thought you said it was a nice dog, Mommy."

"Flash is very nice. And he likes children. He's just happy to see you, but you wait, he'll calm down." Bethany glanced at Sloan expectantly.

"Okay, boy, time to sit and mind your manners." Sloan crouched next to Flash and kept up a firm tone. The dog knew he meant what he said, and dutifully sat next to Sloan, but kept his eyes on Heidi.

"I like dogs," Heidi told Sloan, "but not the jumping."

"We'll make sure Flash gets that."

Heidi frowned. Bethany chuckled, as Flash came closer and ran his nose around her boots.

"Is it okay if Flash sniffs your shoes, Heidi?" Sloan asked.

"Okay. But he won't eat them, right?"

Amused, Sloan caught Bethany's eye. "Nope. Hey, come with me. I've got something to show you. Do you like peaches?"

Heidi nodded and looked around him and into the kitchen. "Do you have peaches in there?"

"I do. I just need to slice 'em up."

With Flash padding behind, Sloan led them to the kitchen, where he had a breakfast barstool for Heidi at the counter. "Is it okay if I lift you up?"

Heidi considered the question. Then she shook her head. "Mommy can do it."

Sloan was only a little surprised. It made sense that Heidi would still be a little shy around him and need time to size him up. Bethany lifted Heidi and settled her on the stool.

Heidi studied his countertop and smiled at Bethany. "He's got strawberries, too."

Sloan grinned. "I'm glad you approve. I'm going to cut up the fruit. You can supervise."

"She's good at that," Bethany said.

"And help yourself to coffee," Sloan said.

"Coffee, coffee, coffee. Mommy drinks it all day. Grandma Jen, too."

"I plead guilty," Bethany said, pouring herself a cup.

With Heidi paying close attention, Sloan sliced up one peach and started to cut the next one in half. When Flash let out a loud bark, probably at a bird on the porch, Heidi jerked in her seat. In an instant Sloan's focus shifted from his hands to Heidi. The knife veered off the peach and sliced into the edge of Sloan's palm. "Oops, look at that. I cut myself." He grabbed the dish towel at the sink and wrapped it around his hand.

Bethany came to his side. "Let's see."

Sloan lifted the towel. "It's nothing. I'll hunt up a bandage."

Bethany pivoted to the sink and turned on the faucet. "Run it under cold water first. I can't tell how deep it is. It may be a small cut, but it's bleeding a lot."

"Okay." Sloan held his hand under the cold water. "I think my dad has an old first aid kit in that bottom drawer at the end of the counter."

"Does it hurt?" Heidi craned her neck to get a better look.

Sloan scrunched his face and shook his head. "A little sting. Not too much."

He kept rinsing his hand while Bethany rummaged around in the kit and found a bandage the right size to cover the cut. "This ought to do it. Dry your hand, I'll put it on."

Sloan pulled a paper towel off the roll and patted his hand, but it kept bleeding for a bit. He kept his eye on Heidi, who watched his every move. "Good thing your mom is a nurse, huh?"

Heidi frowned. "The blood washes the dirt out."

"Good point." Sloan took the paper towel off the cut and then extended his hand for Bethany to spread the bandage over the cut. When she was done, he showed Heidi his hand. "See? I'm good to go. Let's get this breakfast show on the road."

"Do you want me to slice the peaches?" Bethany asked.

"Oh, I think I can manage." He looked down at Flash. "No barking at birds, buddy. You know better."

Sloan heated the two skillets, one with sausage, and the other for pancakes. He started with small ones for Heidi. Bethany smothered the pancakes with peaches and strawberries and maple syrup. "Eat while it's hot. You can have sausages later if you want to," she told Heidi after she'd cut the pancakes into small pieces. While Heidi got busy, Bethany held the plates while Sloan doled out the hot pancakes.

When they carried their food to the counter, Heidi pointed to Sloan's hand. "Our bandages have bears. But yours doesn't."

Sloan pulled the corners of his mouth down. "You're right. I'll have to talk to my dad about getting nicer ones."

When Heidi giggled at his pretend sad face, Sloan had a sudden but powerful sense that all was right with his world.

Later, they bundled up and walked through the snowy field out back. "The guy who has mowed and plowed these fields for years told me he always maintains clear trails for Dad and Flash." He grinned. "Part of that community spirit that you've been focused on."

Bethany smiled at him.

Now and again the sun broke through the clouds for a minute or two and the snow glistened under the light before the clouds drifted in again. "I never get tired of the fields when they're like this, especially when the sun makes the crystals twinkle like tiny diamonds," he said.

"I look around sometimes and it takes me a minute to realize that this ranch and the cattle defined my dad," Sloan said. "And it certainly helped shape me, even if I didn't want it for myself."

"The way the sheep and my mom's spinning and the herb garden shaped me."

"But you didn't have to leave the state to pursue your own life," Sloan blurted.

"No. And I know you believed you had to."

"I believed it because it was true, Bethany," he shot back.

"I'm sorry. I obviously said the wrong thing."

"It's okay. I didn't mean to snap at you. It's hard for other people to understand what my dad was like back then." Sloan didn't want Bethany apologizing for something she didn't understand. "Your parents were different. The only reason Dad was okay with me going to college was because all my cousins went to college. But he expected me to come back. The idea of ranching with him always hung over my head."

"I never knew that part of your story. I don't think any of us did. Maybe your cousins were aware."

"Having so many cousins helped me out with that." Sloan nodded. "There was always one of the kids who wanted to pick up the ranching life. That's why Dad ultimately realized he could both leave the life behind but keep the acres in the family."

Sloan watched as Heidi ran ahead of them with Flash. "I'm glad she's decided he's a nice dog. But it's good to see her be cautious at first."

"I figured one day we'll get a dog, but I'm in no hurry. I've got enough to do with managing where Heidi and I are supposed to be. My parents help out a lot, but dog sitting would probably push the limit."

"I don't blame you. As easy a dog as Flash is, I still have to make sure I'm home at certain times." Sloan looked at the two of them ahead. Heidi romped along trying to keep up with Flash, but then the dog stopped to wait for her to catch up. He should get on with it and say what he needs to. Soon. "The sight of her with Flash kinda warms my heart."

"Mine, too," Bethany whispered. "I look around at your incredible fields and the woods, and I suppose Lucas will miss all this a little when he moves to his studio—sooner than we imagined. Conversion work starts next week." Bethany suddenly stopped walking. "Uh-oh, I don't see Heidi."

"Me, either." Sloan no sooner said the words than Flash appeared ahead on the path and barked at them, but then hurried back into the lower gully. Sloan broke into a run with Bethany a few steps behind. "Easy, Flash," Bethany said, going past the dog. "Wait a second, there she is. She didn't go far off the trail." Heidi was pulling up her pant leg. No tears yet. "I fell down. I'm bleeding, Mommy."

"Let's see." Bethany exposed both of Heidi's legs, but only one showed a little bit of blood where she'd skinned her knee. She took a tissue out of her jacket pocket and dabbed at it.

"Did you trip on that rock?" Sloan asked.

Heidi nodded. "I wanted to be with Flash." At the sound of his name, Flash's tail started swishing.

"No harm done." Bethany showed Heidi the tissue with a few bloodstains. "See? Hardly any red at all."

"Will you put a bandage on it? Like Sloan's?"

"You want a plain one like mine? No bears?" Sloan had his arm around Flash to hold him back from inspecting Heidi's wound.

Heidi nodded. "Uh-huh." She gave him a sly smile.

"Are you sure?" Bethany smiled up at Sloan. "Do you really need one?"

Heidi nodded. "I'm sure."

"Whaddya say we go back to the house and get that first aid kit out again. Okay?" Sloan winked at Bethany. Her blue eyes were soft when she smiled at him and then turned back to Heidi.

"Sounds good, right, sweetie?"

By the time they got back to the house, Heidi was running along with Flash again, but once they were in the kitchen, she pulled up one leg of her fleece pants.

Sloan retrieved the first aid kit and pulled out a small-size bandage. "Do you want your Mom to put it on you?"

Heidi shook her head. "You do it."

Sloan knelt in front of Heidi. He glanced up at Bethany as he tore the paper off the bandage. She wore the same faint but sweet smile he'd seen before when he was interacting with Heidi. He put the bandage across the little girl's knee. He looked into Heidi's curious, trusting face, and then got to his feet. "There you go. All done."

He wasn't fooling himself, he was sure of it. His heart was full. That other conversation would have to wait.

CHAPTER FIFTEEN

SLOAN COULD SEE Bethany was a little breathless when she settled in the passenger seat. "I'm sorry about this, but I need a favor. Charlie's parents are arriving late tonight, and I told them I'd turn on the heat for them. It completely slipped my mind. I need to stop at my old house."

"That's okay," Sloan said. "We have time before our reservation."

"My in-laws will be here for the holidays, until Heidi's birthday in late January." She put her hand on her chest and blew out air.

"And they stay in your old house?"

"Uh-huh. It's the real reason I've hung on to it. I have no intention of ever living there again. But for as long as Ed and Cheri want to visit, I'll keep it. I can get temporary renters now and then, but I won't sell it." She'd been talking a mile a minute, as if harried.

"Are you okay, Bethany?" he asked. "This is only a little detour. Nothing major."

Bethany rested her head back on the seat. "I'm

really fine. I've been looking forward to our date all day. Ironically, it's a chance to get my mind off Winding Creek and all the details of the cost of converting those rooms into independent-living units. Exciting as this is."

Sloan couldn't resist. "Hey, given what you did with the bunkhouse, it's a known fact that you're really good at building additions."

Bethany responded with a mocking groan. "Oh, really?"

They reached the edge of downtown and Bethany directed him to make the two turns to land on O'Malley Street. Even with only the streetlights to illuminate the neighborhood, when he stopped across the street, Sloan could see the row of classic bungalows and white picket fences. It could have been a movie set representing a small town.

He couldn't clearly see the path to the front door in the dark. "I'll go in with you."

"Sure, you can take a look around. It's a nice little place."

Once inside, Bethany flipped on some lights and Sloan could see it was fully furnished. "It looks one hundred percent ready for guests."

"I called in the cleaning service after the last renters left. I only took a few things with me when Heidi and I moved out." Bethany led the way to the thermostat and turned the switch.

They looked at each other waiting for the comforting whoosh of the furnace cycling on.

"Well, that's a relief," Bethany said as she moved into the center of the living room. "After Charlie died, I was a little concerned that his parents wouldn't want to stay here. But thankfully that wasn't the case."

"It must have been difficult to leave, though." Sloan kept his voice low. She bobbed her head left to right and back again, as if considering her answer. "Let me put it this way. When it was the three of us, it was perfect. It's as no-fuss, no-bother as any house could be. On my own with Heidi, it just wasn't the same." She took a deep breath. "And so, the bunkhouse. And doting grandparents a quick walk away."

"I'm glad you showed this to me," Sloan said softly. "I've wanted to get a feel for the life you once had. To hear you talk about it, it's obvious you were happy."

"Nothing is perfect, Sloan, but we built the life we wanted."

"And that's what you've done pretty well since." He thought about what he'd say next. "I know that being one hundred percent responsible for Heidi can't be easy, but you've made it look seamless. I admire you."

"Well, I appreciate that, even though you're embarrassing me a little."

He closed the space between them and Sloan took her hand. "Shall we go?" He gave her hand a quick squeeze. "I hear this restaurant is pretty good."

"And I'm hungry." She squeezed his hand back. "And by the way, thanks for...for, you know, what you said. It means a lot to me coming from you."

Sloan nodded. She likely had no idea how that touched his heart. At least for now, he wanted to forget about everything else.

BETHANY HAD ALWAYS thought the Rancher's Palace was a bit of a pretentious name for what was essentially a steakhouse, although it was arguably the best restaurant of its kind in the county, maybe in the region. It was called a palace because it was housed in one of Landrum's architectural oddities, a narrow house with a tower that gave it a distinctly royal look. It was also strictly reservation-only, especially on a Friday night.

When the host had seated them at a corner table, Sloan leaned across the table, his dark eyes obviously amused. "The minute we walked in here, I felt so grown-up."

Bethany burst out laughing. "When we opened those heavy, oak castle doors, I was looking at this place through the eyes of a teenager, too. It always seemed like coming here was the big time."

"Exactly." Sloan chuckled. "It still feels a little that way. Here I am, all grown-up and having dinner with a beautiful woman in a pretty red dress."

She smiled, surprisingly not embarrassed by his words. "You're looking pretty good yourself in that gray suit. Fit for a courtroom, too, isn't it?"

"Lucky break. It was the only suit I packed. This is my first chance to wear it."

From the start, Sloan had a way of bringing out her flirtatious side. At first she'd tried to deny it was anything more than fun banter, but that had proved futile. Her train of thought was broken when the server took their drink order, red wine for each of them. She opened the menu, even though she'd order the prime rib special. Her favorite food.

This wasn't the first time she'd had an inner fight with herself over enjoying Sloan a little too much. It had been much easier at first when she assumed he was going back to Denver, or wherever. He hadn't talked about it lately. But even knowing he could leave, she never missed an opportunity to spend time with him. That hadn't seemed important at first, but now it did. Her heart beat a little faster when she decided to break this heady feeling with a touch of reality. She lowered her menu and cleared her throat. "You haven't talked about your plans recently,

Sloan. Do you know what you'll do when Lucas is settled back home, or in a new home?"

"What made you think of that?" Sloan closed his menu and set it aside.

"Time is racing by. Next thing you know it'll be—" She stopped talking when the server delivered a breadbasket and took their order. A moment later, she returned with two glasses of wine. When she left, Sloan smiled and raised a glass. "Let's have a toast."

Bethany raised her glass. "I'm game. What are we toasting?"

"Well, let's start with a toast to a bright future for Winding Creek."

She tapped his glass with hers, then took a sip. And then she looked at him expectantly. "And?"

Glass in hand, he leaned forward. "Well, I've made a decision. I'm staying here in Adelaide Creek."

Bethany tried to will her heart to slow down. "So you're not looking for another firm out of state?" Theoretically, Sloan's decisions had nothing to do with her. But that theory had proved wrong.

"No. I'm going to do what you've done, and Heather and Willow. Quincy, of course, and so many of my other relatives. I'll create a life here."

"You'll join a firm in Landrum? Or perhaps start one yourself? Small-town law may not be as exciting." Or lucrative, she thought.

He shook his head, but slowly and with a thoughtful expression. "No plans to try to join a firm, but I suppose I'll put my shingle up eventually. To start, I'm going to do some work with vets. Help rejuvenate a network so they can collectively support each other."

"That's good." But that didn't answer the question of making a living.

"And Lonnie and I were lamenting the lack of free or low-cost legal services in town, not just for veterans, but for everyone. So I'll set up a day to hold a free legal clinic, maybe meet in a room at the O'Connor Mansion. I can see lots of opportunities developing down the road."

That touched Bethany in a way she couldn't quite define. "Wow, that sounds like a perfect fit with your...I don't know...values." She couldn't believe how perfect.

The muscles in Bethany's neck and shoulders relaxed, as if she'd been waiting for an answer to a question whose importance she hadn't quite appreciated, or admitted. But that relief was short-lived. Sloan wasn't leaving after all. It had been easy to declare herself off-limits, or tell herself that what they were having was a mere flirtation, when the man in question was expected to eventually go away. But now what?

"You played a big part in my decision, you

know," Sloan was saying when she refocused on him. "You and Heidi. And Quincy."

Puzzled, Bethany rolled her hand forward, an invitation to elaborate.

Sloan offered a teasing smile. "You're idealistic, and passionate about what you believe."

She shrugged. "So are you."

Sloan flashed a conciliatory smile. "The way our firm operated, we got paid to be idealistic. We took chances and were sometimes called the David firm facing the Goliath corporation, but on a personal level, we didn't have all that much at stake."

"But you'll have more at stake here in town?"

Sloan looked like he had something he wanted to say, but then their food arrived. Between bites over the next few minutes they made the rounds of topics from the new bands at Tall Tale to the upcoming Christmas Eve caroling at Winding Creek.

"In my little family, all the focus is on Christmas," Bethany said. "Mom volunteered to make elf costumes for the preschool production of their holiday play. It's a Santa's workshop sort of thing. Heidi's looking forward to it."

"She'll be adorable, I'm sure.

"I had fun with her at the Christmas Market." With a faint smile, he added, "I haven't been around many small children, so the magic surrounding Santa and his elves and flying reindeer is new to me. Her birthday is in late January, right?"

"Yes, but really, you don't have to remember my daughter's birthday, Sloan." Oops, she hadn't meant to use that scolding tone of voice.

He reacted by pulling back and tucking his chin. "But I want to. And you can't stop me."

An unexpected answer. With no clever response at hand, she simply said, "Well, then, thank you."

"Your Heidi has been willing to take a few minutes out of her very busy life to tell me about her castle and ranch families. I mean, what with school and doting grandparents, and a great mom, what's a little girl to do?"

Bethany laughed at the characterization, mostly because it was so true. But there was a touch of nervousness too. Sloan had thrown her off-center and upended her neat plan to miss him a little after wishing him well when he left for a new destination. If she missed him, then that was the price she'd pay. She truly hadn't considered how she'd feel if he stayed. Bethany leaned back in her chair and took a sip of wine and changed the subject. "Every table in this section is full," she said. "I hadn't known it was this popular."

"Bridget told me this place has only gotten better. Including their giant pieces of triple chocolate cake." Sloan held up his hands several inches apart. "Maybe that big. Want to try it, maybe split one?"

"Of course," Bethany said, smiling. She'd never been demure about her appetite. And she loved chocolate.

The server arrived to clear their dishes and Bethany ordered dessert. For a second or two she wished she had her own car and that they'd say good-night in the parking lot. It was ridiculous, not to mention taking some of the shine off the evening. This was a real date. Wine and prime rib and chocolate cake on the way.

"This palace has lived up to its reputation in every sense," Sloan said, putting his fork down. "I surrender. I'll burst if I take another bite. It's all yours."

Bethany stuck her fork in the thick frosting. "I've still got a little room left."

"Good for you," Sloan said.

They finished their coffee and were quiet on the drive home. Not wanting the evening to end, Bethany invited Sloan in for coffee or another glass of wine.

"I was hoping you'd ask."

She poured them each a glass of wine. When she brought it to him, Sloan had taken off his suit jacket and was standing by the fireplace.

"Do you dance?" he asked.

Bethany's heart immediately raced. "Uh, well, I do, sort of, but not for ages. How's that for an answer?"

"The same one I'd give." He put his wine on the mantel and held out his hand.

"Uh, there's no music." What came next was so simple. All she had to do was put her hand in his.

"We don't need it. I'll hum in your ear."

She glanced at his hand, open and inviting. And then took it.

He drew her to him. "Let's give it a try. Too bad I don't have my old record album collection. That's going to move with me. I'll share some of my old 1960s and '70s favorites."

"You're a collector?"

"A bit." Sloan took the first slow dancing steps around the living room.

She hadn't danced in a long time, but she recognized Sloan as a skilled, smooth dancer. She relaxed in his arms and went with him as they made a couple of turns in the empty space around the couch and coffee table. He managed to find the rhythm of "At Last," and sang the words softly in her ear.

"It's been so long I forgot how much I enjoy slow dancing," Bethany whispered.

"Me, too. It's about time we remembered." Sloan pulled back and stared into her eyes. With his arms still around her, he lowered his mouth to hers for a soft, gentle kiss. He pulled back, but she eagerly sought his mouth. Nothing seemed to matter except the warmth of his lips. She held on to him and tried to lock this moment in her memory.

He finally broke the kiss. "For a long time now, I've wanted to be here with you and dance and maybe do that."

"Oh, really?" Bethany said, resting her cheek against his shoulder, suddenly shy.

"Since I was maybe seventeen." He stepped back and held her hands. "I always had a crush on you."

She cringed. "That's so long ago."

"Nothing's changed." Sloan smiled. "Except that I'm older and willing to take a chance that you might...you know, like me, too."

He was being honest. It was time for her to be the same. "I do have feelings, Sloan, I do." She took a breath. "But I–"

He drew her close. "Let's leave it at that for tonight. No buts, no qualifiers."

Her resistance to her feelings vanished. "Okay." She extended her arms toward him. "Then sing a new song and let's have another dance."

CHAPTER SIXTEEN

BETHANY KNOCKED BEFORE she went inside Lucas's room. He was standing by the window looking out at the snow coming down. "Quite a sight, Lucas. We'll have ourselves a white Christmas for sure. And here you are, looking fine and doing well."

"Sure am." Lucas's voice exuded a pleasant energy, typical of him these days.

"I don't need the nurses checking me out all the time. Sloan probably told you I don't intend to go back to the ranch. Unless I have to for a little while. If I have Flash, I'm good wherever I am. But I can't go tromping around in the woods anymore and risk falling. Sloan says I can live in an apartment right here."

He waved toward her. "Time to let younger folks take over that big barn of a house."

"You'll be close to family here. Like now, you'll have lots of visitors."

Lucas grinned. "Since Sloan is sticking around, we'll manage."

"I bet you're happy he's not going back to Denver."

"Surprised, too. I never had understood what he was up to there. Didn't know he was such a big-shot lawyer."

Bethany suppressed a smile, thinking what Sloan would say to that term.

"I suppose by now you know my son's got a ton of money. That's why he can hang around Adelaide Creek." Lucas shook his head. "But he tells me he hasn't been idle all this time. He and Lonnie are cooking up plans to help veterans. He said something about setting up some kind of foundation—I guess for the vets."

Bethany didn't try to define what Lucas meant by a ton of money, but she'd heard plans about helping vets, so maybe a foundation was a good idea. Instead of probing, she opted for a quick change of subject. "I'll bet lots of people in your big Lancaster clan will be happy to buy your house."

"Sell the place? No way!" Lucas plunked down in his chair. "Sloan said you and your little girl were out there the other day. He made pancakes and showed you around."

"Oh, yes, Heidi and I were there. We went out for a walk with Flash."

"Then you think you'll like living there?"

Bethany reeled forward. Then she chuckled

nervously. "I think you've got the wrong impression, Lucas."

"Wait a minute." With narrowed eyes, Lucas gave her a long look. "I figured Sloan wanted you to see the place, you know, for after you're married. I suppose the place needs some fixing up—"

"Really, uh, we've never talked about anything like that." Her voice was a little shaky. How had he come up with such a mistaken notion? And when she thought about it, why hadn't Sloan told her he was starting a foundation?

"Maybe I've gotten a little ahead of myself." Lucas suddenly appeared a little flushed. "I suppose I had a feeling about you two."

Bethany wasn't about to argue with that. Not now, when she'd finally given in to the same feeling. "Don't worry about it. Actually, though, it's time for me to be on my way. I've got a couple of stops before I pick up Heidi."

She started for the door, but Lucas called her back. "Bethany, I want to say one thing. I know it's none of my business, but I do believe Sloan would be a real good dad to your Heidi. He gets a big kick out of her." He paused. "'Course, I may be biased and you know best."

Maybe because she'd never expected those words, spoken in such a heartfelt way, Bethany had no immediate response.

Lucas was so right about Sloan, as if she'd needed yet another nudge to truly open herself to new possibilities in her life, and Heidi's. Dancing with Sloan the other night, she'd been certain she'd moved on. Charlie really was her past, a lovely past, but gone now. Picturing Sloan helping her to raise Heidi had strengthened her feelings. At least now she knew what she wanted.

She was still standing with her back against her office door when her phone pinged. She looked at the screen and smiled. Sloan. Of course, Sloan.

SLOAN WAS USED to rehearsing opening and closing arguments. He wrote scripts for direct and cross-examinations. Those skills seemed irrelevant to what he needed to tell Bethany now, had to tell her. He'd put it off, while everything with the foundation and the center was galloping ahead. When he arrived at her house with their pizza dinner, he kissed her cheek and she took the pizza box out of his hand. He put the shopping bag of other food on the counter.

"Come see our tree, come see our tree!" Heidi ran from the living room and tugged on his index finger to pull him into the living room. "It's real. Grandpa got it in the woods."

He let Heidi take him to the corner of the room to see their tree, while Bethany brought out plates and opened two bottles of a local dark beer. When he glanced back, Bethany's gaze was fixed on him and Heidi. Contentment. That was what she exuded.

When Bethany called them to the breakfast bar, they ate the veggie-filled, deep-dish pizza and listened to Heidi chatter about her preschool play. "I can sing 'Santa Claus is Coming to Town.' All the words."

"Yes, you can," Bethany said with a laugh in her voice. "Seems I can't get them out of my head, either."

"So, I guess that's a song in your play, huh?"

Heidi's face lit up. "You can come see it. Can't he, Mommy?"

Bethany looked at Sloan. "Why, yes. We talked about it the other day."

"I'll definitely plan on it." Sloan gestured to the tree. "You have a picture postcard tree," he said. "It's been a while, but we used to cut the trees from our woods. Like a long line of my ancestors."

"We always get our trees from the woods behind the house, too, don't we, Heidi?"

Heidi held up two fingers. "Two trees. The one we got is bigger than Grandpa's."

"My folks avoid a lot of fuss nowadays, so they cut a small one for their home," Bethany said. "The Christmas Day open house is here at my place, so Dad says it only makes sense that they scale down while I'd scale up."

Heidi nodded. "I love Christmas best." She looked up at Sloan. "Real reindeer live way far away. It's very cold there."

Bethany's amused expression told him something was afoot. "I've heard that, Heidi. Did you learn about reindeer in one of your books?"

For some reason Heidi giggled. "Will you read it to me?"

"Consider yourself hoodwinked," Bethany said.

If that was so, bring it on. He'd happily be hoodwinked like that every day. "You bet, I'll read it to you."

"When it's bedtime?"

"That's the best story time."

Bethany cast a helpless smile at Sloan. "I guess you two have a deal."

"In...deed." Sloan dragged out the word and winked at Heidi, enjoying the moment. Logically, he knew kids weren't always this easy. He'd bet Heidi could be stubborn. Likely hard to handle when what she wanted clashed with her mom's agenda. But at this moment, she was simply a cute and lively soon-to-be four-year-old. And his heart had more room for her than he ever could have imagined.

Sloan helped Bethany clean up dinner and store the leftovers, and then she brought out a gingerbread cake topped with a dollop of whipped cream. That and the hazelnut coffee added other aromas to the room already dominated by the competing smells of pizza and the fresh scent of the newly cut pine tree. Heidi skipped off to the living room to examine the tree again.

Bethany took a sip of coffee and wrapped her hands around the mug. "So nice and warm. One of life's little pleasures." She tilted her head toward the living room. "When Dad and I spotted the tree, it was clearly big and showy, but now that it's inside, it turned out to be a giant that's taken over more than its share of the room. Lucky me, I have many strings of white fairy lights. Hope you don't mind helping. Heidi's counting on it."

"Are you kidding? This is fun." For too long, Christmas had been just another day. Sloan couldn't help but add, "It's been years since I've done something as festive as decorate a tree. Lots of people at the firm went skiing for Christmas, or caught flights to see relatives or went off in search of the tropics."

"I'm curious why you didn't drive over to see your dad. I'm not judging…"

"No, no, I get it. Hard to explain, but after Mom died, Dad lost interest and after a couple of years he stopped cutting a tree. I didn't ask him, I suppose because I never knew what reaction I might get. Years later, Jeff and some of our other high school buddies helped me cut one down in the woods and drag it into the house. We found a carton of ornaments that I hadn't seen in years."

Sloan shook his head as the memory sharpened. "I thought maybe Dad objected to the work involved with a tree, but he was indifferent at best when he saw what we'd done. Gave birth to a new nickname, Lumberjack."

Bethany groaned.

"Thankfully, short-lived." Only years later did Sloan figure out that his mom was the catalyst for most of the fun times in their house. Without Polly, Lucas couldn't find a way to be happy.

Sloan abruptly stopped that train of thought. Things had changed with his dad now. He was grateful for that. He finished the last of his coffee and slid off the stool. "Ready when you are."

"Yep, I think Heidi has waited long enough."

Between the two of them, they managed to wind the long ropes of lights around the tree, top to bottom. With every muscle in motion, Heidi moved around the tree and made it her job to point out potential empty spots in the branches. Bethany's sense of humor took over as she made adjustments to earn her pint-size critic's approval.

"Tomorrow Grandma and Grandpa will help us add ornaments. But tonight, we can't forget Santa's sleigh." Bethany pulled back tissue paper from a box and gingerly lifted up an old-fashioned wooden Santa in a sleigh attached to a line of reindeer. "It belonged to my dad's family. And under the tree it goes." As if handling fragile glass, Bethany positioned the elaborate handmade piece, with its red and green and faded gilt paint, under the tree. She snapped a couple of photos with her phone.

"Okay, Heidi, it's time to light it up." Bethany pushed the rocker switch on.

"Fairy lights!"

Sloan swallowed hard. Between the glow from the fire and fairy lights, Bethany's beautiful face was shining and showing her delight in Heidi's excitement. Sloan's feelings came in waves of building intensity. Another mental picture he'd been painting of what he wanted in his future had just played out in front of him.

He put his arm around Bethany's shoulder and she reached up to put her hand on his. "This is really nice, Sloan."

Sloan said the only word he could manage at the moment, "Yes."

TIME TO STEP UP. No more procrastinating. Bethany wished she didn't have to talk to Sloan about something so serious. But she'd watched him settle down to read to Heidi. He'd pulled up a chair and positioned the book so she could read along with him and turn the pages of the oversize picture book. In her heart, she easily quoted

Heather, who'd declared, "This is going somewhere." So it was, but after the clarity she'd had only a few hours ago, she had to get an answer to an important question.

When Heidi drifted off, Sloan left the room while Bethany finished tucking her in. When she came out, Sloan was standing in the living room in front of the tree.

When she joined him, he blurted, "I need to talk with you about something. It's really important."

"I have something on my mind, too." Bethany filled her lungs and on the exhale said, "And it can't wait."

Sloan looked taken aback, or perhaps it was apprehension in his face. "Uh, well, you first."

She took a couple of steps forward and stopped while there was still some distance between them. "Every once in a while, I have a feeling you're keeping something from me. And I need an answer. Are you the anonymous donor? Not Quincy."

Sloan closed his eyes and blew out air.

"It's true!"

His eyes opened wide in surprise. "This is what I planned to talk with you about. I was going to tell you earlier. That day you brought Heidi to my house, but we were interrupted. I need to explain."

"Explain?" In a show of exasperation, Bethany put her hands on her hips. "For almost three months you've listened to me talk about Quincy as the secret donor. Roof repairs are one thing, but a foundation to fund Winding Creek's expansion?" She huffed. "Well, don't I feel foolish?"

"I'm sorry. I really am, Bethany. It started with the roof repairs. I offered the money on impulse." He extended his arms toward her. "It wasn't a big deal for me. Then the rest of it grew from there."

"Oh, right. Bringing out a wad of cash for some decorations is a far cry from advancing thousands of dollars in seed money—"

"To kick off the long-term plan for an independent-living community. Right? A component of your vision." His voice slowed down even as it also rose with each word. "Consider it selfish. Since my dad will benefit, why shouldn't I help fund it?"

Bethany had been thrilled to hear the news about the seed money. Of course, she had, but what about honesty? She thought they had been building something special between them and it all started with that. "Yes, Sloan, it's true. That donation will help us, the board and me, support senior services in Adelaide Creek. It opens doors for us."

Clearly frustrated, Sloan shifted his weight. "Exactly."

"But you kept important information from me. It's as if you were lying to me. I had to learn the truth about who you really are from Lucas. He was the one who bragged about his rich son." Oops, that wasn't fair. She dropped her arms to her sides. "No, wait. I didn't mean that. Lucas wasn't bragging. He was surprised, even a little mystified that you'd kept your wealth a secret from him."

"My success wasn't a secret. I mentioned the cases at the time I was working on them. But no, I didn't mention the settlements and the firm's stake in the cases. I could have been more specific, but I had a feeling he'd get the facts mixed up and the family would get the wrong impression. I finally told him more about myself to get him to understand why I could take such a long leave—and set up a foundation."

Bethany frowned. "But then you decided not to go back at all."

"And that's part of what I wanted to talk to you about. I started a fund, a small not-for-profit, so I can continue to use the money to do some good. Starting with Winding Creek. So, no more anonymity."

"What? You can't be our *bank*, Sloan."

His face reddened instantly. His cheeks were a deep crimson. "Well, that's what foundations do—they *bankroll* beneficial projects. But let's get something straight, Bethany. I'm not Robin Hood. I didn't steal the money."

She sighed, unable to look at him. "That's beside the point."

"Wait, wait...what's beside the point?"

"This is personal. You lied to me."

He waved away her words. "I did no such thing."

"A lie of omission. You let me think Quincy paid for the roof. I went to the town meeting thinking he, or someone he knew, gave us the seed money."

"It wasn't meant to hurt you. But I wasn't ready to reveal that side of me...the financial freedom I have."

"It's the secrecy, Sloan. Only days ago we were dancing and kissing in my living room. Tonight you're reading to my child. It's sweet and wonderful. But meanwhile, you're funneling money into the place I work—the place I run. I'm accountable for everything that goes on there."

"I didn't know what was going to happen between us when I started. And I was going to tell you. I tried to tell you when we were walking with Heidi at the ranch. Then I didn't want to talk shop on our date..." He stopped for a deep breath and to gather his thoughts. "I was still waiting for the details to fall into place. The final paperwork."

Bethany didn't even try to temper her plaintive tone. "I was married to a man who couldn't talk about his work. *Ever.* Whether he was in front of his triple screens in the tiny office in our bungalow or off somewhere in a remote corner of the world, I had no idea what he was actually doing—or even where he was doing it."

Sloan closed his eyes and nodded. But Bethany didn't trust that he truly understood what that meant.

"He had to be secretive. It was part of an oath he took. But it was hard. At times, he could have been in Texas or Thailand. Or an apartment in Berlin." Bethany rubbed her forehead with the tips of her fingers.

"I'm so sorry, I really am." Sloan spoke softly and took a couple of steps toward her.

She put up her hand to stop him. "No, don't. I thought we were, you know, going somewhere, but…"

He stopped abruptly. "That's what I think, too. It's what I want."

"It doesn't matter. It's impossible now."

"Why? Because I didn't tell you I paid for the roof repairs? Or donated the seed money for the expansion?" He paced back and forth. "Sorry. I don't want to wake up Heidi." In a lower voice, he continued to unload what was on his mind. "Are you bothered by the fact that I have the money to fund these kinds of projects? And, full disclosure, it's true, I don't have to find a paying job."

"It's not the money itself. As the director of Winding Creek, I can't have gossip going around about me. The secret man, who later turned out to be the center's *banker*? And now my boyfriend? Wow. The rumors and accusations write themselves."

Sloan shook his head, his wide eyes and slack jaw showing disbelief. Then he headed from the room, grabbing his jacket off the back of a chair by the door.

"Well, what did you expect me to say, Sloan?"

Sloan spun around. "Banker? How about calling me a *donor* and maybe you could say, 'Thanks for the support.'" He turned and grabbed the doorknob, but apparently wasn't done. "I said I was sorry for staying anonymous for so long, Bethany. And I am. But I'm not going to apologize for helping to fund the place where my own dad wants to live now. And I'm sure not apologizing for falling in love with you."

Before she could take in the reality of his words, he was out the door. Through the window she watched him rush to his SUV. He backed up and turned around and started down the long, bumpy drive, his taillights fading as he got farther away. Then he turned onto the road and disappeared.

She hadn't been totally wrong, not about his secrecy, or about a relationship that *could* look bad to an outsider. She played back her words and winced. Standing there, she admitted it. She'd sounded petty and resentful. She was the one who blew it. Her heart sank at the next thought. Maybe it was all for the best.

IF ONLY SHE could believe that.

It hadn't occurred to Sloan to skip Heidi's big day. Whatever had happened between him and Bethany, he couldn't let Heidi down. Now he was likely to be late and the program would start without him. He hadn't considered that the update with his dad's doctor would run so long. Even worse, he was stuck at the back of a long line of vehicles at the lowered railroad gates.

He thrummed his fingers on the steering wheel, aware that his rising frustration was a waste of energy. In spite of his impatience, he drifted into a memory of sitting at a railroad crossing with his mom. They passed the time by counting the freight cars as they crossed this side of the road between Adelaide Creek and Landrum. He could almost hear the rattle of the empty cars as they moved down the track. Some things hadn't changed much, like the black pyramids visible over the top of the dozens of identical coal cars. The sight distracted him from counting the minutes he had left to get to the preschool in time for the start of Heidi's play.

Should he text Bethany and let her know he was on his way? Nah. She was probably busy making sure Heidi's costume was perfect, and enjoying this happy time with Jen and Dan. The way things stood, she would find his call more annoying than welcome.

Foolishly, Sloan had allowed his imagination to soar ahead to being at Heidi's school events and parents' nights. Maybe Heidi would play soccer or basketball, and with any luck, be better at it than him. In spite of everything, that thought amused him. He might have fallen in love with Bethany, but Heidi also claimed a piece of his heart. It wasn't only for Bethany that he wanted to be at this preschool play. It was for Heidi, too. Building trust was important. He knew that all too well. This misunderstanding, or breakup, or whatever he called it, wouldn't change that.

Looking to his right from his spot at the end of the line, Sloan caught a glimpse of the last car and sighed in relief. A few minutes later, the dozen or so cars were on their way again. Half a mile later, he followed an SUV into the parking lot of the school. In the fading light of late afternoon, the school building was lit with red and green lights bordering the windows and the doorway. Snow creatures of various shapes and sizes dotted the side yard and transformed it into a winter sculpture garden.

He held the door for the latecomers in the SUV, a woman and children barely out of preschool themselves. The room was quiet when they entered, with every seat filled. The scents of pine cones and cinnamon filled the air. He'd arrived just as two teachers had finished arranging the little kids in their spots on the makeshift set. Sloan joined a couple of other adults who were standing along the side wall.

The room wasn't so big that the kids weren't able to see their special members of the audience no matter where they were. And it was easy to spot Heidi in her green-and-white elf costume. She sat at a miniature workbench with other kids who each held a toy tool. Other kids wore reindeer costumes, and Santa, whoever he really was, sat poised in a large office chair decorated with reins and garland at the front of Santa's sleigh. A deep wooden wagon painted red and draped with silver garland was attached to the chair with a rope.

Sloan watched Heidi beam when she found Bethany and her grandparents in the audience. Such a happy smile and an excited wave. But Heidi and her friends weren't distracted for long, because their teachers started their performance with "Santa Claus is Coming to Town." He hadn't predicted that a couple of dozen off-key voices had the power to grab hold of his heart. Did anyone sing with greater earnestness than those three- and four-year-olds?

About the time they got to the part about Santa

checking his list, not once but twice, Heidi recognized him standing against the wall. Her face transformed when she smiled and waved energetically. He waved back but tried to be subtle about it.

He willed himself not to glance Bethany's way, but out of the corner of his eye, he caught Jen's subtle nod to acknowledge him. Aware of how close Bethany and her mom were, he assumed that whether or not she'd shared the specifics about their situation, Jen would sense trouble between them, anyway.

When the play called for the kids to show a toy they'd made in Santa's workshop, Heidi held up a wooden airplane high over her head. Poise seemed like a much too serious word to use for a not-quite-four-year-old's performance, but Sloan saw that quality in her. She was her mother's child, all right.

The play ended with the troop of elves packing Santa's wagon attached to his sleigh. The kids dressed in reindeer costumes then pulled Santa off the stage to begin delivering his load of toys. The kids sang "Deck the Halls," and stretched out the last "la la la" so long everyone in the audience laughed while they applauded the cast.

Sloan stayed put while the kids ran to their families and the teachers and a couple of volunteers brought out the refreshments. When he was the lone person standing at the side wall, he moved closer to Bethany and her family. Heidi was pulling on Dan's hand to lead him to the cookie table.

"Hey, Heidi, look who's here." Dan turned his head to look at Sloan over his shoulder.

"I know, Grandpa, I saw him." Swinging Dan's hand now, Heidi smiled at him. "I waved, right?"

"Yes, you did. You did a fine job as an elf." Sloan briefly exchanged a glance with Dan. "I'm really glad I got to see you and your friends. I bet you'll be in lots of school programs from now until you're grown up."

Heidi's face turned thoughtful, as if she was seriously considering his remark. "I hope so. It's fun."

"I always knew she'd be a little performer," Bethany said, coming alongside him. "Thanks for making it here."

"I said I'd be here." Had she thought he'd forget?

"I know, but I wouldn't have blamed you if you'd stayed away."

He wasn't sure how to interpret Bethany's words or the quiet tone. He didn't have time to think about it because Heidi appeared in front of him.

"You like frosting on cookies, don't you, Sloan?"

"You bet I do. Do you want to show me where they are?"

Heidi nodded and he followed her to the table where she pointed to a tray of frosted cookies. "Better get one now. They'll be gone soon. Everyone likes 'em."

Sloan picked up a Christmas tree cookie covered with a thick layer of bright green frosting. "Do you want to share this one? I can break it in two."

"Okay." Heidi giggled.

Sloan laughed, too, thinking that he'd surprised Heidi. She was probably getting an extra treat. He broke the cookie into two pieces. Fairly even ones, too. Not bad. "You choose which half you want."

"Better pick fast, Heidi. We're getting ready to go." Dan smiled at Heidi. And once she made her choice, Dan took her free hand and started to walk away.

Heidi waved and said goodbye. Sloan watched as they joined Jen and headed for the door.

A familiar female voice came from behind him. "So, I'll see you tomorrow. Always a good day for Lucas when you can bring Flash."

"Sure. Tomorrow."

Sloan waited to leave until Bethany had disappeared with her family.

CHAPTER SEVENTEEN

"BETHANY HAS DONE it again. With your help. Can't forget that." Quincy spoke to Sloan, as they stepped into Winding Creek's festive lobby and hub. "Those three trees against the wall with the red, green and white lights, they look like real trees in the woods. Beautiful."

It took effort, but Sloan managed to keep his voice neutral when he responded. "All set up for Christmas Eve. The kids did a great job dressing the lobby and the hub." He'd taken a second trip to the party store with Cooper and Tori, plus a couple of students they'd brought with them. Bethany had set him and the kids loose to decorate the lobby and patients' lounge, along with the cafeteria. Sloan was sure she'd stayed out of this phase of the first Christmas at Winding Creek because she wanted to avoid him.

"Don't be modest. You had a hand in all this." Quincy glanced down to take a quick look at his watch.

"She'll be here, Quincy. Don't worry. C'mon,

let's sit down and wait for her." They claimed a couple of chairs in the lobby where they could watch for Lonnie coming across the lot and through the revolving doors.

Quincy guffawed. "I'm not worried, kiddo, I'm eager."

"I'm aware of that because Lonnie told me so. She's every bit as excited about getting her new life underway as you are." Adelaide Creek's newest couple had finally opened up about the spark that had ignited into a blazing and life-changing romance. Like Sloan himself, Lonnie was wrapping up her work at the firm and moving on. To Adelaide Creek. To be with Quincy.

After establishing she was welcome to stay with Sloan for as long as she'd like, Lonnie pointed out that they'd be a team again, first to help vets. After that, it remained to be seen, but one day, Adelaide Creek could have a new legal clinic.

"I don't think Lonnie and I will wait too long to make it official." Quincy lightly elbowed Sloan. "What do you think of your old uncle getting married again after all these years?"

"You're certainly in a hurry." It was only a few days ago that he'd hoped he and Bethany would take that big step, *eventually*. "But, naturally, I think it's wonderful—and you have great taste in women."

Quincy scoffed. "We don't have to make all kinds of adjustments like you and Bethany face. For one thing, you have to build a strong bond with Heidi. I suppose that's your priority right now."

Sloan raised his hand in a clear halt sign. "Quincy, no. Stop. That's not going to happen."

His expression blank, Quincy stared at him for a couple of seconds. "Since when? I thought you two were, you know, getting close."

"We are. Or were. But..." Sloan stopped. He'd leave it at that. This wasn't the time or place for a conversation about him. "Never mind. Let's focus on you. Do you have a wedding date in mind?"

"Well, since you ask," Quincy said, "Willow and Tom got married on New Year's Eve. It was a great wedding. But Lonnie still has things to do at the firm before she can come here permanently. For now, I'm thinking about Valentine's Day."

Sloan smiled. "You sound like a teenager, but sure that's a perfect day."

"And you'll be my best man? Right?"

Sloan's surprise left him reeling. So much had happened since the wet, dreary day he'd arrived in Adelaide Creek, including that happy twist of fate that brought Lonnie and his uncle together. And now, not quite three months later, they were discussing wedding dates.

"Sloan? Why are you taking so long to answer me?" Quincy grabbed his shoulder. "I assume you approve."

"Yes, yes, of course. I'm stunned. It's happening so fast. I'm honored to be your best man. Congratulations."

Quincy pointed around the room. "Wow, I've been so preoccupied, I haven't paid attention to what's going on here. The music is starting soon. Lots of families are here."

Sloan smiled. "My job was watching them do the work."

The three artificial trees against the wall gave the hub a homey, welcoming feel. At the moment, Erin Hunnicutt with her fiddle and her brother Tom Azar with his guitar were talking to the high school kids who were behind the refreshment table. The caroling would start soon. The hub held dozens of patients and their families, some of whom Sloan had come to know during his dad's stay at Winding Creek. Whether that was for a few weeks of rehab or for permanent care, Sloan was sure Bethany remembered every patient's name and probably their family members' and friends' names as well.

"Look at this group, Sloan," Quincy said. "Your cousins and old friends are here. The people you grew up with, plus the new families they've created over the last few years."

Sloan had the same reaction when he surveyed the crowd. He'd made his choice, and he was home to stay. But in some ways, he was one of the newcomers now. Heidi was sitting with Jen and Dan, and a couple he assumed were Charlie's parents, Cheri and Ed. Heather and Matt and their twins sat with Olivia and Jeff. Olivia's daughter Jillian, now Jeff's daughter, too, was following her stepbrother Carson around as he videotaped the event for the website. Bridget and her teenagers were in the crowd. He hadn't formally met Erin's boyfriend, Mack, one of Tall Tale's owners, who was at the refreshment table with his young son, Liam. But like Erin, Mack and his boy were now linked to all Sloan's old friends, and relatives.

However briefly, Sloan had begun to count himself among that group of young families. Prematurely, as it turned out. But he'd committed himself to Adelaide Creek, regardless of messing things up with Bethany. He could put up arguments for his choice to stay anonymous, but they weakened by the day. Her side of the issue, especially the emotions behind even the whisper of secrecy, made sense. But the idea that a personal relationship would somehow compromise Bethany's position as director? No one, not even someone like Hayes, would ever believe that. Bethany's record would always withstand scrutiny. He had to find a way to prove that to her. Maybe not today or tomorrow, when her family celebrated Christmas, but soon.

When Quincy left to mingle with the crowd, Sloan got to his feet. Out of the corner of his eye, Sloan saw Willow coming his way. She held Naomi's hand, and pushed the empty stroller with the other. She gave him one of her warmest smiles. "I see all of Adelaide Creek was invited to this Christmas shindig."

"Seems so." He waved at Naomi, who'd scooted behind Willow, but then stuck out her head to reward Sloan with a shy smile. "But I hadn't expected so many people to show up." In a silly voice, he added, "Right, Naomi?" That brought on a giggle as she hid her face again.

"Speaking of good news, congratulations are in order, my friend. Tom and I heard about Winding Creek's expansion. You and Bethany, and the board, managed not only to save this place, but improve it." Willow gave him a scrutinizing look. "Here you are, doing all sorts of good things for your little hometown."

"Providing the seed money to make these changes wasn't a huge deal for me, Willow. Really. And trust me, Quincy gets a lot of the credit."

Willow flashed a sly smile. "Your life is changing in lots of ways, or so I hear. Heather filled me in. I'm really happy for you and Bethany. We weren't sure she'd ever open her heart again. But when she did, I'm glad it was for you."

Sloan squared his shoulders and blurted, "Oh, no, no. This was all premature. It's not like that now, Willow." He spilled the words as fast as possible to get this over with. "I mean, it didn't work out with Bethany. But we're still friends, I hope. I'm back for good, though. Lots to do." Listening to himself spout those defensive, stock phrases—staccato style—he knew they rang hollow.

Willow's smile gave way to a skeptical expression. "Okay. I won't argue—or probe. Not on Christmas." She lifted her chin a notch. "But something about this doesn't add up."

"Hey, Willow, I'll take all the credit I deserve for bringing Lonnie to town."

"Yes, my friend, brag away. I'm really happy for my dad." Willow turned her head to the sound of Erin's voice. She'd begun singing "Little Drummer Boy" a cappella, but Tom quickly joined in. The blending of the two voices and the haunting melody brought a hush to the crowd. The singers from the high school soon joined in and the tempo and the volume gradually increased.

When Naomi started to climb in the stroller by herself, Willow got the hint and whispered, "I better keep moving."

When his cousin took off, Sloan meandered across the space to get closer to his dad, who was with Andre and some other patients arranged on the outer edges of the circle. Heidi saw him and smiled as he walked by. Then, when the singing stopped, she turned around and pointed to him. "Sloan came to my play." That got everybody's attention, including the two in-law grandparents who responded with curious expressions.

Sloan settled for returning Heidi's bright smile. His dad beckoned him over. Erin and Tom shifted the mood by starting an up-tempo pop holiday song, and some of the teenagers broke off into smaller groups and sang while they walked through the halls.

"What is it, Dad?" Sloan asked when he'd reached him.

"Let's go back to my room. The singing is really nice, but I need to talk to you. It's important." Lucas took off, albeit at a snail's pace. Sloan followed, impressed still with his dad's improved mobility. "Slow and steady, right, Dad?"

"You know it. This place has made all the difference."

Sloan then got to the point. "I know what you want to talk about. Pretty exciting about Quincy and Lonnie, isn't it?"

"Sure, sure, but that didn't come as a surprise. Ever since my brother met your friend, he couldn't stop talking about her. You did good as the matchmaker."

"Okay, then what is it? We're making plans to move you into a studio here at Winding Creek as soon as possible."

"Looking forward to it," Lucas said. "Flash is, too." As soon as Lucas was inside the room he spoke his mind. "What happened with you and Bethany? I get it that she doesn't want to live in our house way out at the ranch."

"Dad, Dad...stop."

"Not until I have my say. I was thinking you two were getting along really well. You seem like a good pair. Take it from me, son, you can't beat smart and pretty." Lucas narrowed his eyes. "Did you do something to drive her away?"

"Come on, it's more complicated than that." Even as far away as his Dad's room, Erin's voice singing "What Child is This?" was as clear as a bell. Another haunting melody that stirred his emotions. He'd hoped to avoid any talk of Bethany, at least until he'd had a chance to try to patch things up. Start again. Or as Lonnie sometimes said of his opening or closing statements, "Edit the script, Sloan."

"But you don't just like her! You *love* her. Anyone can see that in the way you look at her."

No sense trying to hide it. "Yes, Dad, I do, but Bethany is angry that I kept my donations to the center a secret. It embarrassed her. She'd assumed it was Quincy and felt foolish being kept in the dark." That wasn't the whole story, but it would have to do for now.

"You can say you're sorry. That ought to help things."

What could he say? His dad meant well. "It's a good start."

"She's a good woman. Like your mom." Lucas pumped his fist. "You gonna put up a fight?"

Sloan didn't trust himself to speak. This guy was the dad he could have used earlier in his life. A dad who might have helped him during that awkward teenage time when he was too shy to ask Bethany out on a date. His voice cracked a little when he said, "That's my plan." Sloan would have confided in his dad about the details, but he wasn't exactly sure of them himself.

"Listen to me now. Back when you were born, I gave Polly a real pretty ring." His dad chuckled. "My little brother was always smarter about these things, you know, about women and romance. Quincy said a little gift was a good idea. He helped me pick it out. Anyway, the stone is Wyoming jade. It's in a nice gold setting."

Sloan's chest tightened. That ring. He remembered it. His mother wore it all the time. He'd never known it was a gift from his dad. As a little kid he'd never thought to ask.

"Anyway, I want you to give it to Bethany." Lucas flapped his hand in the air. "For when you two settle things. It's not an engagement ring. It's not fancy enough. Too early for that, I imagine. But for when you've shown her the good man you've become. The good father you'll be to her little girl." Lucas laughed. "She's a busy little bee, isn't she?"

"Are you trying to give Heidi another grandpa?" Sloan barely got the words out.

Lucas's eyes opened wide. "Wouldn't mind a bit. Now, the ring is in a little box in the bottom drawer of that small chest in my closet."

"You've kept it all these years." It was a statement, not a question. And another glimpse into the way his dad felt about his mom. Maybe he hadn't been indifferent all those years. Maybe it was the way he wore his sadness.

"At first I kept it for myself, because, you know, just to have it because I missed her so much." Lucas smiled sadly. "Then I kept it for you to give to the right woman. When you didn't find one for so long, I kept it anyway. Glad I did."

His dad waved his hand again, this time to the door. "Let's join the others. Lots going on out there today."

Sloan struggled to transition from the dad who'd just showed him his heart to the all-business dad ready for more Christmas cheer.

"Okay, you're the boss." Sloan took in a breath and hugged his father. "Merry Christmas, Dad. And thanks."

"You're welcome, son. Just make things right."

"I will, Dad." In a teasing tone he added, "You need to give me a little time."

Not too much time. He held images of Bethany's bright smiles when she'd see him approaching her, or how she laughed at his quips, or her warmth when he'd held her in his arms. The sweet kisses.

He had to act. Now.

BETHANY CIRCULATED THROUGH the room, greeting everyone, including her parents and her in-laws, but when Lonnie and Quincy joined the caroling in the hub, and then Sloan and his dad came back, she slipped off to her office. Call it hiding out, but her mood was less than festive. The last time she checked on her little girl, Heidi was in heaven with all four grandparents and a bunch of friends.

Her mind jumped back a few days to the last time she'd seen Sloan. She'd been thinking up what to tell Heidi if she noticed Sloan hadn't come to her preschool program after all. But when the cute Santa's workshop play was over and Bethany prepared to leave, there he was, standing alone along the back wall of the main room at the preschool. He was giving Heidi a big thumbs-up. Heidi was giggly and beaming in her elf costume. He'd kept his promise. Of course, he had.

Bethany sat at her computer and clicked on the folder that held Quincy's paperwork and drawings for the new, independent-living suites. Maybe she was missing a surge of Christmas spirit, but she had the satisfaction of her vision coming to life. Thanks to Sloan. But that couldn't erase the changes within her. She'd chosen to lock her heart, but it turned out her heart had a mind of its own. It won the battle and overrode all her logical reasons why it shouldn't happen, and she'd fallen in love again, anyway.

Bethany opened her day planner and picked up a pen, not for any particular reason, but she looked busy with something while her brain shuffled through memories of Sloan. She couldn't help herself.

A knock on the door startled her, and she called out, "Come in."

Cheri? The last person she expected to see. "Hey, this is a surprise." She gestured to the chair. "Join me. We haven't had a chance to catch up. It's been busy around here."

"With Dan and Ed, plus your mom, Heidi is well occupied," Cheri said. "I thought I'd come to see you."

Bethany had always gotten on well with her mother-in-law, a down-to-earth woman who'd trusted her son's choice of a partner.

Cheri filled a couple of minutes with small talk about Heidi and Winding Creek, and what Jen had told her about the recent developments. "You've done an amazing job here."

"Thanks, but it's a team in the real sense of the word. But no matter what, Heidi is always my priority." Why had she said that?

Cheri frowned and rested her forearms on her side of the desk and leaned forward. "Ed and I have never doubted that, not for a second. We see Heidi and we know what kind of mom you are. You never have to explain your life to us."

Bethany swallowed hard, her emotions rising not only from the words, but from Cheri's firm but loving tone. She was about to respond when Cheri sat back in the chair and gave her a pointed look.

"Your mom tells me there's a man around now. A very good man, Jen says." Cheri's eyes grew misty. "This is absolutely none of my business, but I hope you don't pass up a chance to have love in your life again."

"But Heidi…" Bethany fumbled around to figure out what she wanted to say.

Cheri shrugged. "You've always shown good judgment. You'll know what to do." Clearly not expecting an answer, Cheri stood and hurried to the door. "You should trust yourself, Bethany. The rest of us do." Cheri smiled as she stepped into the hall. "People are starting to drift away. We'll probably leave soon. So, we'll see you later this evening."

Bethany stayed in the chair and, with the door open now, listened to Erin and Tom leading the gathering in an energetic version of "Joy to the World." Judgment, Cheri had said, intending it as a compliment, and Bethany would take it that way. But Sloan had taught her a few things about another kind of judgment. She'd judged him for his secrecy, but also failed to fully understand what he was willing to do for the community. She was the one at fault, so she'd be the one to make the first move to fix it.

She picked up her phone and was figuring out what she wanted to say in her text, when her phone pinged. A new text. From Sloan.

can I see you tonight...late is ok...nd to talk

Her hands trembled from the strong shot of relief.

was abt 2 text u...yes, yes...bunkhouse

She had a second chance.

CHAPTER EIGHTEEN

Sloan stood at the side of the SUV and reached inside his coat to pat his blazer pocket. There it was, the little velvet box with the jade ring. He'd rehearsed—multiple times—the story he'd pass on about it, including his dad insisting that Sloan give it to Bethany now.

He'd waited hours at the house with Flash, and it was almost ten o'clock when Bethany texted that she was in the bunkhouse after Christmas Eve dinner with her parents and in-laws. Heidi was finally asleep. Flash had stood by the door when Sloan put on his coat. He cocked his head, obviously confused by this unscheduled event. "Okay, you can come with me. Bethany likes you. But no barking. We can't wake up Heidi."

Minutes later, he let Flash out of the SUV. "Let's go, boy. And wish me luck. Hey, she opened the door without me knocking. That's a good sign, right, Flash?"

"Hi there." Bethany opened the door wider to let him and Flash inside.

Sloan reached out to give her a hug, but she hurried into the living room. He followed her and before Flash could get there, she lifted a plate of cookies off Heidi's play table.

"Ooh, close call," she said with a laugh. "Santa's sugar cookies would be a big temptation for our canine friend."

"I never thought of that. I brought him along because he was confused when I got ready to leave." Sloan chuckled. "His circadian clock knew this was not a typical departure time. He's up way past his bedtime. I didn't think you'd mind if I brought him along."

He followed her when she carried the plate back to the kitchen and put it on the counter. The dog stayed behind and curled up in front of the fireplace. Flash would be snoring soon.

"On the other hand, the sugar cookies must be gone before Heidi's up in the morning, so we can give him one or two at least." When she looked up at Sloan, her blue eyes were sparkling. "Wine? Or, I have some of that cider I know you like?"

"Can I have cider another time?"

"Good choice." She picked up the open bottle of wine and the two glasses she had on the counter and headed to the living room. "That implies there will be another time." Bethany's voice was low.

"I sure hope so." He lifted the bottle from her hand and filled the two glasses.

"Then you forgive me?"

"That was my line," Sloan said. "I was hoping you'd forgive me for keeping secrets. You've done nothing wrong."

Bethany smiled. "I'm apologizing, anyway. So there. Besides, I was judgmental. Unreasonable. My mistakes."

"I should have trusted you with the truth." Now wasn't the time to explain his reasons. "One day soon I'll tell you about the cases we took on and why I've been able to start this foundation." He held up his hands defensively. "So you know, I set up the foundation to create a wall between my personal assets and the foundation. No room for confusion there."

"However you arrange it, you're a part of a major improvement in Adelaide Creek. More than one. And I can't begin to predict all the good you and Lonnie can do for vets."

"I'll concede that point. And the way I set up the funding, I'm a silent partner in your vision." He held out his glass, and she tapped it with hers.

She let out a happy sigh. "A Christmas Eve toast to our town and Winding Creek."

Sloan was a little nervous now. This was going so well. "Bethany—"

"Sloan, I—"

"Ah, oops, you first, Bethany."

"I only want to say this once, Sloan, and then we never have to discuss it again." She took a sip of her wine and then put her glass on the table. "I never thought I'd feel this way again. Fall in love and hope for a new future. I thought when Charlie died my chance for that was behind me." She shook her head. "I was wrong. I've fallen in love with you."

Sloan closed his eyes and ran those words through his head. "And I love you back. It's true, I've always had feelings for you." He reached for her hand. "You know how I feel about Heidi, right?"

Bethany nodded. "But about that," she said. "You do understand it will take time…to know you, adjust to you."

"Oh, I'm way ahead of you." Sloan wanted to get the words right, to move past his surging emotions and deliver the necessary message. "Heidi already stole a big piece of my heart. Watching her as an elf in the play, and going along with the bandage game, her beautiful imaginative Sylvie-the-mermaid… But I want her to want me to become her daddy. It doesn't matter how long it takes."

Bethany's eyes filled with tears. "You do know how to say the right thing."

"Enough words for now." He got to his feet and held out his hand. "Come dance with me."

"I'd thought you'd never ask. And will you hum 'At Last' again?" She took his hand and he led her to the empty space in front of the fireplace. "We better watch out for Flash this time."

When he took her in his arms, it was as if everything that came before fell away, and this moment and only the next days and months and years mattered. He hummed the tune and they slowly moved in a circle behind the couch and back to the fireplace. When he stopped, she tightened her arms around him, and starting with kissing her cheek, he made his way to her mouth. She accepted his lips eagerly. Intoxicating kisses... Everything about her captivated him.

When he thought of the ring in the box, he decided this was the moment to seal his promise. He broke the kiss and loosened his arms. "I want to give you something."

"Now?"

"It's the best time. Trust me." He reached into his pocket and took out the ring box. When her eyes popped open, he rushed to explain. "This isn't what it looks like. You can breathe again."

She let out a light laugh. "Okay."

He opened the box, and when she saw the ring he was rewarded with a happy smile. "My dad gave my mom this ring when I was born. Apparently, Quincy helped him pick it out."

"It's beautiful, Sloan. Wyoming jade. One of my favorite stones."

"I'm not asking you to marry me…yet. But I'm promising to do everything I can to build on what we have…you and me. And Heidi."

She looked into his eyes. "Right here, right now, I'm making the same promise to you."

Sloan took the ring out of the box. "Here, try it on."

She took the ring and slipped it on her slim finger. "Hey, a perfect fit."

"Like us," he said.

"We're good dancers, that's for sure," Bethany said, reaching for his shoulder and hand. "Hum another tune. Let's dance 'til dawn."

"Okay." He pretended to think hard. "Remember that singer our grandparents used to talk about? Had a different sort of name. Elvis, maybe?"

Bethany laughed. "Oh, Sloan. Too funny."

He drew her close and began a little combination of humming and singing. Maybe they could dance the night away, after all, he thought, as he softly crooned, "I Can't Help Falling in Love with You."

When he'd run out of words, he swung her out to his side and then brought her back to give her another kiss. It might have happened, too, if Flash hadn't decided that was the moment to wiggle his body between them, his tail wagging wildly.

"Ha! I think Flash is ready for a sugar cookie. And a little attention," Sloan said.

"He's not going to leave us alone until we give in." Bethany took Sloan's hand and they walked to the counter. She grabbed the plate with two cookies and put it on the kitchen floor. "I've got plenty hidden away for Santa."

As they watched the dog happily devour the treats, Sloan put his arm around Bethany and she rested her head on his shoulder.

"Merry, merry Christmas, Sloan."

"Best of all, Bethany, Happy New Year."

* * * * *

For more Adelaide Creek romances from acclaimed author Virginia McCullough and Harlequin Heartwarming, visit www.Harlequin.com today!

Get up to 4 Free Books!

We'll send you 2 free books from each series you try PLUS a free Mystery Gift.

FREE Value Over $25

Both the **Harlequin® Special Edition** and **Harlequin® Heartwarming™** series feature compelling novels filled with stories of love and strength where the bonds of friendship, family and community unite.

YES! Please send me 2 FREE novels from the Harlequin Special Edition or Harlequin Heartwarming series and my FREE Gift (gift is worth about $10 retail). After receiving them, if I don't wish to receive any more books, I can return the shipping statement marked "cancel." If I don't cancel, I will receive 6 brand-new Harlequin Special Edition books every month and be billed just $6.39 each in the U.S. or $7.19 each in Canada, or 4 brand-new Harlequin Heartwarming Larger-Print books every month and be billed just $7.19 each in the U.S. or $7.99 each in Canada, a savings of 20% off the cover price. It's quite a bargain! Shipping and handling is just 50¢ per book in the U.S. and $1.25 per book in Canada.* I understand that accepting the 2 free books and gift places me under no obligation to buy anything. I can always return a shipment and cancel at any time by calling the number below. The free books and gift are mine to keep no matter what I decide.

Choose one:
- ☐ **Harlequin Special Edition** (235/335 BPA G36Y)
- ☐ **Harlequin Heartwarming Larger-Print** (161/361 BPA G36Y)
- ☐ **Or Try Both!** (235/335 & 161/361 BPA G36Z)

Name (please print)

Address _____ Apt. #

City _____ State/Province _____ Zip/Postal Code

Email: Please check this box ☐ if you would like to receive newsletters and promotional emails from Harlequin Enterprises ULC and its affiliates. You can unsubscribe anytime.

Mail to the Harlequin Reader Service:
IN U.S.A.: P.O. Box 1341, Buffalo, NY 14240-8531
IN CANADA: P.O. Box 603, Fort Erie, Ontario L2A 5X3

Want to explore our other series or interested in ebooks? Visit www.ReaderService.com or call 1-800-873-8635.

---

*Terms and prices subject to change without notice. Prices do not include sales taxes, which will be charged (if applicable) based on your state or country of residence. Canadian residents will be charged applicable taxes. Offer not valid in Quebec. This offer is limited to one order per household. Books received may not be as shown. Not valid for current subscribers to the Harlequin Special Edition or Harlequin Heartwarming series. All orders subject to approval. Credit or debit balances in a customer's account(s) may be offset by any other outstanding balance owed by or to the customer. Please allow 4 to 6 weeks for delivery. Offer available while quantities last.

Your Privacy—Your information is being collected by Harlequin Enterprises ULC, operating as Harlequin Reader Service. For a complete summary of the information we collect, how we use this information and to whom it is disclosed, please visit our privacy notice located at https://corporate.harlequin.com/privacy-notice. Notice to California Residents – Under California law, you have specific rights to control and access your data. For more information on these rights and how to exercise them, visit https://corporate.harlequin.com/california-privacy. For additional information for residents of other U.S. states that provide their residents with certain rights with respect to personal data, visit https://corporate.harlequin.com/other-state-residents-privacy-rights/.

HSEHW25